LOOK HOMEWARD, ANGEL

AND OTHER MODERN PLAYS

LOOK HOMEWARD, ANGEL

AND OTHER MODERN PLAYS

LOOK HOMEWARD, ANGEL
by Ketti Frings
from the novel by Thomas Wolfe

MARTY
by Paddy Chayefsky

ALL THE WAY HOME
by Tad Mosel
from the novel A DEATH IN THE FAMILY
by James Agee

SCHOLASTIC BOOK SERVICES
NEW YORK • TORONTO • LONDON • AUCKLAND • SYDNEY • TOKYO

THREE FACES OF LOVE

The three plays in this anthology are variations on the theme of love. Love is a funny word. When you are lonely, it sounds like the greatest thing in the world. But love can also be stifling. You have probably experienced the two sides of love in your relationship with your parents. The security of home can be comforting. If you fail a test, if you catch the flu, if you break up with your girl friend, it is good to know that someone stands by you. On the other hand, your parents' love can be suffocating. Sometimes you want to do your own thing. you resent having to answer to anyone, you long to be on your own, at work or at college. There is a wide range of emotion between loneliness and love, between love and the desire for freedom, which these plays explore with honesty and sensitivity.

Marty is a simple story of two lonely people who find one another. As a love story, it is modern in tone because the lovers are so unglamorous. ("I set out in *Marty*," Chayefsky says, "to write the most ordinary love story in the world. I didn't want my hero to be handsome, and I

I didn't want the girl to be pretty. I wanted to write a love story the way it would literally have happened to the kind of people I know.") One of these people is Marty, the butcher, a thirty-six-year-old bachelor. His mother and his customers constantly plague him with the question, "When you gonna get married?" Marty would like to get married. He is lonely, and he is sick of hanging around the bar Saturday nights with his best friend, Angie. But Marty thinks of himself as a "fat little ugly man" that no woman would look at twice. One night at a dance hall, he meets a school teacher. A wallflower like himself, she understands his pain and his sense of rejection. The two approach each other with awkward gestures that may strike you as all too familiar.

(*Marty tries to kiss the girl.*)

GIRL: No, Marty, please.

MARTY: I like you, I like you, I been telling you all night I like you. . . .

GIRL: No. . .

MARTY: Please. . .

GIRL: No. . .

MARTY: All right! I'll take you home! All right! All I wanted was a lousy kiss! What am I, a leper or something?!

GIRL: I just didn't feel like it, that's all.

MARTY: Well, that's the history of my life. I'm a little short, fat, ugly guy. Comes New Year's Eve, everybody starts arranging parties, I'm the guy they gotta dig up a date for. I'm old

6

enough to know better. Let me get a packa cigarettes, and I'll take you home.

GIRL: I'd like to see you again, very much. The reason I didn't let you kiss me was because I just didn't know how to handle the situation. You're the kindest man I ever met. The reason I tell you this is because I want to see you again very much.

MARTY: Wadya doing tomorrow night?

So goes modern love in New York City, according to Chayefsky. It is a bit awkward perhaps, but it is tender and hopeful. For all Chayefsky's disclaimers, he has in one sense written a romantic play. He has faith in love and the possibility of closeness. There are questions about love he never asks, questions that lie at the heart of Tad Mosel's *All the Way Home*. Where Chayefsky sees a cure for loneliness, Mosel wonders if the cure is ever found. Is the gulf between two people ever bridged? In the long run, are we not all thrown back upon ourselves?

All the Way Home is the story of Jay and Mary Follet, a young married couple who live just outside Knoxville, Tennessee, in the spring of 1915. They have one six-year-old son, Rufus, and are expecting a second child. The marriage is a loving one, but for all their closeness, Jay and Mary continually stumble on gulfs that separate them. Jay used to be a drinker, one great barrier between him and his religious, abstaining wife. Even after Jay swears off liquor, he has strange absences. He disappears into the hills to talk with the old country people. He goes off at night to eat in all-night diners. "He'd feel himself being closed in," Mary explains, "watched by the superintendents, he'd say and — There was

7

always a special quietness about him afterward, when he came home, as if he were very far away from where he'd been, but very far away from me, too, keeping his distance, but working his way back."

When Jay is killed in a car crash, Mary must come to terms with the loneliness that always threatened her. She realizes that, in the long run, we are always left alone. "People fall away from us," she tells her Aunt Hannah, in a quiet moment before Jay's funeral, "and, in time, others grow away from us. That's simply what living is, isn't it?" Almost, but not quite. In her love for Jay, Mary reaches out across the gulf and grants him, in death, the freedom she could never grant him in life. She hopes that, at the moment of the crash, Jay was drunk, if not with liquor, then with the sheer joy of being alive. "If he was drunk, Hannah, I hope he loved being. Speeding along in the night — singing at the top of his lungs — racing because he loved to go fast — racing to us because he loved us. And for the time, enjoying — revelling in a freedom that was his, that no place or person, that nothing in this world could ever give him or take away from him."

Freedom is the reverse side of the coin of love. The individual needs room to breathe; the child to grow. *Look Homeward, Angel,* by Ketti Frings, is a play about this need for freedom. Eugene Gant, a seventeen-year-old growing up in Altamont, North Carolina, longs to go to college and be a writer. Unfortunately, his ambition collides with the will of his mother, Eliza Gant, a strong-minded, practical woman who runs a boarding house. She wants to keep Gene at home, under her thumb. And she has little patience with his "scribbling and dreaming." She thinks Gene should work in his father's stone-cutting shop and earn his keep.

Eliza and Gene love each other, but they don't understand each other. The mother's values lie in the realm of money, security; the son's in the realm of creativity and expansiveness. In order to fulfill himself, Gene must work free of this real but oppressive love. The struggle is not an easy one, for Gene is emotionally tied, not only to his mother, but to his exuberant irresponsible father, and to a young woman named Laura. As he breaks these ties and leaves for college, Gene looks back for the lost security of childhood. He reaches for the old loves which are already receding. "I've already forgotten the old faces. I forget the names of people I knew for years. I get their faces mixed. . . . There is something I have lost and can't remember." And he hears his brother's voice answering, "The things you have forgotten and are trying to remember are the child that you were. He's gone, Gene. And will never return. No matter where you search for him, in a million streets, in a thousand cities."

EUGENE: Ben, help me! You must have an answer. Help me, and I won't go searching for it.

BEN'S VOICE: You little fool, what do you want to find out there?

EUGENE: *I want to find the world. Where is the world?*

BEN'S VOICE: The world is nowhere, Gene. . . .

EUGENE: Ben, wait! Answer me!

BEN'S VOICE: The world is nowhere, no one, Gene. *You* are your world.

Gene is left, finally, with himself — a loneliness that is frightening in its actuality but exciting in its potential. When, like Gene, you leave home, and the close circle of your high school friends, you may remember Ben's words, and remember, too, that they are full of promise.

Sara Sheldon

LOOK HOMEWARD, ANGEL

by Ketti Frings

Based on the novel by Thomas Wolfe

CHARACTERS

Eugene Gant
Ben Gant
Helen Gant Barton
Eliza Gant
Will Pentland
The Boarders
Marie "Fatty" Pert
Jake Clatt
Mrs. Clatt
Florry Mangle
Mrs. Snowden
Miss Brown
Laura James
Dr. Maguire
W. O. Gant
Mr. Tarkington
Madame Elizabeth
Luke Gant

SYNOPSIS

The action takes place in the town of Altamont,
North Carolina, in the Fall of 1916

ACT I
Scene I That day
Scene II That evening

ACT II
Scene I A week later
Scene II The next night

ACT III
Two weeks later

ACT I

Scene 1

The Dixieland Boarding House
The house is a flimsily constructed frame house
of fifteen drafty various-sized rooms. It has a
gabled, unplanned, and rambling appearance,
and is painted a dirty yellow. Most of its furni-
ture is badly worn and out of style. The beds are
chipped enamel-covered iron. There are accor-
dian hat trees, cracked mirrors, an occasional
plant. On the typically southern veranda which
embraces the front and one side of the house, there
are chairs, rockers, and a wood box. There is a
sign above the door, electrically lighted at night:
DIXIELAND — ROOM AND BOARD. In the
center of the house, slightly raised, is a turntable
on which all the bedroom scenes are played. At
the back of the house a walk approaches the rear
of the veranda. There is a side door and near it a
circular yard seat. Also down front is a table and
a chair.
The street itself has a feeling of great trees hang-
ing over it. Occasionally during the play the
stillness is broken by the rustle of autumn leaves,
and the poignant wail of a train whistle. The

curtain rises in darkness. After a moment we hear
EUGENE's *voice coming from his room. Seated, his*
back to the audience, he is only partially
glimpsed, writing, surrounded by books.

EUGENE *(Reading):* "Ben, by Eugene Gant. . .
My brother Ben's face is like a piece of slightly
yellow ivory . . .

> (*Lights from up on the veranda where*
> BEN GANT, *30, delicate and sensitive, the*
> *most refined of the* GANTS, *and forever*
> *a stranger among them, is seated on the*
> *front steps reading a newspaper. He is*
> *sometimes scowling and surly, but he is*
> *the hero protector of those he loves,*
> *with quiet authority and a passion for*
> *home which is fundamental. At times*
> *he speaks to the side over his shoulder,*
> *in a peculiar mannerism of speech, as*
> *though he were addressing a familiar*
> *unseen presence.*)

EUGENE: His high, white forehead is knotted
fiercely by an old man's scowl. His mouth is
like a knife. His smile the flicker of light across
the blade. His face is like a blade, and a knife,
and a flicker of light. And when he fastens his
hard white fingers and his scowling eyes upon
a thing he wants to fix, he sniffs with sharp
and private concentration.

> (*Lights reveal* MARIE "FATTY" PERT, *43,*
> *seated near* BEN *in her rocker. She is a*
> *generous, somewhat boozy woman, knit-*
> *ting a pair of men's socks and tenderly*
> *regarding* BEN.)

Thus women looking, feel a well of tenderness for his pointed, bumpy, always scowling face. . . ."

(EUGENE *continues writing*.)

BEN: Somebody's got to drive the Huns from the skies. Poor old England can't be expected to do it alone.

MRS. PERT: It's their mess, isn't it?

BEN: It says here there's an American flying corps forming in Canada.

MRS. PERT: Ben Gant, what are you thinking of?

BEN: All my life in this one little burg, Fatty! Besides getting away, I'd be doing my bit.

MRS. PERT: Would they take you so old?

BEN: This article says eighteen to thirty-two.

MRS. PERT: Aren't the physical standards pretty high?

BEN: Listen to her! I'm in good condition!

MRS. PERT: You're twenty pounds underweight! I never saw anyone like you for not eating.

BEN: Maguire gave me a thorough checkup this spring!

MRS. PERT: How would your family feel, if you went?

BEN: What family? The batty boarders? Apologies, Fatty. I never associate you with them.

Except for Gene, nobody'd know I was gone.
(*Looks up, dreamily*) To fly up there in the
wonderful world of the sky. Up with the angels.

(HELEN GANT BARTON *and her husband*
HUGH *enter from the house.* HELEN *is
gaunt, raw-boned, in middle twenties,
often nervous, intense, irritable, and
abusive, though basically generous, the
hysteria of excitement constantly lurk-
ing in her. It is a spiritual and physical
necessity for her to exhaust herself in
service to others, though her grievances,
especially in her service to her mother,
are many.* HUGH *is a cash register salesman, simple, sweet, extremely warm-
hearted. He carries a tray with a coffee
pot and cups and saucers which* HELEN
*helps him set on the table. They have
been arguing.*)

HUGH: We should never have agreed to live here
for one day — that's the answer. You work yourself to the bone — for what?

HELEN: Mrs. Pert, the other boarders have almost finished dinner!

MRS. PERT: What's the dessert, Helen?

HELEN: Charlotte Russe.

HUGH: They're like children with a tape worm.

BEN: Fatty, I told you you'd better get in there!

MRS. PERT: I was trying to do without, but I'm
afraid that calls me. See you later, Ben.

HELEN: Ben, where is Mama?

BEN: How should I know?

HELEN: I've had to serve the entire dinner alone!

HUGH: Look at me, holes in my socks, a trouser button missing — and before I married you I had the reputation of being "dapper."

HELEN: I bet she's off somewhere with Uncle Will, and *I'm* left in the kitchen to slave for a crowd of old cheap boarders! That's her tactic!

HUGH: "Dapper Hugh Barton" — it said so in the newspaper when we were married.

HELEN (*To* BEN, *who pays no attention*):   You know that, don't you, *don't you?* And do I ever hear her say a word of thanks? Do I get — do I get as much as a go-to-hell for it? No. "Why, pshaw, child," she'll say, "I work more than anybody!" And most time, damn her, she does.

BOARDER: (*Off stage, calling, ringing the service bell*):   Helen! Helen!

HELEN: You come in, Hugh, and help me!
              (HELEN *exits into the house.*)

BEN: How are the cash registers selling, Hugh?

HUGH: Putting the cigar box out of business. I got a good order in Raleigh last week. I've already put away nine hundred dollars toward our own little house.

BEN: You ought to have one, Hugh. You and Helen.

HUGH (*Looking at part of the newspaper*): I guess they don't have to advertise the good jobs do they? The really big jobs . . . they wouldn't be here in the newspaper, would they?

BEN: Why?

HUGH: If there was something good here in town . . . not on the road so much . . . maybe then I could talk Helen into moving away. Ben, you hear things around the paper —

HELEN (*Off*): Hugh! Hugh!

BEN: I'll keep my ears open, Hugh.

HUGH: Well, I guess I don't want to make Helen any madder at me. Thanks, Ben.
> (*Exits inside. An automobile is heard off, driving up, stopping.* BEN *moves down to the yard seat, reads, his newspaper. The car door slams.*)

ELIZA (*Off*): I'll vow I never saw such a man. What little we have got, I've had to fight for tooth and nail, tooth and nail!
> (ELIZA GANT *enters with* WILL PENTLAND, *her brother.* ELIZA, *57, is of Scotch descent, with all the acquisitiveness and fancied premonitions of the Scotch. She is mercurial, with dauntless energy, greed, and love. She has an odd way of talking, pursing her lips, and she characteristically uses her right hand in a*

point-making gesture, fist enclosed, fore-finger extended. These mannerisms are often imitated by those who hate and love her. ELIZA *is carrying some fall leaves and a real estate circular.* WILL *is punchy, successful, secure, a real estate broker. They do not notice* BEN.)

ELIZA: Like the fellow says, there's no fool like an old fool! Of course Mr. Gant's been a fool all his life. Pshaw! If I hadn't kept after him all these years we wouldn't have a stick to call our own.

WILL: You had to have an *artistic* husband.

ELIZA: Artistic. I have my opinion about that. Why, Will, the money that man squanders every year on liquor alone would buy all kinds of good downtown property, to say nothing of paying off this place. We could be well-to-do people now if we'd started at the very beginning.

WILL: You've given him every opportunity.

ELIZA: He's always hated the idea of owning anything — couldn't bear it, he told me once — 'cause of some bad trade he made when he was a young man up in Pennsylvania. If I'd been in the picture then, you can bet your bottom dollar there'd been no loss.

WILL (*Chuckling*):   Or the loss'd been on the other side.

ELIZA: That's a good one! You know us Pent-

lands! Well, I'm going to get after Mr. Gant
right today about that bank offer.

WILL: Let me know when you've warmed him
up enough for me to talk to him.

ELIZA: It'll take a good deal of warming up, I
can tell you. He's so blamed stubborn about
that precious old marble yard, but I'll do it!

WILL: Give me a jingle when you want to look
at that farm property. I'll drive you out there.

ELIZA: Thanks, Will! I appreciate it. (WILL *exits.* ELIZA *starts into the house, sees* BEN.) Ben!
What are you doing home at this hour?

BEN: I'm working afternoons this week.

ELIZA: Oh. (*Somewhat worriedly*) Will you get
dinner downtown?

BEN: I usually do.

ELIZA: You always sound so short with me, Ben.
Why is that? You don't even look at me. You
know I can't stand not being looked at by the
person I'm talking to. Don't you feel well?

BEN: I feel good.
          (*A train whistle is heard in the dis-
          tance.*)

ELIZA: Oh, pshaw, there's the midday train
now! Has Eugene gone to the station?

BEN: How should I know?

ELIZA (*Calling up to* EUGENE's *room*):   Eugene,
are you up in your room? Eugene? (EUGENE

GANT, *hearing his mother's voice, rises from his chair, turns toward the window, but he doesn't answer, and* ELIZA *does not see him.* EUGENE *is 17, the youngest of the* GANTS, *tall, awkward, with a craving for knowledge and love. During the following he leaves his room.*) Eugene! I'll vow, that boy. Just when I need him . . . (*Notices* MRS. PERT's *knitting*) Ben, I hope you haven't been lying around here wasting time with that Mrs. Pert again?

BEN: Listen to her! It's the nicest time I spend.

ELIZA: I tell you what: It doesn't look right, Ben. What must the other boarders think? A woman her age . . . a drinking woman . . . married. Can't you find someone young and pretty and free to be with? I don't understand it. You're the best looking boy I've got.

BEN (*More pleasantly*): If it'll make you feel better, Mama, I'll look around.
(*Relieved by the change in his mood,* ELIZA *smiles. She also notices the sprawled newspaper.*)

ELIZA: That's Mr. Clatt's newspaper. You know he's finicky about reading it first. Fold it up before you go.
(*During the above,* EUGENE *is seen coming down the stairs from his room. Now limping slightly, he starts to sneak out the side door, but* ELIZA *spots him.*)

ELIZA: Eugene, where are you sneaking to? Come out here.

EUGENE (*Comes out*):   Yes, Mama?

ELIZA: The train's just coming in. Now you hurry over to that depot.

EUGENE: Today? I did it yesterday.

ELIZA: Every day until every room is filled. The advertising cards are on the hall table. Go get them. (EUGENE, *disgruntled, goes into the entry hall to get the cards from the small stand.* ELIZA *strips some dead leaves off a plant.*) I declare, seventeen is an impossible age. I don't know why he complains. He hasn't anything else to do. Spending his time up there scribbling, dreaming.

BEN: The other boarding houses send their porters to the trains.

ELIZA: Never you mind, Ben Gant, you used to do it. It's little enough I've ever asked of you boys. (*To* EUGENE *as he comes from the hall*) Have you got the cards?

EUGENE: In my pocket.

ELIZA (*Holding out her hand*):   Let me see them. Let me see them!

EUGENE (*Takes cards from pocket, reads*):   "Stay at Dixieland, Altamont's Homiest Boarding House." — It should be homliest.

ELIZA: Eugene!

EUGENE: I hate drumming up trade! It's deceptive and it's begging.

ELIZA: Oh my . . . my! Dreamer Eugene Gant, what do you think the world is all about?

We are all . . . all of us . . . selling something. Now you get over to the depot right this
minute. And for heaven's sake, boy, spruce up,
shoulders back! Look like you are somebody!
(EUGENE *starts off*.) And smile! Look pleasant!
(EUGENE *grins, maniacly*.)

BEN (*Suddenly, as he watches* EUGENE *limping*):
What are you walking like that for?

EUGENE: Like what?

BEN *(Rises)*:   What are you limping for? My
God, those are my shoes you've got on! I threw
them out yesterday!

ELIZA: They're practically brand new.

BEN: They're too small for *me*, they must be
killing him.

EUGENE: Ben, please!

ELIZA: Maybe you can afford to throw out
brand new shoes.

BEN: Mama, for God's sake, you ask him to
walk straight, how can he? His toes must be
like pretzels!

EUGENE: They're all right. I'll get used to them.

BEN (*Throwing down his paper*):   My God, it's
a damned disgrace, sending him out on the
streets like a hired man . . . . Gene should be
on that train, going to college!

ELIZA: That's enough — that's just enough of
that! You haven't a family to provide for like
I have, Ben Gant. Now I don't want to hear
another word about it! Gene will go to college

when we can afford it. This year he can help his
Papa at the shop.

BEN: I thought you were going to warm up
Papa, so he'll sell the shop.

ELIZA: Ben Gant, that wasn't intended for your
ears. I'd appreciate it if you wouldn't mention
it to Mr. Gant until I have. Hurry off now,
son, get us a customer!

EUGENE: Why should Papa sell his shop?

ELIZA: Now you're too young to worry about my
business. You tend to yours.

EUGENE: What business do I have to attend to,
Mama ?

ELIZA: Well, get busy, get busy! Help your Papa at the shop.

EUGENE: I don't want to be a stonecutter.

ELIZA: Well, go back to delivering newspapers.
Work for Uncle Will in his real estate office.
But keep the ball rolling, child. Now hurry on
or you'll be late!
          (EUGENE *exits.*)

HELEN (*Entering*):   Mama, dinner's practically
over! I'm no slave!

ELIZA: I'll be right in, Helen. (HELEN *exits, slamming door.* ELIZA *sighs. For a moment, left
alone with* BEN, *she becomes herself, a deeply
troubled woman.*) What's the matter with him,
Ben? What's wrong with that boy? What's the
matter with all of you? I certainly don't know.
I tell you what, sometimes I get frightened.

Seems as if every one of you's at the end of something, dissatisfied, and wants something else. But it just can't be. A house divided against itself cannot stand. I'll vow, I don't know what we're all coming to. (*Approaches side door, pauses*) If you like, this once, as long as you're home, why don't you eat here? I'm sure there's plenty left over.

BEN: No thank you, Mama.
(*He starts off.*)

ELIZA: A good hot meal!

BEN: I've got to get over there.

ELIZA: Ben, are you sure you feel all right?

BEN: I feel fine.

ELIZA: Well, have a nice day at the paper, son. (BEN *exits.* ELIZA *looks after him, then hearing the voices of the boarders, exits into the house by the side door. The boarders, ushered by* HELEN, *enter through the front door. They are:* JAKE CLATT, *30, an insensitive boor;* MRS. CLATT, *60,* JAKE'S *mother, with a coarse smile and dyed hair. She is deaf and carries a cane;* FLORRY MANGLE, *29, wistful, humorless, interested in* JAKE; MRS. SNOWDEN, *50, quiet, unobtrusive, lonely;* MISS BROWN, *36, prim on the surface, but with the marks of the amateur prostitute;* MR. FARREL, *60, a retired dancing master, new to* DIXIELAND.)

MRS. CLATT: I ate too much again.

HELEN (*Loudly to* MRS. CLATT):   Help yourself to coffee, please, Mrs. Clatt. I'm short-handed to-day.

MRS. CLATT (*Brandishing her cane at* MR. FARREL, *who is about to sit*): Not there, that's my chair! That one's free, since the school teacher left.

MISS BROWN: You're a teacher too, aren't you, Mr. Farrel?

MR. FARREL: Of the dance. Retired.

MISS BROWN: I hope you'll stay with us for a while. Where are you from?

MR. FARREL: Tampa.

MISS BROWN: Do you know the Castle Walk, Mr. Farrel? I'd love to learn it!
          (*They stroll down to the yard seat.*)

MRS. CLATT: I don't know what Mrs. Gant makes this coffee of. There isn't a bean invented tastes like this.

JAKE: Couldn't you make it for us sometime, Helen?

HELEN: My mother always makes the coffee here.
          (HUGH *and* MRS. PERT *enter. The others seat themselves.*)

MRS. PERT: That was scrumptious dessert, but oh dear!
          (*Sits in her rocker*)

JAKE: Yes, it was good, if only the servings were bigger.

MRS. CLATT: I'm told the best boarding house food in town is down the street at Mrs. Haskells'.

JAKE: That's right, mother. That's what I heard.

HUGH: Then move in to Mrs. Haskells'!

HELEN (*With a shove*): Hugh!
(*She exits.*)

MISS MANGLE: I spent one season there, but I prefer it here. It's more informal and entertaining.

JAKE: Not lately. It's been over a month since Mrs. Gant had to have Mr. Molasses Edwards and his two Dixie Ramblers evicted for not paying their rent. She certainly loves to see the police swarm around!
(LAURA JAMES, *23, carrying a suitcase and a* DIXIELAND *advertising card, enters. She is attractive, but not beautiful. She advances to the steps.*)

MISS MANGLE: Don't you?

JAKE: I like excitement — why shouldn't I?

MISS MANGLE: Other people's excitement. Don't you ever want excitement of your own? I do.
(MRS. CLATT *sees* LAURA, *nudges her son into attention*)

LAURA: Good afternoon!

HUGH (*Crosses to her*): Good afternoon!

LAURA: Is the proprietor here?

HUGH: I'll call her. (*Calls inside*) Mrs. Gant!
Customer! (*To* LAURA) Please come right up.

JAKE (*Leaping to* LAURA):   Here, let me take that
suitcase. It must be heavy for you.

LAURA: Thank you.

> (JAKE *takes* LAURA's *suitcase. The other
> boarders look her over, whisper.* ELIZA,
> *wearing an apron, places some leaves in
> a vase on the hall table, enters. At first
> raking glance she doubts that* LAURA,
> *so young and different, is a true
> prospect.*)

ELIZA: Yes?

LAURA: Are you the proprietor?

ELIZA: Mrs. Eliza Gant — that's right.

LAURA: I found this card on the sidewalk.

ELIZA (*Takes card*):   On the sidewalk! And
you're looking for a room?

LAURA: If you have one for me.

ELIZA: Of course I have, dear — a nice quiet
room. You just sit down here and have yourself a cup of my *good* coffee, while I go and
open it up, so I can show it to you. Hugh, you
take care of the young lady. This is Mr. Barton, my son-in-law.

LAURA: How do you do, Mr. Barton? I'm Laura
James.

ELIZA: Laura — why that's a good Scotch name.
Are you Scotch?

LAURA: On one side.

ELIZA: Pshaw! I could have told you were
Scotch the minute I laid eyes on you. I'm
Scotch too. Well, isn't that nice? (*Makes intro-
ductions*) Miss James, Mr. Clatt . . . (*Each
acknowledges the introduction according to
personality.*) . . . his mother, Mrs. Clatt, Mrs.
Snowden, Miss Mangle, Mr. Farrel, (*Disap-
provingly notices* MISS BROWN *with* MR. FAR-
REL.) . . . Miss Brown . . . *Miss* Brown!
And Mrs. Pert. Where do you come from,
dear?

LAURA: I live in Richmond.
            (MISS BROWN *and* MR. FARREL *exit, prac-
            ticing the Castle Walk, eventually reap-
            pear at the rear of the veranda.*)

ELIZA: Richmond! Now that's a pleasant city
— but hot! Not like it is here, cool and refresh-
ing in these hills. You haven't come to Altamont for a cure, have you dear?

LAURA: I'm healthy, if that's what you mean.
But I've been working hard and I need a rest.
            (HUGH *approaches with coffee.*)

ELIZA: Here's your coffee.

LAURA (*Takes coffee*):   Thank you, Mr. Barton.
What are your rates, Mrs. Gant?

EUGENE (*Off*):   Mama! Mama!
            (EUGENE *runs up the back walk, around
            the veranda.*)

ELIZA: Suppose I show you the room first.

EUGENE: Mama!

ELIZA: I declare, that child either crawls like a snail or speeds like a fire engine. . . .

EUGENE (*Pulls* ELIZA *away from the others*): Can I speak to you, Mama?

ELIZA: I don't see you limping *now*, when you're not trying to get sympathy. Don't think I don't know your little tricks to . . .

EUGENE (*Urgently*): Mama, Papa's been at Laughran's again. Doctor Maguire is trying to steer him home now.

ELIZA (*Momentarily stabbed*): The doctor? Is he sick or is he drunk?

EUGENE: He's rip roaring! He's awful. He kicked Uncle Will again!
> (*From offstage come the sounds of a small riot approaching. The occasional bull yell of* GANT, *children chanting "Old Man Gant came home drunk," a dog barking, etc.*)

ELIZA (*Weakly*): I don't think I can stand it again. A *new* young lady, too. (EUGENE *turns to see* LAURA, *who, with the other boarders, has heard the approaching* GANT.) Oh Eugene, why do they keep bringing him home? Take him to a state institution, throw him in the gutter, I don't care. I don't know what to do any more. What'll I do, child?

EUGENE: At least it's been a month this time.

GANT (*Off*):   Mountain Grills! Stay away from me!

JAKE CLATT: My God, Mr. Gant's on the loose again!

MISS MANGLE: Oh dear, oh dear —

MRS. CLATT: What? What is it?

JAKE CLATT (*Shouting*):   The old boy's on the loose again!

EUGENE (*Crossing up to the boarders*):   Would you go inside, all of you, please?

MRS. CLATT: I haven't finished my coffee.

EUGENE: You can wait in the parlor. Please, just until we get him upstairs!

JAKE CLATT: And miss the show?

MISS BROWN: Come along, Mr. Farrel. Let's clear the deck for the old geezer.

MR. FARREL: Perhaps there is some way I can help?

MISS BROWN: I wouldn't recommend it, Mr. Farrel.

JAKE CLATT: Look at him, he's really got a snootful this time!

> (EUGENE *urges several of the boarders inside, where they cram in the hallway,* JAKE *and* MRS. CLATT *remain on the porch.* LAURA, *not knowing where to go, remains with* HUGH *outside.*)

GANT (*Bellowing, off*):   Mountain Grills! Moun-

tain Grills! Fiends, not friends! Don't push
me! *Get away from me!*

DOCTOR MAGUIRE (*Off*):   All right then, Gant, if
you can walk, walk!
> (ELIZA *stands downstage, stiff and
> straight.* W. O. GANT, *60, clatters up the
> back steps, his arms flailing, his power-
> ful frame staggering, reeling. At heart
> he is a far wanderer and a minstrel, but
> he has degraded his life with libertinism
> and drink. In him still, though, there is
> a monstrous fumbling for life. He is ac-
> companied by* DR. MAGUIRE, *unkempt
> but kind, and by* TARKINGTON, *a dis-
> reputable crony, also drunk but navi-
> gating, and by* WILL PENTLAND.)

DR. MAGUIRE: Here we are, Gant, let's go in the
back way.
> (GANT *pushes the doctor aside, plunges
> headlong along the veranda, scattering
> rockers, flower pots, etc.*)

GANT: Where are you? Where are you? The
lowest of the low — boarding house swine!
Merciful God, what a travesty! That it should
come to this!

EUGENE: Papa, come on. Papa, please!
> (EUGENE *tries to take* GANT *by the arm;*
> GANT *flings him aside.*)

GANT (*With a sweeping gesture*):
"Waken lords and ladies gay
On the mountain dawns the day —"

Don't let me disturb your little tete-a-tete. Go
right ahead, help yourself! (MRS. CLATT *screams
and dashes into the hall.*) Another helping of
mashed potatoes, Mrs. Clatt? Put another tire
around your middle —

> (EUGENE *tries to catch his father's flail-
> ing arms, is flung into* MRS. PERT'S
> *rocker.*)

ELIZA: Mr. Gant, I'd be ashamed. I'd be
ashamed.

GANT: Who speaks?

ELIZA: I thought you were sick.

GANT: I am not sick, madame, I am in a wild,
blind fury.

> (*Raises a chair aloft, threatening* ELIZA.
> EUGENE *and the* DOCTOR *grab it away
> from him.*)

ELIZA: Dr. Maguire, get him in the house.

DR. MAGUIRE: Come on, Gant, let me help you.

GANT (*Plunging down the steps*): Just one moment! You don't think I know my own home
when I see it? This is not where I live. I reside
at *92 Woodson Street.*

DR. MAGUIRE: That was some years ago. This is
your home now, Gant.

GANT: This barn? This damnable, this awful,
this murderous and bloody barn — home? Holy
hell, what a travesty on nature!

WILL: Why don't we carry him in?

DR. MAGUIRE: You keep out of this, Pentland.
You're the one who enrages him.

GANT: Pentland — now that's a name for you!
(*Pivots, searching for him*) You're a Mountain
Grill! Your father was a Mountain Grill and
a horse thief, and he was hanged in the public
square.
      (*While* HUGH *holds* GANT, EUGENE *brings
a cup of coffee.*)

EUGENE: Papa, wouldn't you like some coffee?
There's some right here.

GANT: Hah! Some of Mrs. Gant's *good* coffee?
(*He kicks at the coffee cup.*) Ahh! I'll take some
of that *good* bourbon, if you have it, son.

DR. MAGUIRE: Get him a drink! Maybe he'll pass
out.

GANT: Drink!
      (EUGENE *starts into the house.*)

ELIZA: Gene! Dr. Maguire, you know there isn't
a drop of alcohol in this house!

LAURA: I have some. (*As all stare at her,* LAURA
*quickly opens her handbag, takes from it a
small vial, crosses to the doctor.*) I always carry
it in case of a train accident.

GANT: Well, what are we waiting for, let's have
it!

DR. MAGUIRE (*Taking the vial*):   Good God, this
won't fill one of his teeth.

GANT (*Roars*):   Well, let's have it!
      (LAURA *backs away in fear.* HELEN *en-*

*ters, the joy of being needed shining on
her face.*)

DR. MAGUIRE: You can have it, Gant, but you'll
have to come up onto the veranda to drink
it —

GANT: Mountain Grills! Vipers! Lowest of the
low! I'll stand here until you take me home.
Isn't anybody going to take me home?

HELEN: Papa! Why have you been drinking
again when you know what it does to you?

GANT (*Weakens, leans against her*): Helen — I
have a pain right here.

HELEN: Of course you do. Come with me now.
I'll put you to bed, and bring you some soup.
(HELEN *takes the huge man's arm, leads
him toward the veranda.* HELEN's *suc-
cess with* GANT *etches itself deeply into*
ELIZA's *face.*)

GANT: Got to sit down — (*Sits on edge of veranda*) Sit down, Helen, you and me. Sit and
talk. Would you like to hear some Keats . . .
beautiful Keats?

ELIZA (*Crossing up to veranda, angrily*): He's
got his audience now. That's all he wants.

EUGENE: Mama, he's sick!

ELIZA: Mr. Gant, if you feel so bad, why don't
you act nice and go inside! The whole neighborhood's watching you.

GANT (*Wildly sings*): "Old Man Gant came

home drunk . . . (TARKINGTON *joins him.*) Old
Man Gant came home drunk. . . ."

TARKINGTON (*Singing, waving his arms*): "Old
Man Gant came home. . ."
(*His joy fades as he see* ELIZA *glaring at
him.*)

ELIZA: Were you drinking with him too, Mr.
Tarkington?

TARKINGTON: Sev-ereal of us were, Mrs. Gant, I
regret to say.

ELIZA (*Pulling* TARKINGTON *to his feet*): I'll have
Tim Laughran thrown in jail for this.

TARKINGTON: He started out so peaceable
like. . . .

ELIZA (*Pushing him toward rear exit of veranda*): I warned him for the last time.

TARKINGTON: Just on beer!

ELIZA: *Get off my premises!*
(TARKINGTON *exits.* GANT *groans.*)

HELEN: Dr. Maguire's here to give you something for your pain, Papa.

GANT: Doctors! Thieves and bloodsuckers!
"The paths of glory lead but to the grave." —
Gray's Elegy. Only four cents a letter on any
tombstone you choose, by the master carver!
Any orders? (*Groans, weak with pain*) It's the
devil's own pitchfork. Don't let them put me
under the knife — promise me, daughter. Promise me!

(HELEN *nods. With a giant effort,* GANT *pulls himself up.*)

GANT: "Over the stones, rattle his bones! He's only a beggar that nobody owns."

MAGUIRE: Good God, he's on his feet again!

EUGENE: Hugh, let's get him in the house.

GANT (*Throwing off* HUGH *and* EUGENE): I see it! Do you see the Dark Man's shadow? There! There he stands — the Grim Reaper — as I always knew he would. So you've come at last to take the old man home? Jesus, have mercy on my soul!

> (GANT *falls to the ground. There is an agonized silence.* EUGENE, THE DOCTOR, *and* HUGH *rush to him.*)

ELIZA (*Anxiously*): Dr. Maguire?

> (DR. MAGUIRE *feels* GANT'*s heart.*)

MAGUIRE: He's just pased out, Mrs. Gant, Men, let's carry him up!

> (HUGH, WILL, MAGUIRE, *and* EUGENE, *lift the heavy body, quickly carry* GANT *inside.* HELEN *follows.* ELIZA, *saddened and miserable, starts to gather up the coffee cups.* LAURA *picks up her suitcase and starts off.* ELIZA *turns, sees her.*)

ELIZA: Oh, Miss James. I was going to show you that room, wasn't I?

> (*Seizes* LAURA'*s suitcase*)

LAURA: Hmmmmm?

ELIZA: I think you'll enjoy it here. It's quiet and peaceful — oh, nobody pays any mind to Mr.

Gant. I'll tell you what; we don't have occur-
rences like this every day.

LAURA: Well, how much is it?

ELIZA: Twenty — fifteen dollars a week. Three
meals a day, and the use of electricity and the
bath. Do you want me to show it to you?

LAURA: No, I'm sure it will be all right.

ELIZA (*Starting in, turns back*):   That's in advance, that is.

> (LAURA *opens her purse, takes out a roll
> of dollar bills, puts them one by one in-
> to* ELIZA's *outstretched hand.*)

LAURA: One, two, three — I always keep my
money in one dollar bills — it feels like it's
more.

ELIZA (*Almost cheerful again*):   Oh, I know what
you mean.

> (MR. FARREL *enters by the side door
> with his suitcase. He is hoping to sneak
> out.*)

ELIZA (*Sees him as the paying business continues*):   Mr. Farrel! Where are you going? Mr.
Farrel, you've paid for a week in advance!

> (MR. FARREL *wordlessly gestures that it's
> all too much for him, exits.*)

ELIZA: Well, they come and they go. And you're
here now, isn't that nice?

LAURA: . . . Nine . . . . ten . . .

> (BEN *enters from the other direction,
> hurriedly.*)

BEN: I heard about father — how is he?

ELIZA: Drunk. Dr. Maguire's taking care of him now. Ben, this is Miss James . . . this is my son, Ben Gant.

BEN (*Impressed by her looks, nods*):   Miss James.

LAURA (*Barely looking at* BEN, *nods*):   — fourteen, fifteen. There.

ELIZA (*Puts the money in bosom of her dress*): Thank you dear. Miss James is going to stay with us awhile, we hope! I'll take you up, dear. You'll be cozy and comfortable here. (*They start inside.*) I'll show you the rest of the house later.

LAURA (*Turning in doorway*):   Nice to have met you, Mr. Gant.
            (ELIZA *and* LAURA *exit.*)

BEN (*Imitating* LAURA's *disinterest, as he picks up cup of coffee*):   Nice to have met you, Mr. Gant.
            (*Shrugs, drinks coffee.* WILL *enters from the house, still sweating.*)

WILL: That father of yours. Do you know he kicked me? I don't want to tell you where. Why don't you watch out for him more, Ben? It's up to you boys, for your mother's sake — for Dixieland. I warned her about him . . . a born wanderer like he is, and a widower. But you can't advise women — not when it comes to love and sex. (*He starts off, stops.*) You might thank me for my help. No one else has.

BEN: Thank you, Uncle Will.

WILL: Bunch of ungrateful Gants. You're the only one of them who has any class.
(WILL *exits.* BEN *lights a cigarette.* EUGENE *enters.*)

EUGENE: Did you hear about it, Ben?

BEN: There isn't a soul in town who hasn't.

EUGENE: What's it all about? It doesn't make sense. Can you figure it out, Ben? Why does he do it?

BEN: How should I know? (*Drinks his coffee*) Is Maguire almost through?

EUGENE (*Hurt, not understanding* BEN'*s preoccupation*): Ben, remember in the morning when we used to walk together and you were teaching me the paper route? We talked a lot then.

BEN: Listen to him ! We're talking.

EUGENE: If he hates it so much here, why does he stay?

BEN: You stupid little fool, it's like being caught in a photograph. Your face is there, and no matter how hard you try, how are you going to step out of a photograph? (DOCTOR MAGUIRE *enters.*) Shut up now, will you. Hello, Doc.

DR. MAGUIRE: Your sister sure can handle that old goat like a lamb! The funny thing though is that people like him. He's a good man, when sober.

BEN: Is he all right?

DR. MAGUIRE: He's going to be.

BEN: Can I speak to you a minute about me? If you have a minute.

DR. MAGUIRE: Shoot, Ben.

BEN (*To* EUGENE): Haven't you got something else to do?

EUGENE (*Seating himself*): No.

DR. MAGUIRE: What's the matter — you got pyorrhea of the toenails, or is it something more private?

BEN: I'm tired of pushing daisies here. I want to push them somewhere else.

DR. MAGUIRE: What's that supposed to mean?

BEN: I suppose you've heard there's a war going on in Europe? I've decided to enlist in Canada.

EUGENE (*Rises*): What do you want to do that for?

BEN (*To* EUGENE): You keep out of this.

DR. MAGUIRE: It is a good question, Ben. Do you want to save the world? This world?

BEN: In Christ's name, Maguire, you'll recommend me, won't you? You examined me just a couple of months ago.

DR. MAGUIRE (*Puts down his bag*): Well, let's see, for a war the requirements are somewhat different. Stick out your chest. (BEN *does so;*

THE DOCTOR *looks him over*.) Feet? Good arch, but pigeon-toed.

BEN: Since when do you need toes to shoot a gun?

DR. MAGUIRE: How're your teeth, son?

BEN: Aren't you overdoing it, Doc?
                (BEN *draws back his lips and shows
                two rows of hard white grinders. Un-
                expectedly*, MAGUIRE *prods* BEN's *solar
                plexis with a strong yellow finger and*
                BEN's *distended chest collapses. He sinks
                to the veranda edge, coughing*.)

EUGENE: What did you do that for?

DR. MAGUIRE: They'll have to save this world without you, Ben.

BEN *(Rises, grabs* THE DOCTOR*)*:   What do you mean?

DR. MAGUIRE: That's all. That's all.

BEN: You're saying I'm not all right?

DR. MAGUIRE: Who said you weren't all right?

BEN: Quit your kidding.

DR. MAGUIRE: What's the rush? We may get into this war ourselves before too long. Wait a bit. (*To* EUGENE) Isn't that right, son?

BEN: I want to know. Am I all right or not?

DR. MAGUIRE: Yes, Ben, you're all right. Why, you're one of the most all right people I know. *(Carefully, as he feels* BEN's *arms)* You're a little run down, that's all. You need some meat on those bones. (BEN *breaks from him, moves away*.) You can't exist with a cup of coffee in one hand and a cigarette in the other. Besides the Altamont air is good for you. Stick around. Big breaths, Ben, big breaths.

> (*Picks up his bag*)

BEN: Thanks. As a doctor, you're a fine first baseman.

DR. MAGUIRE: Take it easy. Try not to care too much.

> (*Exits*)

EUGENE: He's right. You should try to look after yourself more, Ben.

> (EUGENE *tries to comfort* BEN. BEN *avoids his touch, lurches away*.)

BEN: He doesn't have any spirit about this war, that's all that's the matter with him.

> (BEN *recovers his coffee, drinks.* EUGENE *studies him.*)

EUGENE: I didn't know you wanted to get away from here so badly.

BEN (*Looks over at* EUGENE, *puts down coffee*): Come here, you little bum. (EUGENE *approaches close.*) My God, haven't you got a clean shirt? (*He gets out some money.*) Here, take this and go get that damn long hair cut off, and get some shoes that fit, for God's sake. You look like a lousy tramp. . . .

EUGENE (*Backing away*): Ben, I can't keep taking money from you.

BEN: What else have you got me for? (*The brothers roughhouse playfully with the money,* EUGENE *giggling. Then, with sudden intense ferocity,* BEN *seizes* EUGENE's *arms, shakes him.*) You listen to me. Listen to me. You go to college, understand? Don't settle for anyone or anything — learn your lesson from me! I'm a hack on a hick paper — I'll never be anything else. You can be. Get money out of them, anyway you can! Beg it, take it, steal it, but get it from them somehow. Get it and get away from them. To hell with them all! (BEN *coughs.* EUGENE *tries to help him.* BEN *escapes, sits tiredly on the veranda's edge.* EUGENE *disconsolately sinks into a nearby chair.*) Neither Luke, nor Stevie, nor I made it. But you can, Gene. I let her hold on and hold on until it was too late. Don't let that happen to you. And Gene, don't try to please everyone — please yourself. (BEN *studies* EUGENE, *realizes his confusion and depression. Then, noticing* LAURA's *hat which she has left on the yard table, he points to it.*) Where's she from?

EUGENE (*Follows* BEN's *gaze to* LAURA's *hat, picks it up, sniffs it*): I don't know. I don't even know her name.

BEN: Miss James. I'll have to announce her arrival in my society column. (*Takes hat from* EUGENE, *admires it*) The firm young line of spring . . . budding, tender, virginal. "Like something swift, with wings, which hovers in a wood — among the feathery trees, suspected, but uncaught, unseen." Exquisite. (*Returns hat to table, rises*) Want to walk downtown with me? I'll buy you a cup of mocha.

EUGENE: Maybe I ought to stay here.

BEN (*Ruffling* EUGENE'*s hair*):   With her around I don't blame you. I dream of elegant women myself, all the time.

EUGENE (*Rising*):   You do? But, Ben, if you dream of elegant women, how is it . . . well —

BEN: Mrs. Pert? Fatty's a happy woman — there's no pain in her she feels she has to unload onto someone else. Besides, she's as adorable as a duck. Don't you think so?

EUGENE: I guess you're right. I like her — myself . . . sure.

BEN: Someday you'll find out what it means. I've got to get back to work.

EUGENE: Ben, I'm glad they won't take you in Canada.

BEN (*With that upward glance*):   Listen to him! I was crazy to think of going. I have to bring you up first, don't I?
>   (BEN *exits.* EUGENE *walks about restlessly, looks up at* LAURA'*s window.* MISS BROWN, *dressed for a stroll, carrying a parasol, enters from the house.*)

MISS BROWN: Gene! You haven't even said hello to me today.

EUGENE: Hello, Miss Brown.

MISS BROWN: My, everything's quiet again. Lovely warm day, isn't it?

> (MISS BROWN *sings and dances sensu-*
> *ously for* EUGENE.)

"Pony boy, pony boy,
Won't you be my pony boy?
Don't say no, can't we go
Right across the plains?

> (MISS BROWN *approaches* EUGENE; *he*
> *backs away from her, stumbling against*
> *table.*)

Marry me, carry me
Far away with you!

> (*She starts out through rear veranda.*)

Giddy-ap, giddy-ap, giddy-ap. Oh!
My pony boy!"

> (MISS BROWN *exits.* EUGENE *sits on the*
> *yard seat, takes off one shoe and rubs*
> *his aching toes.* LAURA *enters, picks up*
> *her hat, sees* EUGENE. EUGENE *hides his*
> *shoeless foot.*)

MISS BROWN (*Off stage, fainter*):
Mmmm, mmm, mmmm—Mmmmm,
   mmmm, mmmm,
Marry me, carry me
Far away with you!
Giddy-ap, giddy-ap, giddy-ap. Oh!
My pony boy."

> (*At the door,* LAURA *looks again at*
> EUGENE, *smiles, exits.*)

                 Curtain

ACT I

Scene 2

The Dixieland Boarding House
   The night is sensuous, warm. A light storm is threatening. Long, swaying tree shadows project themselves on the house. Seated on the side veranda are JAKE, MRS. CLATT, FLORRY, MISS BROWN, *and* MRS. SNOWDEN. MRS. PERT *is seated in her rocker,* BEN *on the steps beside her. They are drinking beer.* MRS. PERT *measures the socks she is knitting against* BEN's *shoe.* JAKE CLATT *softly plays the ukelele and sings.* EUGENE *is sitting on the side door steps, lonely, yearning.*

JAKE (*Singing*):
   "K-k-katy, K-k-katy" (*etc.*)
        (*As* JAKE *finishes,* FLORRY *gently applauds.* JAKE *starts softly strumming something else.*)

MRS. PERT (*To* BEN, *quietly*): I know you talked to the doctor today. What did he say? Tell Fatty.

BEN: I'm out before I'm in. Oh, I know you're pleased, but you don't know how it feels to be

47

the weakling. All the other members of this
family — they're steers, mountain goats, eagles.
Except father, lately — unless he's drunk. Do
you know, though, I still think of him as I
thought of him as a little boy — a Titan! The
house on Woodson Street that he built for
Mama with his own hands, the great armloads
of food he carried home . . . the giant fires he
used to build. The women he loved at Madame
Elizabeth's. Two or three a night, I heard.

MRS. PERT: It's nice for parents to have their
children think of them as they were young.
(*As* BEN *chuckles*) I mean, that's the way I'd
like my children to think of me. Oh, you know
what I mean.

BEN (*Laughs with his typical glance upward*):
Listen to her!

MRS. PERT: Ben, who are you always talking to,
like that?
    (*Imitates* BEN *looking up over his
    shoulder*)

BEN: Who, him? (*She nods.*) That's Grover, my
twin. It was a habit I got into, while he was
still alive.

MRS. PERT: I wish you'd known me when I was
young. I was some different.

BEN: I bet you weren't half as nice and warm
and round as you are now.

MRS. PERT: Ben, don't ever let your mother hear
you say those things. What could she think?

BEN: Who cares what she thinks?

MRS. PERT: Dear, I only hope when the right girl comes along you won't be sorry for the affection you've lavished on me.

BEN: I don't want the *right girl*. Like some more beer? I've got another bottle.

MRS. PERT: Love some more, honey.
                (BEN *rises, searches under the yard table for the bottle he has hidden, realizes it's not there, suspiciously looks at* EUGENE. EUGENE *innocently gestures, then reaches behind him and tosses the beer bottle to* BEN. BEN *and* FATTY *laugh.* BEN *returns with the beer to* FATTY *as* LAURA *enters from the house.*)

JAKE (*Rising expectantly*):   Good evening, Miss James.

LAURA: Good evening.

JAKE: Won't you sit down?

MRS. CLATT (*As* LAURA *seems about to choose a chair*):   That's Mr. Farrel's. Your's is back there!

JAKE (*Loudly*):   Mr. Farrel has left, Mother.

MRS. CLATT: What?

JAKE: Never mind. (*To* LAURA) No sense in being formal. Won't you sing with me, Miss James?

LAURA: I love music, but I have no talent for it.

(LAURA *moves toward rear of veranda,
away from the others.*)

FLORRY (*To* JAKE): I love to sing.

(JAKE *ignores* FLORRY, *follows after*
LAURA, FLORRY *tugging at* JAKE's *coat.*)

MRS. SNOWDEN (*To* JAKE *as he passes*): Do you
know "Indiana Lullaby"? It's a lovely song.

(JAKE *and* LAURA *exit.*)

BEN: I'm comfortable when I'm with you, Fatty.

MRS. PERT: That's good, so'm I.

BEN: People don't understand. Jelly roll isn't
everything, is it?

MRS. PERT: Ben Gant, what kind of a vulgar
phrase is that?

BEN: It's a Stumptown word. I used to deliver
papers there. Sometimes those Negro women
don't have money to pay their bill, so they pay
you in jelly roll.

MRS. PERT: Ben — your little brother's right over
there listening!

BEN (*Glances toward* EUGENE): Gene knows all
about jelly roll, don't you? Where do you
think he's been all his life — in Mama's front
parlor?

EUGENE: Oh, come on, Ben!

BEN (*Laughs*): There's another word I remember in the eighth grade. We had a thin, anxious
looking teacher. The boys had a poem about
her.

(*Quotes*)
"Old Miss Groody
Has good Toody."

FATTY: Ben, stop it!
(*They both laugh.* LAURA *has managed to lose* JAKE, *and has strolled around the back of the house. She enters to* EUGENE *from the side door.*)

LAURA: Good evening.

EUGENE: What!

LAURA: I said good evening.

EUGENE (*Flustered*): Goodyado.

LAURA: I beg your pardon?

EUGENE: I mean — I meant to say good evening, how do you do?

LAURA: Goodyado! I like that much better. (*They shake hands,* LAURA *reacting to* EUGENE's *giant grip.*) Don't you think that funny?

EUGENE (*Sits on yard seat*): It's about as funny as most things I do.

LAURA: May I sit down?

EUGENE (*Leaping up*): Please.

LAURA (*As they both sit*): I'm Laura James.

EUGENE: I know. My name's Eugene Gant.

LAURA: You know, I've seen you before.

EUGENE: Yes, earlier this afternoon.

LAURA: I mean before that. I saw you throw those advertising cards in the gutter.

EUGENE: You did?

LAURA: I was coming from the station. You know where the train crosses the street? You were just staring at it. I walked right by you and smiled at you. I never got such a snub before in my whole life. My, you must be crazy about trains.

EUGENE: You stood right beside me? Where are you from?

LAURA: Richmond, Virginia.

EUGENE: Richmond! That's a big city, isn't it?

LAURA: It's pretty big.

EUGENE: How many people?

LAURA: Oh, about a hundred and twenty thousand, I'd say.

EUGENE: Are there a lot of pretty parks and boulevards?

LAURA: Oh yes . . .

EUGENE: And fine tall buildings, with elevators?

LAURA: Yes, it's quite a metropolis.

EUGENE: Theatres and things like that?

LAURA: A lot of good shows come to Richmond. Are you interested in shows?

EUGENE: You have a big library. Did you know it has over a hundred thousand books in it?

LAURA: No, I didn't know that.

EUGENE: Well, it does. I read that somewhere. It would take a long time to read a hundred thousands books, wouldn't it?

LAURA: Yes, it would.

EUGENE: I figure about twenty years. How many books do they let you take out at one time?

LAURA: I really don't know.

EUGENE: They only let you take out two here!

LAURA: That's too bad.

EUGENE: You have some great colleges in Virginia. Did you know that William and Mary is the second oldest college in the country?

LAURA: Is it? What's the oldest?

EUGENE: Harvard! I'd like to study there. First Chapel Hill. That's our state university. Then Harvard. I'd like to study all over the world, learn all its languages. I love words, don't you?

LAURA: Yes, yes, I do.

EUGENE: Are you laughing at me?

LAURA:. Of course not.

EUGENE: Are you smiling a lot!

LAURA: I'm smiling because I'm enjoying my self. I like talking to you.

EUGENE: I like talking to you, too. I always talk better with older people.

LAURA: Oh!

EUGENE;   They know so much more.

LAURA: Like me?

EUGENE: Yes. You're very interesting.

LAURA: Am I?

EUGENE: Oh yes! You're very interesting! (JAKE
CLATT *approaches,* FLORRY MANGLE *hovering
anxiously on the veranda.*)

JAKE CLATT: Miss James?

LAURA: Yes, Mr. Platt?

JAKE CLATT: Clatt.

LAURA: Clatt.

JAKE CLATT: Jake Clatt! It's a lovely evening.
Would you like to take a stroll?

LAURA: It feels to me like it's going to rain.

JAKE CLATT (*Looking at the sky*):   Oh, I don't
know.

EUGENE (*Rising, moving in between* LAURA *and*
JAKE):   It's going to rain, all right.

JAKE CLATT: Oh, I wouldn't be so sure!

LAURA: Perhaps some other time, Mr. Clatt.

JAKE   CLATT: Certainly. Good night, Miss
James. Good night, sonny. (EUGENE *glares after* JAKE, *who returns to the veranda. The
other boarders have disappeared.* JAKE *and*
FLORRY *exit.* FATTY *and* BEN *still sit on the*

steps. A train whistle moans mournfully in
the distance. EUGENE *cocks an ear, listens.)*

LAURA: You do like trains, don't you?

EUGENE: Mama took us on one to St. Louis to
the Fair, when I was only five. Have you ever
touched one?

LAURA: What?

EUGENE: A locomotive. Have you put your
hand on one? You have to feel things to fully
understand them.

LAURA: Aren't they rather hot?

EUGENE: Even a cold one, standing in a station
yard. You know what you feel? You feel the
shining steel rails under it . . . and the rails
send a message right into your hand — a message of all the mountains that engine ever
passed — all the flowing rivers, the forests, the
towns, all the houses, the people, the washlines
flapping in the fresh cool breeze — the beauty
of the people in the way they live and the way
they work — a farmer waving from his field, a
kid from the school yard — the faraway places
it roars through at night, places you don't
even know, can hardly imagine. Do you believe
it? You feel the rhythm of a whole life, a whole
country clicking through your hand.

LAURA (*Impressed*):   I'm not sure we all would.
I believe you do.

> (*There is a moment while* LAURA *looks*
> *at* EUGENE. BEN *moves up to the veranda*
> *and the phonograph, plays the record*

"Genevieve." EUGENE *and* LAURA *speak simultaneously.*)

EUGENE: How long do you plan to . . .

LAURA: How old are you . . . ?

EUGENE: I'm sorry — please.
(*Draws a chair close to* LAURA, *straddles it, facing her*)

LAURA: No, you.

EUGENE: How long do you plan to stay here, Miss James?

LAURA: My name is Laura. I wish you'd call me that.

EUGENE: Laura. It's a lovely name. Do you know what it means?

LAURA: No.

EUGENE: I read a book once on the meaning of names. Laura is the laurel. The Greek symbol of victory.

LAURA: Victory. Maybe someday I'll live up to that (*After a second*) What does Eugene mean?

EUGENE: Oh, I forget.

LAURA: You, forget?

EUGENE: It means "well born."

LAURA: How old are you?

EUGENE: Why?

LAURA: I'm always curious about people's ages.

EUGENE: So am I. How old are you?

LAURA: I'm twenty-one. You?

EUGENE: Nineteen. Will you be staying here long?

LAURA: I don't know exactly.

EUGENE: You're only twenty-one?

LAURA: How old did you think I was?

EUGENE: Oh, about that. About twenty-one, I'd say. That's not old at all!

LAURA (*Laughs*):   I don't feel it is!

EUGENE: I was afraid you might think I was too young for you to waste time with like this!

LAURA: I don't think nineteen is young at all!

EUGENE: It isn't, really, is it?

LAURA: Gene, if we keep rushing together like this, we're going to have a collision.

> (LAURA *rises, moves away from* EUGENE. *He follows her. They sit together on the side steps, reaching with whispers toward each other. The turntable revolves, removing* EUGENE's *room and revealing* GANT's *room.*)

FATTY: Ben, what's your full name?

BEN: Benjamin Harrison Gant. Why?

FATTY: I thought Ben was short for benign.

BEN: Benign! Listen to her!
        (*They laugh. The lights come up in*
        GANT's *bedroom.* ELIZA, *carrying a
        pitcher and a glass, enters.* GANT *is in
        bed, turned away from her.*)

GANT: Helen?

ELIZA (*Bitterly*):   No it's not Helen, Mr. Gant.
        (*Pours a glass of water*)

GANT (*Without turning*):   If that's water, take
    it away.

ELIZA: Why aren't you asleep? Do you have any
    pain?

GANT: None but the everyday pain of thinking.
    You wouldn't know what this is.

ELIZA: I wouldn't know?
        (*She starts picking up* GANT's *strewn
        clothing.*)

GANT: How could you? You're always so busy
    puttering.

ELIZA: All the work I do around here, and you
    call it puttering?

GANT: Some people are doers, some are thinkers.

ELIZA: Somebody has to do, Mr. Gant. Some-
    body has to. Oh! I know you look on yourself
    as some kind of artist fella — but personally, a
    man who has to be brought maudlin through
    the streets — screaming curses — if you call that
    artistic!

GANT: The hell hound is at it again. Shut up, woman!

ELIZA: Mr. Gant, I came in here to see if there was something I could do for you. Only pity in my heart. Now will you please turn over and look at me when I talk to you? You know I can't stand being turned away from!

GANT: You're a bloody monster, you would drink my heart's blood!

ELIZA: You don't mean that — we've come this far together, I guess we can continue to the end. You know I was thinking only this morning about that first day we met. Do you realize it was thirty-one years ago, come July?

GANT (*Groaning*):   Merciful God, thirty-one long miserable years.

ELIZA: I can remember like it was yesterday. I'd just come down from Cousin Sally's and I passed by your shop and there you were. I'll vow you looked as big as one of your tombstones — and as dusty — with a wild and danger-ous look in your eye. You were romantic in those days — like the fellow says, a regular courtin' fool — "Miss Pentland," you said, "you have come into this hot and grubby shop like a cooling, summer shower — like a cooling, summer shower." That's just what you said!

GANT: And you've been a wet blanket ever since.

ELIZA: I forgive you your little jokes, Mr. Gant. I forgive your little jokes.

(*Sits beside him, finds needle and thread
under her collar, mends his dressing
gown*)

GANT: Do you? (*Slowly turns and looks at her
finally*) Do you ever forgive me, Eliza? If I
could make you understand something. I was
such a strong man. I was dozing just now,
dreaming of the past. The far past. The people and the place I came from. Those great
barns of Pennsylvania. The order, the thrift,
the plenty. It all started out so right, there.
There I was, a man who set out to get order
and position in life. And what have I come to?
Only rioting and confusion, searching and
wandering. There was so much before, so
much. Now it's all closing in. My God, Eliza,
where has it all gone? Why am I here, now, at
the rag end of my life? The years are all blotted
and blurred — my youth a red waste — I've got-
ten old, an old man. But why here? Why here?

ELIZA: You belong here, Mr. Gant, that's why!
You belong here.
(*She touches his hand.*)

GANT (*Throws away her hand*):   And as I get
weaker and weaker, you get stronger and
stronger!

ELIZA: Pshaw! If you feel that way, it's because
you have no position in life. If you'd ever listened to me once, things would have been different. You didn't believe me, did you, when I
told you that little, old marble shop of yours
would be worth a fortune someday? Will and

I happened to be downtown this morning . . .
(GANT *groans*.) . . . and old Mr. Beecham
from the bank stopped us on the street and he
said, "Mrs. Gant, the bank is looking for a site
to build a big new office building, and do you
know the one we have our eye on?" And I said,
"No." "We have our eye on Mr. Gant's shop,
and we're willing to pay twenty thousand dollars for it!" Now, what do you think of that?

GANT: And you came in here with only pity in
your heart!

ELIZA: Well, I'll tell you what, twenty thousand dollars is a lot of money! Like the fellow
says, "It ain't hay!"

GANT: And my angel, my Carrara angel? You
were going to sell her too?

ELIZA: The angel, the angel, the angel. I'm so
tired of hearing about that angel!

GANT: You always have been. Money dribbled
from your honeyed lips, but never a word
about my angel. I've started twenty pieces of
marble trying to capture her. But my life's
work doesn't interest you.

ELIZA: If you haven't been able to do it in all
these years, don't you think your gift as a stonecutter may be limited?

GANT: Yes, Mrs. Gant, it may be limited. It
may be limited.

ELIZA: Then why don't you sell the shop? We
can pay off the mortgage at Dixieland and
and then just set back big as you please and

live off the income from the boarders the rest of
our lives!

GANT (*Furious, he all but leaps from the bed.*):
Oh holy hell! Wow-ee! The boarders! That
parade of incognito pimps and prostitutes,
calling themselves penniless dancing masters,
pining windows, part-time teachers, and God
knows what all. Woman, have mercy! That
shop is my last refuge on earth. I beg you —
let me die in peace! You won't have long to
wait. You can do what you please with it after
I've gone. But give me a little comfort now.
And leave me my work! At least my first wife
understood what it meant to me. (*He sentimentally seeks the plump pillow.*) Cynthia, Cynthia . . .

ELIZA (*Coldly*): You promised me you would
never mention her name to me again. (*There
is a long silence.* ELIZA *bites the sewing thread.*)
Mr. Gant, I guess I never will understand you.
I guess that's just the way it is. Good night.
Try to get some sleep. (*She rises, tucks the bed
clothes about him.*) I reckon it's like the fellow
says, some people never get to understand each
other — not in this life.

　　　(ELIZA *exits, stands outside* GANT's *door,
　　　trying to pull herself together.*)

GANT (*Moans*): Oh-h-h, I curse the day I was
given life by that blood-thirsty monster up
above. Oh-h-h, Jesus! I beg of you. I know
I've been bad. Forgive me. Have mercy and pity
upon me. Give me another chance in Jesus'
name. . . . Oh-h-h!

(*The turntable removes* GANT's *room replacing it with* EUGENE's *room. Lights come up on the veranda.* LAURA *and* EU-GENE *still sit on the side steps.* FATTY *and* BEN, *as earlier, seated, are softly laughing.* ELIZA, *bitterly warped by her scene with* GANT, *enters. She starts gathering up the boarders' coffee cups and saucers.*)

MRS. PERT (*A little giddy*): Why, if it isn't Mrs. Gant! Why don't you sit down and join us for awhile?

ELIZA (*Her sweeping glance takes in the beer glasses.*): I've told you before, Mrs. Pert, I don't tolerate drinking at Dixieland!

BEN: Oh, Mama, for God's sake . . .

ELIZA (*Angrily turns off the phonograph*): You two can be heard all over the house with your carrying on.

BEN: Carrying on — listen to her!

ELIZA: You're keeping the boarders awake.

BEN: They just went in!

ELIZA: As I came past your door just now, Mrs. Pert, there was a light under it. If you're going to spend all night out here, there's no sense in wasting electricity.

BEN: The Lord said "Let there be light," even if it's only 40 watts.

ELIZA: Don't you get on your high horse with

me, Ben Gant. You're not the one who has to
pay the bills! If you did, you'd laugh out of
the other side of your mouth. I don't like any
such talk. You've squandered every penny
you've ever earned because you've never known
the value of a dollar!

BEN: The value of a dollar! (*Rises, goes into
hall to get his jacket*) Oh, what the hell's the
use of it anyway? Come on, Fatty, let's go for a
stroll.

FATTY (*Rises*):   Whatever you say, Ben, old
Fatty's willing.

ELIZA (*Attacking* MRS. PERT):   I don't want
any butt-ins from you, do you understand?
You're just a paying boarder here. That's all.
You're not a member of my family, and never
will be, no matter what low methods you try!

EUGENE (*Leaving* LAURA, *miserable*):   Mama,
please!

ELIZA (*To* EUGENE):   I'm only trying to keep
decency and order here, and this is the thanks I
get! You should all get down on your knees
and be grateful to me!

BEN (*Coming out of hall, slamming the screen
door*):   What am I supposed to be grateful
for? For what?

FATTY (*Trying to stop it*):   Ben, Ben, come on.

BEN: For selling the house that papa built with
his own hands and moving us into this drafty
barn where we share our roof, our food, our

pleasures, our privacy so that you can be Queen Bee? Is that what I'm supposed to be grateful for?

ELIZA (*Picks up bottle and glasses*): It's that vile liquor that's talking!

EUGENE: Let's stop it! For God's sake, let's stop it! Mama, go to bed, please. Ben . . .
>   (EUGENE *sees that* LAURA *has exited into the house. He frantically looks after her.*)

BEN: Look at your kid there! You've had him out on the streets since he was eight years old — collecting bottles, selling papers — anything that would bring in a penny.

ELIZA: Gene is old enough to earn his keep!

BEN: Then he's old enough for you to let go of him! But no, you'd rather hang on to him like a piece of property! Maybe he'll grow in value, you can turn a quick trade on him, make a profit on him. He isn't a son, he's an investment! You're so penny-mad that —
>   (*Shifting the bottles and glasses into one hand,* ELIZA *slaps* BEN. *There is a long silence. They stare at each other.*)

BEN: Come on, Fatty.
>   (BEN *exits, past* FATTY, *down the street.*)

FATTY: He didn't mean it, Mrs. Gant. (*She follows* BEN.) Ben? Ben, wait for Fatty!
>   (*A moment's pause*)

EUGENE (*Quietly, miserably*):   Mama. Mama. Mama!

ELIZA: Well, she puts him up to it! He never
used to talk to me like that. You stood right
there and saw it. Now I'll just ask you: Was it
my fault? Well, was it?

EUGENE (*Looks after* LAURA):   Mama, Mama, in
God's name go to bed, won't you? Just go to
bed and forget about it, won't you?

ELIZA: All of you. Every single one of you. Your
father, then Ben, now you . . . you all blame
me. And not one of you has any idea, any idea
. . . you don't know what I've had to put up
with all these years.

EUGENE: Oh Mama, stop! Please stop!

ELIZA (*Sinking onto the steps*):   I've done the
best I could. I've done the best I could. Your
father's never given me a moment's peace. Nobody knows what I've been through with him.
Nobody knows, child, nobody knows.

EUGENE (*Sits beside her*):   I know, Mama. I do
know. Forget about it! It's all right.

ELIZA: You just can't realize. You don't know
what a day like this does to me. Ben and I used
to be so close — especially after little Grover
died. I don't think a mother and son were ever
closer. You don't remember when he was a
youngster, the little notes he was always writing me. I'd find them slipped under my door,
when he got up early to go on his paper route
. . . "Good   morning,   Mama!" . . . "Have
a nice day, Mama. . . ." We were so close. . . .

EUGENE: It's late. You're tired.

ELIZA (*Managing to pull herself together, rises*): Well, like the fellow says, it's no use crying over that spilt milk. I have all those napkins and towels to iron for tomorrow.

EUGENE   (*Rises, looking toward* LAURA'*s room*): The boarders can get along without new napkins tomorrow, Mama. Why don't you get some sleep?

ELIZA: Well, I tell you what: I'm not going to spend my life slaving away here for a bunch of boarders. They needn't think it. I'm going to sit back and take things as easy as any of them. One of these days you may just find us Gants living in a big house in Doak Park. I've got the lot — the best lot out there. I made the trade with old Mr. Doak himself the other day. What about that? (*She laughs.*) He said, "Mrs. Gant, I can't trust any of my agents with you. If I'm to make anything on this deal, I've got to look out. You're the sharpest trader in this town!" "Why, pshaw, Mr. Doak," I said (I never let on I believed him or anything), "all I want is a fair return on my investment. I believe in everyone making his profit and giving the other fellow a chance. Keep the ball a-rolling," I said, laughing as big as you please! (*She laughs again in recollection.*) "You're the sharpest trader in this town." That's exactly his words. Oh, dear. (EUGENE *joins her laughter.*) Well . . . I'd

better get at those napkins. Are you coming in,
child ?

EUGENE (*Looks toward* LAURA's *room*): In a
little while.

ELIZA: Don't forget to turn off the sign. Goodnight, son. (EUGENE *turns to* ELIZA. *She kisses
him.*) Get a good night's sleep, boy. You
mustn't neglect your health.
        (*She starts in.*)

EUGENE: Don't work too late.
        (EUGENE *starts toward the side door.*)

ELIZA: Gene, you know where Sunset Terrace
runs up the hill? At the top of the rise? Right
above Dick Webster's place. That's my lot.
You know where I mean, don't you?

EUGENE: Yes, Mama.

ELIZA: And that's where we'll build — right on
the very top. I tell you what, though, in another five years that lot'll bring twice the value.
You mark my words!

EUGENE: Yes, Mama. Now, for God's sake, go
and finish your work so you can get to sleep!

ELIZA: No sir, they needn't think I'm going to
slave away all my life. I've got plans, same as
the next fellow! You'll see. (*Off stage, the
church chimes start to sound the midnight
hour.*) Well, good night, son.

EUGENE: Good night, Mama . . . (ELIZA *exits.*
EUGENE *calls with desperate softness.*) Laura

. . . Laura!! (*Gives up, turns away.* LAURA *enters through the side door.* EUGENE *turns, sees her.*) Did you hear all that? I'm sorry, Laura.

LAURA: What's there to be sorry about?

EUGENE: Would you like to take a walk?

LAURA: It's a lovely evening.

EUGENE: It might rain.

LAURA: I love the rain.
(EUGENE *and* LAURA *hold out their hands to each other.* EUGENE *approaches her, takes her hand. They go off together. For a moment the stage is silent.* ELIZA *enters with an envelope in her hand.*)

ELIZA: See, looky here — I made a map of it. Sunset Terrace goes . . . (*She looks around.*) Gene? Eugene? (*She looks up toward* EUGENE's *room.*) Gene, I asked you to turn out the sign! That boy. I don't know what I'm going to do with him. (ELIZA *goes into the hall, turns out the sign, and stands for a moment. Offstage, a passerby is whistling "Genvieve."* ELIZA *comes down to the edge of the veranda and looks out into the night in the direction taken by* BEN *and* FATTY.) Ben? Ben?

Slow Curtain

ACT II

Scene 1

Gant's Marble Yard and Shop
A week later.

Under a high, wide shed is the sign: W. O.
GANT — STONE CARVER. *The shed is on a back
street, behind the town square. In the distance
can be seen the outline of Dixieland. Inside the
shed are slabs of marble and granite and some
finished monuments . . . an urn, a couchant
lamb, and several angels. The largest and most
prominent monument is a delicately carved angel
of a lustrous white Carrara marble, with an especially beautiful smiling countenance. There is
a cutting area down stage right, protected from
the sun by a shade, where* EUGENE, *wearing one of
his father's aprons, is discovered operating a ped-
alled emery wheel. At the other side of the shed is
an office with grimy desk, a telephone, and a
curtain into another room beyond. A sidewalk
runs between the shed and a picket fence up
stage. Near the office is a stone seat, bearing the
inscription,* "Rest here in peace."

ELIZA *enters from the street. The prim shabbi-
ness of her dress is in contrast to her energetic
mood and walk.*

ELIZA (*Crosses to office, calls inside*):   Mr. Gant! Mr. Gant!

EUGENE (*Stops wheel, calls*):   Papa's not here now, Mama.

ELIZA (*Approaches* EUGENE *just as he accidently blows some marble dust in her face*):Where is he? Gene, you know I can't stand that marble dust — will you step out here where I can talk to you? (*As* EUGENE *ambles out to her*) Besides, I can't stand not to see the face I'm talking to. My goodness, spruce up, boy — how many times do I have to tell you? Shoulders back — like you *are* somebody. And smile, look pleasant. (EUGENE *gives that idiotic grin.*) Oh, pshaw! I hope your father's not over at you-know-where again.

EUGENE: He went to buy a newspaper for the obituaries.

ELIZA: How enterprising of him! But he won't follow up on it. Oh no, he says it's ghoulish to contact the bereaved ones right off. I declare, tombstones are no business anyway, anymore — in this day and age people die too slowly. (*Sinks onto stone seat, leans back, for a brief instant seems actually to rest*) I tell you what, this feels good. I wish I had as much time as some folks and could sit outside and enjoy the air. (*Observes* EUGENE, *looking at her dress as he works lettering a marble slab*) What are you looking at? I don't have a rent, do I?

EUGENE: I was just noticing you have on your dealing and bargaining costume again.

ELIZA: Eugene Gant, whatever do you mean by that? Don't I look all right? Heaven knows, I always try to look neatly respectable.

EUGENE: Come on, Mama.

ELIZA: What! I declare! I might have a better dress than this, but law's sake, there's some places it don't pay to advertise it! Oh, Gene, you're smart, smart, I tell you! You've got a future ahead of you, child.

EUGENE: Mama, what kind of a future have I got if I can't get an education?

ELIZA: Pshaw, boy, you'll get your education if my plans work out! I'll tell you what though — in the meantime, it wouldn't hurt you to work in Uncle Will's office, would it?

EUGENE: I don't know anything about real estate, Mama.

ELIZA: What do you have to know? Buying and selling is an instinct, and you've got it. You've got my eye for looking and seeing and remembering, and that's what's important. Why, there isn't a vital statistic about a soul in Altamont I don't carry right in my head. What they make, what they owe — what they're hiding, what they show! (*She laughs, enjoying her cleverness.*) You see, Eugene, I'm a poet, too — "a poet and I don't know it, but my feet show it — they're longfellows!" (*She leans back, chuckles.*) Oh dear, I can't get a smile out of you this morning. You've been so strange all this last week. (*Rises, slaps him on the back*) Gene, stand with your shoulders back. If you go humped over, you'll get lung trouble sure as you're born. (*Moves upstage, looks toward the town center where she presumes* GANT *is*) That's one thing about your papa: he always carried himself straight as a rod. Of course, he's not as straight now as he used to be — Gene, *what* in the world are you standing on one foot and then the other for? Do you have to go to the bathroom?

EUGENE: Mama! Asking me that at my age!

ELIZA: Then why are you fidgeting? It's not often we have a nice chance to chat like this.

EUGENE: Papa's paying me thirty cents an hour!

ELIZA: Paying you? How did you manage that?

EUGENE: I told him I needed the money.

ELIZA: For heaven's sake, what for? You've got your room and board.

EUGENE: Don't you think I need new clothes for one thing?

ELIZA: Pshaw! The way you're still growing? It doesn't pay. (*She purses her lips, looks at him significantly.*) Has my baby gone and got himself a girl?

EUGENE: What of it? What if it were true? Haven't I as much right as anyone?

ELIZA: Pshaw! You're too young to think of girls, especially that Miss James. She's practically a mature woman compared to you. I don't think you realize how young you are, just because you're tall and read a lot of books. (*Sound of car.* ELIZA *looks off.*) Pshaw! That's your Uncle Will come for me. Say, how long does it take your father to buy a news-paper, anyway?

EUGENE: He said he'd be right back. Is it something important?

ELIZA: Oh, I've got plans, Gene, plans for him, plans for all of us. Well, tell him I'll be back. Second thought, don't tell him, I'll just catch him. I want you to be here too. Work hard, child!

> (ELIZA *exits, the car leaves.* EUGENE *approaches the Carrara angel, touches the draped folds over her breast.* GANT *enters, watches, smiling. He has had a few beers, but he is not drunk.* EUGENE *becomes aware of his father's presence, starts guiltily.*)

GANT: I've done that myself many a time, son. Many a time. Well, what did your mother have to say?

EUGENE: Did you see her?

GANT: I've been sitting over at Laughran's waiting for her to leave. What a longwinded bag!

EUGENE: You promised the doctor you wouldn't go to Laughran's.

GANT (*Putting on his apron*):   What difference does it make? A couple of beers won't hurt what I've got. Was that Will Pentland she went off with?

EUGENE: Yes.

GANT: Aha! And she said she'd be back?

EUGENE: Yes.

GANT: I have a mind what she's up to. She'll be back with freshly drawn up papers tucked in her bosom. Yes, when you touch the breast of Miss Eliza, you feel the sharp crackle of bills of sale, not like the bosom of this angel. She begins to look better after a bath, doesn't she? I've been neglecting her lately. My, how she gleams!

EUGENE (*Sits below angel*): Papa, you were young when you got married, weren't you?

GANT: What?

EUGENE: When did you get married?

GANT: It was thirty-one bitter years ago when your mother first came wriggling around that corner at me like a snake on her belly. . . .

EUGENE: I don't mean Mama. How old were you when you were first married? To Cynthia ?

GANT: By God, you better not let your mother hear you say that name!

EUGENE: I want to know . . . how old were you?

GANT: Well, I must have been twenty-eight. Ah, Cynthia, Cynthia.

EUGENE: You loved her, didn't you, Papa?

GANT: She had a real glowing beauty. Sweet, noble, proud, and yet soft, soft — she died in her bloom.

EUGENE: She was older than you, wasn't she?

GANT: Yes. Ten years.

EUGENE: Ten years! But it didn't make any difference, did it?

GANT (*Confidingly*):   She was a skinny, mean, tubercular old hag who nearly drove me out of my mind!

EUGENE (*Shocked*):   Then why do you talk about her the way you do? To Mama?

GANT: Because I'm a bastard, Gene. I'm a bastard! (LAURA *enters, carrying a picnic basket, her mood somewhat restless.*) Say, isn't this a pretty little somebody looking for you?

EUGENE: Laura!

LAURA: Hello, Mr. Gant.

GANT: Hello!

LAURA: Hello, Gene. So this is your shop!

GANT: This is a real pleasure. It's not often I see *smiling* people around here. Haven't you got fed up with our little resort, young lady?

LAURA: I'm really just beginning to enjoy it here.

GANT: What do you find to enjoy about it?

LAURA: Oh, the countryside is beautiful. Gene and I have had lots of pleasant walks in the hills.

GANT: Oh, so it's Gene who makes it pleasant for you, hey?

EUGENE (*Taking off his apron*): Papa!

GANT: You're fond of Gene, aren't you?

LAURA: He's very nice and intelligent.

GANT: Gene's a good boy — our best.

LAURA (*Looking around*): My, isn't this place interesting? How did you happen to become a stonecutter, Mr. Gant?

> (EUGENE studies LAURA during this, sensing her evasiveness.)

GANT: Well, I guess you'd call it a passion with some people. When I was a boy Gene's age, I happened to pass a shop something like this. (*Of the angel*) And this very angel was there. She's Carrara marble, from Italy. And as I looked at her smiling face, I felt, more than anything in the world, I wanted to carve delicately with a chisel. It was as though, if I could do that, I could bring something of me out onto a piece of marble. Oh, the reminiscences of the old always bore the young.

LAURA: No, they don't.

GANT: So I walked into that shop, and asked the stonecutter if I could become an apprentice. Well, I worked there for five years. When I left, I bought the angel. (*He looks at the angel with longing.*) I've hardly had her out of my sight since. I bet I've started twenty pieces of marble, but I've never been able to capture her . . . I guess there's no use trying anymore. . . .

> (*He becomes silent, morose. Sensitively,* EUGENE *touches his father's shoulder, looks at* LAURA.)

EUGENE: Would you like to look around, Laura?

LAURA: I'm afraid I'm bothering you at your work.

GANT (*Looks at* EUGENE, *coming out of his distant thought and mood*): No, no. Show her about, Gene. (*Suddenly, decisive*) I have some other things I must do. . . . (*Starts toward office, pauses*) — though some people find looking at tombstones depressing. Still, we all come to them in the end.
(GANT *exits.*)

EUGENE: Why do you think you might be bothering me?

LAURA: You are supposed to be working.

EUGENE: You came here to see me. What's happened, Laura? Something's different today.

LAURA: Oh, don't pay any attention to me. I just . . . I don't know.

EUGENE: What's in the basket?

LAURA: I asked Helen to pack us a picnic lunch.

EUGENE: Good! Let's go!

LAURA (*Puts basket on marble slab*): Not now.

EUGENE (*Puts his arm around her*): What is it, Laura? What's the matter? Have I done something wrong?

LAURA (*Shakes her head*): Gene, Helen knows about us! And your father too.

EUGENE: I don't care — I want the whole world to know. (*Picks up basket*) Here, let's go.

LAURA: No. Let's not talk about it. (*Sits on stool, near slab*) This is pretty marble. Where's it from?

EUGENE: Laura, you don't give a damn where that marble came from!

LAURA (*Starts to cry*): Oh, Gene, I'm so ashamed, so ashamed.

EUGENE (*Sits beside her on slab*): Laura, my darling, what is it?

LAURA: Gene, I lied to you — I'm twenty-three years old.

EUGENE: Is that all?

LAURA: You're not nineteen either. You're seventeen.

EUGENE: I'm a thousand years old, all the love I've stored up for you.
　　　(*Again puts his arms around her*)

LAURA (*Struggling away*): I'm an older woman. . . .

EUGENE: In God's name, what does that have to do with us?

LAURA: There have to be rules!

EUGENE: Rules are made by jealous people. They make rules to love by so even those with no talent for it can at least pretend. We don't need rules. We don't have to pretend. Oh, Laura, my sweet, what we have is so beautiful,

so rare .... how often in life can you find
it?

LAURA (*Escaping his arms, rises*): Eugene,
you're a young boy, a whole world just waiting for you.

EUGENE: You are my world, Laura. You always
will be. Don't let anything destroy us. Don't
leave me alone. I've always been alone.

LAURA: It's what you want, dear. It's what
you'll always want. You couldn't stand anything else. You'd get so tired of me. You'll forget — you'll forget.

EUGENE: I'll never forget. I won't live long
enough. (*Takes her in his arms, kisses her*)
Will you forget?

LAURA (*As he holds her*):   Oh my darling, every
word, every touch, how could I?

EUGENE: Then nothing has changed. Has it?
Has it?

MADAME ELIZABETH'S VOICE (*Off*):   Good morning!

> (MADAME ELIZABETH, *38, the town ma-
> dame, enters along the street. She is well
> clad, carries herself stylishly. She sees* EU-
> GENE *and* LAURA, *stops.* EUGENE *and*
> LAURA *break from each other.*)

EUGENE: Good morning, Madame Elizabeth.

MADAME ELIZABETH: Is Mr. Gant here?

EUGENE: He's inside.

MADAME ELIZABETH: Well, don't let me keep you from what you're doing. (*Approaches office, calls*) Mr. Gant!
> (LAURA *and* EUGENE *exit into yard.* GANT, *changed into a better pair of trousers, tying his tie, enters.*)

GANT: Elizabeth, my dear Elizabeth! Well, this is a surprise!
> (*Seizes her hand*)

MADAME ELIZABETH (*Sentimentally looking him over*):   Six years, W.O. Six years — except to nod to. Time, what a thief you are.

GANT: He hasn't stolen from you — you're still as handsome and stylish as ever. Won't you sit down?

MADAME ELIZABETH: Oh, W.O. — you and your gallant manners. But I'm no chicken anymore, and no one knows it better than I do. If you only knew how often we talk about you up on Eagle Crescent. What a man you were! Wild! Bacchus himself. You remember the song you used to sing?

GANT: Life was many songs in those days, Elizabeth.

MADAME ELIZABETH: But when you got liquored up enough — don't you remember? Of course I can't boom it out like you do.
> (*Sings, imitating* GANT. GANT *joins her.*)

"Up in that back room, boys,
Up in that back room,
All those kisses and those hugs,

Among the fleas and bugs.
In the evening's gloom, boys,
I pity your sad doom,
Up in that back room, boys,
Up in that back room."

> (*They both laugh.* GANT *gives her an affectionate fanny clap.*)

GANT: The loss of all that — that's the worst, Elizabeth.

MADAME ELIZABETH (*Sitting on the bench*): Oh, W.O., W.O.! We do miss you.

GANT (*Joining her on the bench*): How are all the girls, Elizabeth?

MADAME ELIZABETH (*Suddenly distressed*): That's what I came to see you about. I lost one of them last night.

> (*Takes handkerchief from her pocket, quietly cries into it*)

GANT: Oh. I'm sorry to hear that.

MADAME ELIZABETH: Sick only three days. I'd have done anything in the world for her. A doctor and two trained nurses by her all the time.

GANT: Too bad. Too bad. Which one was it?

MADAME ELIZABETH: Since your time, W.O. We called her Lily.

GANT: Tch . . . tch . . . tch. Lily.

MADAME ELIZABETH: I couldn't have loved her more if she had been my own daughter.

Twenty-two, a child, a mere child. And not a relative who would do anything for her. Her mother died when she was thirteen, and her father is a mean old bastard who wouldn't even come to her deathbed.

GANT: He will be punished.

MADAME ELIZABETH: As sure as there's a God in heaven — the old bastard! I hope he rots! Such a fine girl, such a bright future for her. She had more opportunities than I ever had — and you know what I've done here. I'm a rich woman today, W.O. Why, not even your wife owns more property than I do. I beg your pardon — I hope you don't mind my speaking of her — (GANT *gestures to go right ahead.*) Mrs. Gant and I both understand that property is what makes a person hold one's head up! And Lily could have had all that too. Poor Lily! No one knows how much I'll miss her.

    (*A moment's quiet.* GANT *is respecting her grief.*)

GANT: I suppose you'll be wanting something for her grave? (*As* MADAME ELIZABETH *nods, he rises.*) Here's a sweet lamb . . . . *couchant* lamb, it's called. *Couchant* means lying down in French. That should be appropriate.

MADAME ELIZABETH: No, I've already made up my mind. . . . (*Rises, moves toward the Carrara angel*) I want that angel.

GANT: You don't want *her* Elizabeth. Why, she's a white elephant. Nobody can afford to buy her!

MADAME ELIZABETH: I can and I want her.

GANT: My dear Elizabeth, I have other fine angels. What about this one? My own carving.

MADAME ELIZABETH: No. Ever since I first saw that angel, I thought, when somebody who means something to me goes, she's going to be on the grave.

GANT: That angel's not for sale, Elizabeth.

MADAME ELIZABETH: Then why should you have her out here?

GANT: The truth is, I've promised her to someone.

MADAME ELIZABETH: I'll buy her from whoever you promised and give them a profit. Cash on the line. Who did you sell it to?

GANT: My dear Madame Elizabeth. Here is a nice expensive Egyptian urn. Your beloved Lily would like that.

MADAME ELIZABETH: Egyptian urns — pah! I want the angel!

GANT (*With growing intensity*):   It's not for sale! Anything you like . . . *everything* you like . . . I'll give it to you. . . . I'll make you a present, for old times' sake. But not my angel!

MADAME ELIZABETH: Now let's not waste any more time over this. How much, W.O.?

GANT: She's a Carrara marble from Italy, and too good for any whore! (*He calls.*) Eugene . . . Eugene!

MADAME ELIZABETH (*Furious*): Why you old libertine, how dare you speak to me like that?

EUGENE (*Entering, with* LAURA): What is it, father? What's the matter?

MADAME ELIZABETH: Your father's a stubborn old nut, that's what!

GANT (*Crosses toward office, turns*): I'm sorry if I've offended you.

MADAME ELIZABETH: You have, W.O., deeply!

GANT: Gene, will you be so kind and see if you can wait upon the Madame?
　　　　(*Exits into the inner room of the office.*)

MADAME ELIZABETH: I've heard the trouble your mother has with the old terror — now I believe it! All I'm asking is that he sells that angel — for one of my dear girls who's gone — a dear, young girl in the flower of her life . . . (*Of* LAURA) . . . like this young girl here.

EUGENE: Madame Elizabeth, I believe Papa is saving that angel for his own grave.

MADAME ELIZABETH (*Sits on bench*): Oh-h-h, why didn't he say so? Why didn't he tell me? Poor, poor W.O. Well, of course in that case . . . (*She partially recovers. To* LAURA) If you were to think of your death, dear — if you can, I mean, and we never know, we never know — is there something here that would appeal to you?

LAURA (*Looks around*): I like the little lamb.

MADAME ELIZABETH: Lambs are for children, aren't they?

EUGENE (*Stoops behind lamb*):   Lambs are for anybody. Put your hand on it. Feel it. (*He takes* MADAME ELIZABETH's *hand, strokes it across the lamb*.) Isn't it cool and content and restful? And you could have a poem engraved on the base.

MADAME ELIZABETH: A poem . . .

EUGENE: Let's see if we can find something you'd like. (*Picks up book*) Here's a book of Fifty Fine Memorial Poems. (MADAME ELIZABETH *still strokes the lamb*. EUGENE *finds a poem*.) See if you like this. . . .
(*Reads*)

"She went away in beauty's flower,
Before her youth was spent;
Ere life and love had lived their hour,
God called her and she went."
           (MADAME ELIZABETH *sobs*.)
"Yet whispers faith upon the wind;
No grief to her was given.
She left your love and went to find
A greater one in heaven."

MADAME ELIZABETH (*Quoting, through her heart-felt tears*):
"She left *your* love and went to find
A greater one in heaven. . . . ."
           (*Rises, addresses* EUGENE)

I hope you never lose someone you love, boy. Well, let me know when the little lying down lamb is ready.

(*She nods with majestic dignity to* LAURA, *exits.* WILL *and* ELIZA *enter, look off in the direction taken by* MADAME ELIZABETH.)

ELIZA: Don't stare after her, Will! You know who that is. (*To* EUGENE) Was that shameless woman here to see your father?

EUGENE: One of the girls at Eagle Crescent died. She bought a monument.

ELIZA: Oh she did! She bought one! Well, your father certainly has to deal with all kinds of people. Will, go in and tell Mr. Gant that we're here. (WILL *exits.* ELIZA *looks at* LAURA.) Oh, Miss James! It's five minutes to dinner time at Dixieland, and you know the rules about being late.

EUGENE (*Crosses to pick up basket*):   Laura and I are going on a picnic.

ELIZA: Not now you're not. (*To* LAURA) My dear, I want to talk privately to Mr. Gant — to Eugene, too, and I've asked Ben to join us.

EUGENE: We've made plans, Mama.

ELIZA: Son, this is a family conference.

LAURA: Gene, please — I'll wait for you over at Woodruff's. Please.

(LAURA *and* EUGENE *stroll off, whispering.* WILL *enters from office, paring his nails.*)

ELIZA: Is he in there?

WILL: He's there. We've got him cornered.
(*They chuckle.*)

BEN (*Looking feverish and ill, enters*):   Hello,
Uncle Will. Hello, Mama — you look like you
just swallowed fifty or a hundred acres. What
did you buy today?

ELIZA: Now, Ben, it happens that today we're
selling — I hope we are anyway.

BEN: What's it all about?

ELIZA: You just sit down there. I may not need
you, but I want you to be here.

BEN (*Sits beneath the angel*):   I hope it won't
take long.
> (GANT *enters. He wears a coat of care-
> fully brushed black wool, tie, and carries
> his hat which he leaves just inside the
> office.*)

GANT: Good morning, Miss Eliza.

ELIZA: My, how elegant! Aren't we burning a
river this morning?

GANT: I heard you were out here, Miss Eliza.
I so seldom have a visit from you!
> (*He gestures the tribute.*)

ELIZA: That's most gracious. You may all sit
down now. Gene! Will! (EUGENE *enters, sits.*
WILL *sits on office step.* GANT *moves a chair
center.*) Now, Mr. Gant. . .

GANT (*As he sits*):   This isn't one of your temperance meetings?

ELIZA (*A bit surprised*):   Our private temperance
   problem — that's a part of it, yes. Mr. Gant,
   how old are you?

GANT: I've lost track.

ELIZA: You're sixty years old in December. And
   if Dr. Maguire were here, he could tell
   you . . . .

GANT: I've heard what Doc Maguire has to tell
   me. I shouldn't be lifting these marbles. I
   shouldn't be drinking liquor. I should take a
   nice, long rest.

ELIZA: Then you save me a great deal of argu-
   ment about that. Now, Gene . . .

EUGENE: Yes, Mama?

ELIZA: You want to go to college, don't you?

EUGENE: Very much.

ELIZA: Well, I figure that four years at Chapel
   Hill will cost thirty-four hundred dollars —
   but of course you'll have to wait on tables.
   Otherwise it would be forty-four hundred dollars, which is ridiculous — at the moment we
   don't even have thirty-four hundred dollars.

GANT: Oh, for God's sake, get to the point, Miss
   Eliza. Have you got the papers from the bank?

ELIZA (*Stands in front of him*):   Why, what do
   you mean, what papers?

GANT: You know what I mean. Fish for them,
   woman! (*Pointing to her bosom*) Go ahead,
   fish for them.

(ELIZA *turns her back, from her bosom
fishes out a large envelope.* GANT *laughs,
a roaring bitter laugh, leaps up to*
EUGENE, *who joins the laughter.*)

ELIZA (*Angrily*):   What in the world are you
two hyenas laughing at?

GANT: Oh, as you would say, Miss Eliza, that's a
good one, that's a *good* one.

ELIZA: Well, I am glad to see you in a *good
mood*.

GANT: So the bank wants this little old lot, here?
That's what you told me, didn't you? Though
I can't for the life of me see why?

WILL: There's a new business street going
through here in a few months.

GANT: Let me see the check.

ELIZA (*Takes check from envelope, hands it to
him*):   Well, its for twenty thousand dollars.
Will had to guarantee it personally for me to
bring it here. Did you ever see anything like it.
Two-zero-comma,   zero-zero-zero-decimal-zero-
zero!

GANT: W. O. Gant. It seems to be in good order
all right.

ELIZA: Well, it is — and Will's looked over this
deed, and it's all in order too, isn't it, Will?
(*Hands the deed to* GANT) Give me your pen,
Will.

WILL (*Hands* ELIZA *the pen*):   And I just had it
filled.

GANT (*Examining the deed*): This fine print . . . I really do need glasses.

ELIZA (*Puts pen on work table*): You can trust Will. He's been all over it, Mr. Gant!

GANT (*Looks at angel*): What about the marble stock and the monuments?

ELIZA: They're not included.

EUGENE: Papa — the years you've spent here . . . all your fine work. Please don't give it up!

ELIZA: Now, Gene, your father knows what he's doing.

EUGENE: But he's such a fine stonecutter!

GANT: You think my work is fine, son?

EUGENE: Isn't it, Ben?
(GANT *crosses down right into the marble yard, looking about.*)

ELIZA: Your father knows his duty to all of us — and to himself.

EUGENE: There isn't a cemetery in the state that isn't filled with his work — you can always recognize it. Clean, and pure, and beautiful. Why should he give it up?

ELIZA: Why, law, I don't say he should give it up entirely. He can have another little shop further out of town.

EUGENE: But he's too old to transplant now, Mama. This is his street. Everyone knows him here. People pass by. Mr. Jannadeau's shop next door, and Woodruff's across the way — all the people and places Papa knows.

GANT: And Tim Laughran's down the block!

ELIZA (*Crosses down to* GANT):   Oh, yes. That's another reason for getting rid of this place. Put yourself out of temptation's way, Mr. Gant.

GANT (*Sits on slab*):   I certainly do love it here.

EUGENE: Don't give it up, Papa!

BEN: What do you want to do to him, Mama?

ELIZA: Now looky here, you are a fine stone-cutter — why, haven't I always said so? But it's time you rested. You want to live a long time, don't you?
   (*Sits beside him on slab*)

GANT: Well, sometimes I'm not sure.

ELIZA: Well, you do — and I want you to live a long time — we all want to! People can talk about a short but sweet life, but we all want to live! Look at me, I'm fifty-seven years old. I've borne nine children, raised six of them, and worked hard all my life. I'd like to back up and rest a little myself. And we can, Mr. Gant. If you'll just sign that little slip of paper. I guarantee, in a year from now, you'll have completely forgotten this dingy, crooked, dusty yard. Won't he, Ben? Won't he? Ben!

BEN: Some people have trouble forgetting some things, Mama.

ELIZA: Why, pshaw, I'm going to *see* to it that

he forgets it. I'll have time to look after you. Won't I, Mr. Gant?

GANT: You're right about one thing, Miss Eliza, that I can't dispute. You have worked hard. (*Rises, moves to center work table*)

EUGENE: Papa, please, don't do it.
      (GANT *sits at work table, signs the deed.* ELIZA *crosses to him, picks it up.*)

ELIZA: Thank you, Mr. Gant. Now the check. You know what I'm going to do? I'm going to plan a great, glorious celebration. (*Gives the deed to* WILL, *speaks to* EUGENE) We'll ask your brother Luke to come home, if the Navy will let him out. And we'll invite Stevie, and Daisy and her husband, too, except if she brings those whiny children of hers. (*Notices* GANT *just looking at the check*) Turn it over, Mr. Gant. Sign it on the back.

GANT: Why do I have to sign it?

ELIZA: Endorse it, that's all. W. O. Gant, like it's written on the front of the check.

GANT: That can wait until I offer it, can't it?

ELIZA: To clear the check, Mr. Gant!

GANT: I'm not used to these things. How do you clear it?

ELIZA: You sign it — I'll deposit it in the Dixie-land account, then we draw checks on it.

GANT: We?

ELIZA: Yes. You draw what you want. I'll draw what we need for Gene's college — for Dixieland, and for anything else we need.

GANT (*Rises, crosses to office*):   I think I'll wait to cash it until I get to Chapel Hill. The bank has a branch there, doesn't it, Will?
(*Gives* WILL *his pen*)

ELIZA: Why would you want to cash it in Chapel Hill?

GANT: This is my check, isn't it? I'm the one who had the foresight to buy this little pie-cornered lot thirty-one years ago for four hundred dollars . . . money from the estate of Cynthia L. Gant, deceased. I guess I'm entitled to the profit.

ELIZA: Now, Mr. Gant, if you're thinking to get my dander up . . .

GANT (*Picks up hat, puts it on*):   Miss Eliza, I've been wanting to get away from here for a long time. I'm taking Gene with me. (*Crosses to* EUGENE.) I'm going to put him in that college there at Chapel Hill.

EUGENE: Now?

GANT: Now! And then I'm going to travel . . . and when Gene's free in the summer, we'll travel together. (*Crosses back to* ELIZA) And there's nothing in this whole wide world that you're going to do to stop me. And I can just see the word Dixieland forming on your cursed lips. What about Dixieland? Nothing for Dixieland? *No, not one Goddamn red cent!* You've plenty of property of your own you can sell. If it's rest and comfort you really want, sell it, woman, sell it! But I think you like working hard, because then that makes us all feel sorry for you. And I do feel sorry for you too, from the bottom of my heart. (*Puts check in pocket*) Well, Eugene?

EUGENE: Papa, I can't go now.

GANT: Why not? You haven't got any better clothes . . . so you might as well go as you are. I guess we'll say our good-byes. (*Addresses the angel*) So long, dear Carrara angel. I'll arrange for us to be together again some day. (*Shakes hands with* BEN) Good-bye, Ben — tell Helen — tell Helen I'll write to her.

ELIZA (*Leaping at* GANT): I won't let you do this. I won't let you.

EUGENE: *Mama!*

ELIZA (*Seizes check from* GANT's *pocket, tears it up, flings it on the ground*): All right, all right, all right! There's your check. I guess there's nothing to prevent you from going to the bank and trying to get another check, but it won't work because I'm going to put an injunction against you. I'll prove you're not responsible to sell this property, or even to own it. I'll get guardianship over you! Everyone knows the times you've been to the cure — the threats you've made to me . . . the times you've tried to kill me — I'll tell them. You're a madman, Mr. Gant, a madman. You're not

going to get away with this. I'll fight you tooth
and nail, tooth and nail. And I'll win.

> (*Trembling, she picks up her hand-
> bag from the stone seat.*)

GANT: All the things you've said about me are
true, Eliza. I've only brought you pain. Why
don't you let me go?

ELIZA: Because you're my husband, Mr. Gant!
You're my husband. Thirty-one years together
and we'll go on — we must go on. A house divided against itself cannot stand. We must try
to understand and love each other. We must
try. . . .

> (ELIZA *exits.*)

GANT (*Quietly*):   Take her home, will you,
Will?

> (WILL *hurries after* ELIZA. *A long mo-
> ment.* BEN, *weak and feverish, dries his
> forehead with his handkerchief.* GANT
> sinks into a chair.*)

GANT: Eugene, go over to Laughran's and get
me a bottle. You heard me.

EUGENE: No, Papa.

GANT: Are you still padding along after your
mother?

BEN: Leave Gene alone. If you want to get sick,
do it yourself.

GANT: Ungrateful sons! Oh, the sad waste of
years, the red wound of all our mistakes.

(GANT *rises, exits,* EUGENE *looks after his father.*)

BEN: The fallen Titan. He might have succeeded if he hadn't tried to take you. He could still make it, but he won't try again.

EUGENE: They loved each other once. They must have had one moment in time that was perfect. What happened? It frightens me, Ben. How can something so perfect turn into this torture?

BEN: They're strangers. They don't know each other. No one ever really comes to know anyone.

EUGENE: That's not true. I know you — I know Laura.

BEN: Listen to him! No matter what arms may clasp us, what heart may warm us, what mouth may kiss us, we remain strangers. We never escape it. Never, never, never.
    (*Closes eyes, leans back*)

EUGENE: Ben! Hey, Ben? (*Worriedly crosses down to* BEN, *feels his face*) Ben, you're burning up! Come on. . . . (*Tries to lift him*) Put your arms around me. I'm going to take you home.

BEN (*Sinks back*): Can't. It's all right, I'm just tired.

EUGENE: Why didn't you tell somebody you're sick, you crazy idiot!
    (EUGENE *again tries to lift* BEN.)

BEN: To hell with them, Gene. To hell with them all. Don't give a damn for anything. Nothing gives a damn for you. There are a lot of bad days, there are a lot of good ones — (EUGENE *rushes into the office, picks up the telephone.*) that's all there is . . . a lot of days. . . . My God, is there no freedom on this earth?

EUGENE (*Into telephone*): Get me Dr. Maguire quickly. *It's my brother Ben!*

BEN (*Stirs, in anguish, looks up at the Carrara angel*): And still you smile . . .
Curtain

ACT II

Scene 2

The Dixieland Boarding House
It is the next night; a painful tenseness grips the house.

LAURA *and* EUGENE *sit together on the yard seat.* MRS. PERT *sits motionless in her rocker near the front door.* HUGH *slowly walks about. The inside hall is lighted, as is* BEN's *room, which we see for the first time. There* DR. MAGUIRE *and* HELEN *are hovering over* BEN's *still body.* GANT *is at the hall telephone.*

GANT (*Shouting into telephone*): Second class seaman, Luke Gant. G-A-N-T — Gant! (*Angrily*) I don't know why you can't hear me.

HUGH (*Crosses to door*): W.O., you don't have to shout because it's long distance.

GANT: Shut up, Hugh, I know what I'm doing. (*Into telephone*) Do what? I am standing back from the telephone. All right, all right . . . (*Moves telephone away from him, lower*) Can you hear me now? Of all the perversities. Very well, I will repeat. Yesterday I sent a telegram

to my son, Luke Gant, to come home, that his
brother Ben has pneumonia. Can you tell me
if — oh, he did leave? Why didn't he let us
know? All right! Thank you. Thank you very
much.

> (*Hangs up, joins the others on the ve-
> randa*)

HUGH: They gave him leave?

GANT: If he made good connections he ought
to be here by now.

HUGH: Ben'll be all right, W. O.

GANT: I remember when little Grover was ill in
St. Louis, and Eliza sent for me. I didn't get
there on time.

> (*Sits on yard stool.* ELIZA *enters from
> the house.*)

ELIZA: Did you reach him?

GANT: He's on his way.

ELIZA: It's all nonsense, of course. Ben is far
from dying. But you do like to dramatize, Mr.
Gant. Still, it will be good to see Luke. . . .

EUGENE: (*Crosses to* ELIZA):   Mama, when can I
see Ben?

ELIZA: When the doctor says. I'll tell you what:
When you go in there, don't make out like
Ben is sick. Just make a big joke of it —
laugh as big as you please —

EUGENE (*Groans*):   Mama!

ELIZA: Well, it's the sick one's frame of mind that counts. I remember when I was teaching school in Hominy township, I had pneumonia. Nobody expected me to live, but I did . . . I got through it somehow. I remember one day I was sitting down — I reckon I was convalescing, as the fella says. Old Doc Fletcher had been there — and as he left I saw him shake his head at my cousin Sally. "Why, Eliza, what on earth," she says, just as soon as he had gone, "he tells me you're spitting up blood every time you cough; you've got consumption as sure as you live!" "Pshaw!" I said. I remember I was just determined to make a big joke of it. "I don't believe a word of it," I said. "Not one single word." And it was because I didn't believe it that I got *well*.

GANT (*Quietly*):   Eliza, don't run on so.

HELEN (*Appears on veranda*):   The doctor says Mama can come in for a few minutes, but no one else yet.

EUGENE: How is he?

HELEN: You know Dr. Maguire. If you can get anything out of him . . .
> (ELIZA *takes a big breath; she and* HELEN *go into house.*)

GANT: Oh God, I don't like the feel of it. I don't like the feel of it.

BEN (*Weakly*):   Maguire, if you don't stop hanging over me I'll smother to death.

MAGUIRE (*To* ELIZA *and* HELEN *as they enter*): With both of you in here soaking up oxygen, leave that door open.

> (ELIZA *advances slowly to* BEN, *swallows a gasp at the sight of the tortured, wasted body.* BEN's *eyes are closed.*)

HELEN: Mama's here, Ben.

ELIZA (*Speaking as though to a baby*): Why hello, son — did you think I wasn't ever coming in to see you?

HELEN (*After a pause*):   Ben, Mama's here.

ELIZA (*To* MAGUIRE): Can't he talk? Why doesn't he look at me?

MAGUIRE: Ben, you can hear what's going on, can't you?

BEN (*Quietly, his eyes still closed*):   I wish you'd all get out and leave me alone.

ELIZA: What kind of talk is that? You have to be looked after, son!

BEN: Then let Mrs. Pert look after me.

HELEN: Ben!

BEN: Maguire, where's Fatty? I want to see Fatty.

HELEN: Ben, how can you talk that way? Your mother and your sister? If it weren't for that woman you wouldn't be sick now. Drinking, carousing with her night after night —

BEN (*Yells with dwindling strength*): Fatty! Fatty!

(*On the veranda,* MRS. PERT *stands quickly, then enters house.*)

HELEN (*To* BEN): You ought to be ashamed of yourself!

DR. MAGUIRE: Mrs. Gant, we need some more cold cloths. Why don't you . . .

HELEN (*Angrily to* MAGUIRE): Fiend! Do you have to add to her misery? When you need something, ask me.

> (ELIZA, *starting out of* BEN'S *room, meets* MRS. PERT *in doorway.* MRS. PERT *hesitates.*)

DR. MAGUIRE: That's all right, Mrs. Pert.

BEN (*Immediately turns toward her*): Fatty?

DR. MAGUIRE: Ben seems to want you here, that's all I care about. (*To* HELEN) You'll be called if you're needed.

HELEN: This is the last time you come into this house, Dr. Maguire!

> (HELEN *leaves the room. Outside* BEN'S *door* ELIZA *hands some cold cloths to* HELEN. HELEN *reenters* BEN'S *room, places them on the bureau.*)

BEN: Fatty, stay by me. Sing to me. "A Baby's Prayer at Twilight" . . .

FATTY (*Sitting beside him*): Sh-h-h, Ben. Be quiet, dear. Save yourself.

BEN; Hold my hand, Fatty.

FATTY (*Takes his hand, sings*):

"Just a baby's prayer at twilight
When lights are low
A baby's years
Are filled with tears
Hmmmm hmmmm hmmmm."

> (*Hearing the voice,* EUGENE *stands, looks up toward* BEN's *room.* HELEN *and* ELIZA *appear on the veranda,* HELEN *comforting her mother.*)

EUGENE: How does he seem. Mama?

ELIZA: He couldn't stand to see me worrying. That's what it was, you know. He couldn't stand to see me worrying about him.

GANT (*Groaning*):   Oh Jesus, it's fearful — that this should be put on me, old and sick as I am —

HELEN (*In blazing fury*):   You shut your mouth this minute, you damned old man. I've spent my life taking care of you! Everything's been done for you — everything — and you'll be here when we're all gone . . . so don't let us hear anything about your sickness, you selfish old man — it makes me furious!

DR. MAGUIRE (*Appearing on veranda*):   If any of you are interested, Ben is a little better.

EUGENE: Thank God!

HELEN: Ben is better? Why didn't you say so before?

ELIZA: I could have told you! I could have told you! I had a feeling all along!

DR. MAGUIRE (*Crosses down steps*):   I'll be back in a little while.

GANT: Well! We can all relax now.

DR. MAGUIRE (*Motions* EUGENE *away from the others*):   Eugene, it's both lungs now. I can't tell them. But see to it that they stay around. I'm going next door and phone for some oxygen. It may ease it a little for him. It won't be long.

> (*He gives* EUGENE *a fond, strengthening touch, exits.*)

GANT: What about Luke? Luke'll be furious when he finds out he came all this way for nothing!

ELIZA: For nothing? You call Ben's getting well "for nothing"?

GANT: Oh, you know what I mean, Miss Eliza. I'm going to take a little nap.

ELIZA: You're going to take a little nip, that's what you mean.

GANT: You can come up and search my room if you don't believe me.

> (*Exits into house.* EUGENE *stands, dazed and miserable. He forces himself during the following scene.* JAKE *and* FLORRY *enter from rear veranda.*)

ELIZA (*Excitedly*):   Mr. Clatt, Miss Mangle — did you hear? Ben is getting better! The crisis is past!

JAKE: We're so happy for you, Mrs. Gant.

ELIZA: I knew all along — something told me.

Oh, not that he didn't have a very high fever
— I admit that — but my second sense . . .

LUKE (*Off*):   Hello — o — there!

ELIZA (*Peering off*): Luke! (*Rushes down
steps*) Luke! Luke Gant!
> (*The boarders melt into the back-
> ground as* LUKE GANT, *wearing a Navy
> uniform, carrying a lightly packed duf-
> fle bag, enters. He is attractive, slight,
> lighted by an enormous love of humor
> and life, and adored by everyone. He is
> the son who got away early, but he still
> carries the marks of a distressing child-
> hood; he stutters sometimes.*)

LUKE: Mama, Mama!
> (*Swings her around*)

HUGH: Well, if it isn't the sailor himself! How
are you?

LUKE (*Shaking hands with* HUGH): I'm fine,
Hugh! How goes it?

ELIZA: Aren't you going to kiss your old mother?

LUKE: Old? You're getting younger and stronger by the minute.
> (*Kisses her*)

ELIZA: I am, I am, son. I feel it — now that
Ben's going to get well.

LUKE: The old boy is better?

HELEN: Luke!

LUKE: Helen!

HELEN (*Leaps into his arms*):   How's my boy?

LUKE: S-s-slick as a puppy's belly. I thought you all might need cheering up. I brought you some ice cream from Woodruff's!
(*Gives carton of ice cream to* HELEN)

HELEN: Naturally, you wouldn't be Luke Gant if you didn't!

EUGENE (*Crosses to Luke*):   Welcome home, Luke!

LUKE (*They shake hands*):   My God, doesn't anybody buy you any clothes — and look at that hair. Mama, he looks like an orphan! Cut off those damn big feet of his, he'd go up in the air!

EUGENE: How long have you got, Luke?

LUKE: Can you s-s-stand me for twenty-four hours? (*Sees* LAURA) Who's this?

ELIZA: That's Miss James from Virginia. Laura, this is another of my sons, Luke Gant.

LAURA (*Shaking hands*):   How do you do, Mr. Gant?

LUKE: How do you do?

ELIZA (*Drawing* LUKE *away*):   All right, just come along here, and behave yourself.

HELEN: I'd better dish up the ice cream before it melts.
(*Exits into house*)

LUKE (*Calling after* HELEN):   Maybe Ben would like some. I got pistachio especially for him.

ELIZA: Tell your father the admiral is here!

LUKE: Can I see Ben, now?

ELIZA: Well, the truth is, that Mrs. Pert is in there with him now.

LUKE: Mrs. Pert is?
        (*Looks at the others*)

HUGH: I wouldn't go into it, Luke. It's a some-what "fraught" subject.

LUKE: Oh boy, oh boy, I know what that is! Still the same old happy household?
        (LUKE *and* ELIZA *sit on the veranda edge.*)

ELIZA: Nonsense. I have nothing against the woman except she's getting too many ideas that she's a fixture here. First thing in the morning I'm going to ask her to move.

LUKE: Doesn't she pay her rent?

ELIZA: Oh, she pays it.

LUKE (*Laughs*):   Then you're never going to ask her to move — don't kid me! The paying customers are what count around here! Aren't they, Mama?

ELIZA: Luke Gant, there are certain standards I have to keep up, for the reputation of Dixie-land!

LUKE (*Never unkindly*):   What kind of standards? The old dope fiend who hung himself in the same bedroom where Ben had to sleep for eight years after he cut him down? And all those amateur femme fatales who bask under your protection here, waylaying us in the hall, the bathroom — Mama, we never had a s-s-safe moment! And people think you find out about life in the Navy!

ELIZA (*Playfully*):   I'm warning you, Luke! It's a good thing I know you're teasing.
          (HELEN *enters with plates, dishes up ice cream.*)

LUKE: Remember the early morning when Ben and Gene and I used to take the paper route together, remember, Gene? Old Ben used to make up stories for us about all the sleeping people in all the sleeping houses! He always used to throw the papers as lightly as he could because he hated to wake them. Remember, Gene?

HELEN: And that book of baseball stories Ben used to read to us by the hour — what was it, Gene?

EUGENE (*In tears*):   *You know me, Al,* by Ring Lardner.

ELIZA (*Leaping to* EUGENE):   Eugene. Child, what is it? What is it!
          (MRS. PERT *enters hurriedly.*)

MRS. PERT: Mrs. Gant! Mrs. Gant!

HELEN: What is it, Mrs. Pert?

MRS. PERT: He can't get his breath!

HUGH: Gene, get the doctor!
        (HELEN *and* ELIZA *follow* MRS. PERT *into the house.*)

ELIZA: You ridiculous woman! The doctor said he was better.
        (EUGENE *exits to get* MAGUIRE. GANT *enters through side door.*)

GANT: What the hell's all the commotion about? (*Sees* LUKE) Luke! Welcome home!

LUKE (*As they shake hands*):   Papa — Ben's not doing so well.

GANT: Jesus, have mercy! That I should have to bear this in my old age. Not another one — first Grover, now Ben . . .

LUKE: For God's sake, Papa, try to behave decently, for Ben's sake!
        (EUGENE *and* DOC MAGUIRE *enter hurriedly.*)

GANT (*Seizing the doctor*):   Maguire, you got to save him — you got to save him.
        (MAGUIRE *pushes past* GANT *into the house, enters* BEN's *room where the three women are gathered,* MRS. PERT *standing nearest* BEN *at the head of the bed.*)

MAGUIRE: You women step back, give him air.
        (*Bends over* BEN)

GANT (*Collapsing onto the steps*): When the old die, no one cares. But the young . . . the young . . .

EUGENE (*Sits beside him*): I would care, Papa.

BEN: It's one way — to step out of — the photograph — isn't it, Fatty?

FATTY: Hush, Ben, don't say that!

HELEN (*To the doctor*): There must be something you can do!

MAGUIRE (*Straightens up*): Not all the king's horses, not all the doctors in the world can help him now.

HELEN: Have you tried everything? Everything?

MAGUIRE: My dear girl! He's drowning! Drowning!

ELIZA (*In a deep pain*): Mrs. Pert, you're standing in my place. . . .
> (MRS. PERT *moves away.* ELIZA *steps close to* BEN, *sits.*)

ELIZA: Ben — son.
> (*She reaches to touch him. His head turns toward her, drops. There is a last rattling, drowning sound.* BEN *dies.* MAGUIRE *checks his heart.*)

MAGUIRE: It's over. It's all over.
> (HELEN, *racked, exits toward the veranda.* MRS. PERT *puts the socks she has been knitting at* BEN's *feet and exits upstairs.* HELEN *enters the veranda, tries to stifle her sobs.*)

HELEN: He's gone. Ben's gone.

> (HELEN *falls into* EUGENE'*s arms.* MA-
> GUIRE, *carrying his doctor's bag, appears
> in the hall, puts a match to his chewed
> cigar.*)

EUGENE (*Crossing up to* MAGUIRE):   Did he say anything? Did he say anything at the end?

MAGUIRE: What were you expecting him to say?

EUGENE: I don't know. I just wondered.

MAGUIRE: If he found what he was looking for? I doubt that, Gene. At least he didn't say anything.

> (EUGENE *leaves and goes into* BEN'*s
> room.* MAGUIRE *comes out onto the ve-
> randa.*)

LUKE: How long have you known, Doc?

MAGUIRE: For two days — from the beginning. Since I first saw him at three in the morning in the Uneeda Lunch with a cup of coffee in one hand and a cigarette in the other.

GANT: Was there nothing to be done?

MAGUIRE: My dear, dear Gant, we can't turn back the days that have gone. We can't turn back to the hours when our lungs were sound, our blood hot, our bodies young. We are a flash of fire — a brain, a heart, a spirit. And we are three cents worth of lime and iron — which we cannot get back. (*He shakes his head.*) We can believe in the nothingness of life. We can believe in the nothingness of

death, and of a life after death. But who can
believe in the nothingness of Ben?

HELEN: Come on, Papa, there's nothing more
to sit up for. Let me put you to bed. Come
along.

> (*She takes the old man and leads him
> gently into the house, as the* DOCTOR
> *exits.* HUGH *and* LUKE *exit after* HELEN
> *and* GANT. *Only* LAURA *is left, still sit-
> ting on the yard seat.* EUGENE, *who has
> been standing in the corner in* BEN's
> *room, goes to his mother, who is hold-
> ing* BEN's *hand tightly.*)

EUGENE: Mama?

ELIZA: He doesn't turn away from me any more.

EUGENE (*Takes her hand, tries gently to disen-
gage* BEN's): Mama, you've got to let go.
You've got to let go, Mama!

> (ELIZA *shakes her head, her rough clasp
> tightening.* EUGENE *leaves the room,
> comes out to the veranda. There, slow-
> ly, he sinks to his knees, prays.* LAURA
> *watches him, her heart going out to
> him.*)

EUGENE: Whoever You are, be good to Ben tonight. Whoever You are, be good to Ben tonight . . . Whoever You are . . . be good to
Ben tonight . . . be good to Ben tonight. . . .
Slow Curtain

ACT III

The Dixieland Boarding House

Two weeks later.

The house is seen in a soft early light. From offstage, a newsboy, whistling, throws four tightly wadded newspapers onto the veranda — plop — plop — plop — plop. The whistling and his steps fade away. The lights come up dimly in LAURA's *room.* LAURA *is in bed in her nightgown.* EUGENE *is at the foot of the bed by the window, looking out. He takes his shirt from the bedpost, puts it on.*

LAURA (*Stirring*): Gene? What was that?

EUGENE: Soaks Baker with the morning papers. Plop — plop — plop — plop — how I used to love that sound. Every time the heavy bag getting lighter. I'll always feel sorry for people who have to carry things. (*Sighs*) It's getting light, it's nearly dawn.

LAURA: Don't go yet.
(*Reaches for his hand*)

EUGENE: Do you think I want to on your last morning here? Mama gets up so early. Do you

114

know that every morning before she cooks breakfast she visits Ben's grave?

(*Sits on bed, takes her in his arms*)

LAURA: Gene, Gene.

EUGENE: Oh, Laura, I love you so. When I'm close to you like this, it's so natural. Are all men like me? Tell me.

LAURA: I've told you I've never known anyone like you.

EUGENE: But you have known men? It would be strange if you hadn't. A woman so beautiful, so loving. You make me feel like I only used to dream of feeling. I've hardly thought to daydream in weeks — except about us.

LAURA: What did you used to dream?

EUGENE: I always wanted to be the winner, the general, the spearhead of victory! Then, following that, I wanted to be loved. Victory and love! Unbeaten and beloved. And I am that now, truly! Laura, will you marry me?

LAURA (*Moving away*):   Oh darling!

EUGENE: You knew I was going to ask you, didn't you. You knew I couldn't let you go even for a day.

LAURA: Yes, I knew.

EUGENE: You're happy with me. You know I make you happy. And I'm so complete with you. (*He draws her back into his arms.*) Do you know that three hundred dollars Ben left

me? He would want me to use it for us. I'll go
with you to Richmond today. I'll meet your
parents, so they won't think I'm an irresponsible fool who's stolen you. That may be a little
hard to prove — but there is a job I can get.
Would you mind living in Altamont?

LAURA: I don't care where I live. Just keep holding me.

EUGENE: I am going to have to tell Mama first.

LAURA: Let's not worry about that now. Tell me
about us.

EUGENE: All the treasures the world has in store
for us? We'll see and know them all. . . . All
the things and the places I've read about.
There isn't a state in this country we won't
know. The great names of Arizona, Texas,
Colorado, California — we'll ride the freights
to get there if we have to. And we'll go to
Europe, and beyond . . . the cool, green land
of Shakespeare, the gloomy forests of Gaul, the
great Assyrian plains where Alexander feasted
. . . the crumbling walls of Babylon, the pal-
aces of the kings of Egypt, the towering white
crags of Switzerland . . . My God, Laura
there might not be time enough for all!

LAURA: There will be time enough, darling.
         (*They kiss longingly. From a far dis-*
         tance, they hear the whistle of a train as
         it passes.)

EUGENE: The Richmond train leaves at noon.
I'll have to get packed.

LAURA: You do love trains, don't you?

EUGENE: I love only you. Will you have confidence in me, the unbeaten and beloved?

LAURA: Yes, darling, I will have confidence in you.

EUGENE: I'll never have to sneak out of this room again.
>   (EUGENE *rises, moves to the door.* LAURA, *on her knees, reaches toward him.*)

LAURA: Eugene! (*He comes back to her*) I will love you always.
>   (*They kiss.* EUGENE *exits.* LAURA *leaps from the bed, hurries after him.*)

LAURA: Gene!
>   (ELIZA *has come out the side door. She takes flowers out of a bucket preparing to take them to* BEN'S *grave.* EUGENE *enters the hallway, lifts the phone receiver. He doesn't see* ELIZA. *Lights dim down on* LAURA's *room as she dresses.*)

EUGENE (*Into telephone*):   Good morning, 3-2 please. Hello, Uncle Will? This is Eugene. Yes, I know how early it is. . . . You know that position you offered me? I've decided to take it.

ELIZA (*Pleased, to herself*):   Well, can you imagine!

EUGENE (*Into telephone*):   I've thought it over and that's what I'd like to do, for a while anyway. That's right. That's fine. . . . Well, you see, I'm getting married . . . . (ELIZA *freezes in pain.*) Yes, married — to Miss James. We're going to Richmond for a few days. We're leaving on the noon train. Thanks, Uncle Will. Thanks a lot.

> (EUGENE *hangs up. He starts to go back upstairs.*)

ELIZA: Eugene!

EUGENE (*Coming out to her slowly*):   Well, now — with your second sense, I thought you would have guessed it, Mama.

ELIZA: First Grover, then Ben, now you . . . Why didn't I know, why didn't I see?

EUGENE: I'm sorry, Mama, but we couldn't wait any longer.

ELIZA: Gene, child, don't make this mistake. She's so much older than you. Don't throw yourself away, boy!

EUGENE: Mama, there's no use arguing. Nothing you can say will change my mind.

ELIZA (*Desperately*):   And my plans for you? What of my plans for you?

EUGENE: Mama, I don't want your plans, I've got my own life to live!

ELIZA: But you don't know! Gene, listen, you know that Stumptown property of mine? I sold it just yesterday so you could go to Chapel Hill — you know I've always wanted you to have an education. You can have it now, child, you can have it.

EUGENE: It's too late, Mama, it's too late!

ELIZA: Why law, child, it's never too late for anything! It's what Ben wanted, you know.

EUGENE: Laura and I are leaving, Mama. I'm going up to get packed.
>   (*He briefly kisses her, exits into house.*)

ELIZA: Gene! (ELIZA *stands looking after him a moment, then quickly enters the hall, lifts the telephone receiver.*) Three-two, please.
>   (HELEN *enters from the kitchen with a broom. She sweeps the veranda.*)

HELEN: What are you calling Uncle Will so early for?

ELIZA (*Into phone*):   Will? No, no, I know — I heard. . . . Yes, I know it's early. . . . Listen, Will, I want you to do something for me. You know my Stumptown property? I want you to sell it. . . . Now, this morning. Will, don't argue with me — I don't care what it's worth. Call Cash Rankin, he's been after me for weeks to sell. . . . Well, I know what I want to do — I'll explain it to you later — just do what I say and let me know.
>   (*She hangs up.*)

HELEN: Well, it's never too early in the morning to turn a trade, is it? What are you selling?

ELIZA: Some property I own.

HELEN: Maybe you can put a little of that money into getting somebody else to help you at that altar of yours, the kichen stove.

ELIZA: Helen, get breakfast started, will you?
I'll be in later. And if Gene comes down, keep
him in there, will you?

HELEN: Oh, all right. You let me know when I
can let him out!
            (*Exits into house.* ELIZA *appears at
            door of* LAURA's *room.* LAURA *is dressed
            and is packing her suitcase.* ELIZA
            knocks.)

LAURA (*As* ELIZA *enters*):   Oh, Mrs. Gant. I've
been expecting you. Come in.

ELIZA: I should think you would.

LAURA: Mrs. Gant, before you say anything . . .

ELIZA: I'll vow, I can't believe a mature woman
— at a time of trouble like this — would take
advantage of a child, a mere child. . . .

LAURA: Mrs. Gant, will you please listen.

ELIZA: I will listen to nothing. You just pack
your things and get out of this house. I should
have known what you were from the first minute I set eyes on you. . . . "I'm looking for a
room, Mrs. Gant. . . ." Why, butter wouldn't
melt in your mouth. . . .

LAURA (*Slowly, distinctly*):   Mrs. Gant, I am
not marrying Eugene. I'm not. I wish with all
my heart I could.

ELIZA: You can't lie out of it. Gene just told me.

LAURA: I am engaged to be married to a young
man in Richmond.

ELIZA: What kind of a wicked game are you playing with my child?

LAURA: Mrs. Gant, this isn't easy. I should have told Gene long ago . . . but I didn't. A girl about to get married suddenly finds herself facing responsibilities. I never liked responsibilities. Gene knows how I am. I like music, I like to walk in the woods, I like . . . to dream. I know I'm older than Gene, but in many ways I'm younger. The thought of marriage frightened me. I told my fiancé I needed time to think it over. I fell in love with Eugene. I found the kind of romance I'd never known before, but I've also found that it isn't the answer. Gene is a wonderful boy, Mrs. Gant. He must go to college. He must have room to expand and grow, to find himself. He mustn't be tied down at this point in his life. He needs the whole world to wander in — and I know now that I need a home, I need children — I need a husband. For people like me there are rules, very good rules for marriage and for happiness — and I've broken enough of them. I telephoned Philip last night. He's arriving at the depot on that early train. We're going on to Charleston together, and we'll be married there. He loves me, and I will love him too after awhile. (*Takes note from desk*) I left this note for Eugene. I couldn't just tell him. (*Gives it to* ELIZA) Will you say good-bye to Mr. Gant for me, and tell him I hope he feels better? And my good-byes to Mr. Clatt and the others? And to Helen. Especially to Helen. She works so hard. (*Looks around*) Good-bye, little room, I've

been happy here. (*Picks up suitcase, faces*
ELIZA) Some day you're going to have to let
him go. Good-bye, Mrs. Gant.

> (*She exits. During the above* HUGH *has
> entered the veranda, is seated, reading
> the newspaper.* LAURA *enters from the
> house, looks back lingeringly, then hear-
> ing the approaching train, hurries off
> toward the station.* HELEN *enters, drink-
> ing coffee.*)

HELEN: Mama? Now where on earth . . .
Hugh, have you seen Mama?

HUGH: Umph.

HELEN: Do you know she was on the phone just
now selling some property? Imagine — at this
hour! And she leaves me to slave in the kitch-
en. . . . Do you know where she is?

HUGH: You know, they don't advertise the good
jobs in here, not the really big ones.

GANT (*Entering in his suspenders, sleepily rub-
bing his jaw*): Isn't breakfast ready yet?

HELEN: Papa, how many times has Mama told
you, you wait until the boarders have had
theirs! And don't you dare appear in front of
them in your suspenders, do you hear?

GANT: Merciful God! What a way to greet the
day!

> (*He exits.*)

HELEN (*Calling after* GANT): Papa, do you
know where Mama is?

(HELEN *exits after* GANT. EUGENE *enters downstairs, carrying his suitcase, stops at* LAURA'S *door, knocks.* ELIZA *has just laid* LAURA'S *letter on the bed.*)

EUGENE: Laura? Laura? (EUGENE *enters to* ELIZA.) Mama! Where's Laura? Where is she?

ELIZA: She's gone.

EUGENE: Gone? Where?

ELIZA: She just walked out on you, child. Just walked out on you. (*Shakes her finger at him*) I could have told you, the minute I laid eyes on her —

EUGENE (*Seizing* ELIZA'S *hand*): You sent her away.

ELIZA: I never did. She just walked out on you, child.

(EUGENE *breaks for the door.* ELIZA *picks up the letter, runs after him.*)

ELIZA: Gene! Eugene! Wait!

EUGENE (*Runs down to the veranda*): Laura . . . (*Looks up street*) Laura . . . (*As* HUGH *points towards station, starts off that way*) Laura . . .

ELIZA (*Entering, waving the letter*): Wait! Wait! She left you this. Gene! (EUGENE *turns, sees the letter.*) She left you this. Read it, child.

(EUGENE *crosses to* ELIZA, *takes the letter, tears it open, reads it.*)

ELIZA: You see, it's no use. It's no use.

        (EUGENE *crosses slowly to the yard seat, sits.* ELIZA *watches him.* HELEN *enters through the front door.*)

HELEN: Mama, there you are! Where have you been? We've got to start getting breakfast. (*As* ELIZA *waves her to silence*) What's the matter?

ELIZA: That Miss James. She and Eugene . . .

HELEN (*Laughs*):   Oh my God, Mama, have you just found out about that? What about it?

ELIZA: She's gone.

HELEN: What?

ELIZA: She just walked out on him.

HELEN (*Crosses to* EUGENE):   Oh ho, so that's it, is it? Has your girl gone and left you, huh? Huh? (*Tickles his ribs. He turns, clasps her knees.*) Why, Gene, forget about it! You're only a kid yet. She's a grown woman.

ELIZA: Helen's right. Why, child, I wouldn't let a girl get the best of me. She was just fooling you all the time, just leading you on, wasn't she, Helen?

HELEN: You'll forget her in a week, Gene.

ELIZA: Why, of course you will. Pshaw, this was just puppy love. Like the fellow says, there's plenty good fish in the sea as ever came out of it.

HELEN: Cheer up, you're not the only man got fooled in his life!

HUGH (*From behind his paper*):   By God, that's the truth!

>   (HELEN *and* ELIZA *glare at* HUGH.)

ELIZA: Helen, go inside, I'll be in in a minute.

HELEN: Oh, all right. Hugh, you come in and help me.

>   (HELEN *exits, followed by* HUGH.)

ELIZA (*Sits beside* EUGENE, *his back still turned to her*):   Gene. You know what I'd do if I were you? I'd just show her I was a good sport, that's what! I wouldn't let on to her that it affected me one bit. I'd write her just as big as you please and laugh about the whole thing.

EUGENE: Oh, God, Mama, please, leave me alone, leave me alone!

ELIZA: Why, I'd be ashamed to let any girl get my goat like that. When you get older, you'll just look back on this and laugh. You'll see. You'll be going to college next year, and you won't remember a thing about it. (EUGENE *turns, looks at her.*) I told you I'd sold that Strumptown property, and I have. This year's term has started already but next year . . .

EUGENE: Mama, *now! Now!* I've wasted enough time!

ELIZA: What are you talking about? Why you're a child yet, there's plenty of time yet. . . .

EUGENE (*Rises, walks about her*):   Mama, Mama, what is it? What more do you want from me? Do you want to strangle and drown me completely? Do you want more string? Do you want me to collect more bottles? Tell me what you want! Do you want more property? Do you want the town? Is that it?

ELIZA: Why, I don't know what you're talking about, boy. If I hadn't tried to accumulate a little something, none of you would have had a roof to call your own.

EUGENE: A roof to call our own? Good God, I never had a bed to call my own! I never had a room to call my own! I never had a quilt to call my own that wasn't taken from me to warm the mob that rocks on that porch and grumbles.

ELIZA (*Rises, looking for an escape*): Now you may sneer at the boarders if you like . . .

EUGENE: No, I can't. There's not breath or strength enough in me to sneer at them all I like. Ever since I was this high, and you sent me to the store for the groceries, I used to think, this food is not for us — it's for them! Mama, making us wait until they've eaten, all these years — feeding us on *their* leftovers — do you know what it does to us — when it's you we wanted for us, *you* we needed for us. Why? Why?

ELIZA (*Trembling*): They don't hurt me like the rest of you do — they wouldn't talk to me like you are, for one thing.
        (*Starts toward side door*)

EUGENE: Because they don't care — they're strangers. They don't give a damn about you!

They'll talk like this about you behind your
back — I've heard them do that plenty!

ELIZA (*Turns*): What? What? What kind of
things do they say about me?

EUGENE: What does it matter what they say —
they say! Doesn't it matter to you what I say?
(*Takes her in his arms, holds her*)

ELIZA (*Beginning to weep*): I don't understand.

EUGENE (*Releases her, moves away*): Oh it's
easy to cry now, Mama, but it won't do you
any good! I've done as much work for my
wages as you deserve. I've given you fair value
for your money, I thank you for nothing.
(*Crosses up to veranda*)

ELIZA: What's that? What are you saying!

EUGENE: I said I thank you for nothing, but I
take that back. Yes, I have a great deal to be
thankful for. I give thanks for every hour of
loneliness I've had here, for every dirty cell
you ever gave me to sleep in, for the ten million hours of indifference, and for these two
minutes of cheap advice.

ELIZA: You will be punished if there's a just
God in Heaven.

EUGENE: Oh, there is! I'm sure there is! Because I have been punished. By God, I shall
spend the rest of my life getting my heart back,
healing and forgetting every scar you put upon me when I was a child. The first move I

ever made after the cradle was to crawl for the door. And every move I ever made since has been an effort to escape. And now, at last I am free from all of you. And I shall get me some order out of this chaos. I shall find my way out of it yet, though it takes me twenty years more — alone.

ELIZA: Gene! Gene, you're not leaving?

EUGENE: Ah, you were not looking, were you? I've already gone.

> (EUGENE *exits into the house, into* LAURA's *room, where he left his valise, He throws his body on the bed, stifles his crying.* ELIZA *sits on the veranda edge, stunned.* GANT, *wearing a vest over his suspenders, enters.*)

GANT: Now do you suppose I can get some breakfast? (ELIZA *doesn't answer.*) Well, do you mind if I make a fire in the fireplace? (*Goes to wood box, muttering*) If I can't get any food to keep me alive, I can get a little warmth out of this drafty barn! (*Starts collecting wood from box*) Some day I'm going to burn up this house — just pile in all the logs that old grate'll hold — and all the furniture — and all the wooden-headed people around here — and some kerosene — till this old barn takes off like a giant cinder blazing through the sky. That would show them — all fifteen miserable rooms — blistering . . .

ELIZA: I wish you would, Mr. Gant. I just wish you would.

GANT: You think I'm joking.

ELIZA: No, I don't.

GANT: If I just get drunk enough, I will!

ELIZA (*Rises, faces house*): Serve it right . . . miserable, unholy house!

GANT: Why, Miss Eliza!

ELIZA: I'll do it myself— (*With demoniacal strength she shakes a newal post by the steps.*) I'll tear you down! I'll kill you, house, kill you! I'll shake you to pieces!
      (*Picks up* MRS. PERT's *rocker, crashes it*)

HELEN (*Entering hurriedly*): Eliza Gant, have you gone mad!

GANT: Let me help you, Mrs. Gant! (*Drops wood, starts tearing at the other post*) Goddamned barn! Thief! Travesty on nature!

ELIZA: Goddamned barn!
      (*Kicks in latticed panels under the veranda*)

HELEN (*Calls inside*): Hugh, come out here!

WILL (*Entering from rear of veranda*): My God, what are they doing?

GANT (*Screaming up at house*): Clatt — Mangle — Brown — Come out of there, you rats, all of you — come out, come out, wherever you are!
      (*The boarders begin to yell and squeal from inside.*)

ELIZA (*Hysterically, imitating* GANT): Come out, come out, wherever you are!

HUGH (*Entering*): What's going on?

GANT (*Breaking off the newel post*): We're tearing down this murderous trap, that's what. Hand me the hatchet, Hugh. It's in the wood box.

HUGH: Fine! Fine!
  (*Dashes to woodbox, takes out hatchet. The boarders enter down the stairs in various stages of undress.*)

MISS BROWN: Call the police.

MRS. CLATT: Let's get to Mrs. Haskell's!

JAKE: Gant's off his nut!

GANT (*Chasing, threatening the boarders*): Squeal, you croaking bastards. Croak and run! Run for your lives!

BOARDERS (*Fleeing*): The house is falling down! It's a tornado! Ladies' Temperance Society, humph! Has anyone called the police?

HUGH: Here's the hatchet, W.O.

GANT (*Leaping for it*): Give it to me.

WILL: Stop it, Gant — stop this! Have you all lost your minds?

ELIZA (*Throwing flower pot after the boarders*): Go to Mrs. Haskell's!

HELEN: Mama!

GANT (*Brandishing hatchet at* JAKE *and* MRS. CLATT *as they exit*):   Look at 'em run! And they haven't even had breakfast. Run, scatter-brains, empty bellies!

JAKE: I'll sue you for this, Gant, I'll sue you for this!

> (*Exits.* MRS. SNOWDEN *enters through front door.* GANT *whirls on her.*)

GANT: So you don't like the food here? So you don't like my wife's coffee!

> (MRS. SNOWDEN, *screaming, hastily retreats.*)

ELIZA (*Lifting a chair to hurl after the boarders*):   Why, law, that's good coffee!

> (HELEN *seizes* ELIZA'S *arms, stops her.* ELIZA'S *sensibilities slowly return.*)

GANT: Look at 'em run! Oh, Miss Eliza, what a woman you are!

> (GANT, *roaring with laughter, crosses down to* ELIZA, *is about to embrace her, sees her sober, shocked face.*)

ELIZA: Mr. Gant, Mr. Gant, what have you done? What have you done?

GANT: What have I done? What have I — Merciful God, woman!

ELIZA: Just look at this mess! And the boarders have all gone!

HELEN: I don't know what got into you, Papa.

GANT: Merciful God! What got into me? Didn't she just stand there herself and . . .

ELIZA: Helen, go get the boarders, tell them he's been drinking, tell them anything, but get them back!

WILL: I never saw such an exhibition.

ELIZA: Will, go with Helen. Tell them we all apologize. They'll listen to you. Hugh, help me clean up this mess.
>   (HELEN *and* WILL *exit after the boarders.*)

GANT: Let them go, Miss Eliza. Let the boarders go!
>   (ELIZA *stands rigid.* GANT *waits anxiously.*)

ELIZA: I just don't know what came over me.

GANT (*Crosses, flings the hatchet in the woodbox*): Merciful God!
>   (EUGENE *enters with his suitcase.*)

GANT: Where are you going?

EUGENE: I'm going to school at Chapel Hill, Papa.

GANT: You are?
>   (*He looks at* ELIZA.)

EUGENE: Mama promised me the money. She sold her Stumptown property.

GANT: Oh? By God, maybe it isn't going to be such a goddamned miserable day, after all! Got any money, son?

EUGENE: I've got Ben's money. Thanks, Papa.

GANT (*Takes money from his pocket, tucks it into* EUGENE's *pocket*): Well go, Gene. Go for both of us. Keep right on going.

EUGENE: I will, Papa. Good-bye.

GANT (*As they shake hands*):   Good-bye, Gene. (*Starts into house, turns*) You're going to bust loose, boy — you're going to bust loose, all over this dreary planet!

> (GANT *exits.* ELIZA *starts picking up the debris.*)

ELIZA: I reckon you've made up your mind all right.

EUGENE: Yes, Mama, I have.

ELIZA: Well, I'll deposit the money in the Chapel Hill Bank for you. I tell you what! It looks mighty funny, though, that you can't just stay a day or two more with Ben gone and all. It seems you'll do anything to get away from me. That's all right, I know your mind's made up and I'm not complaining! It seems all I've ever been fit for around here is to cook and sew. That's all the use any of you have ever had for me. . . .

EUGENE: Mama, don't think you can work on my feelings here at the last minute.

ELIZA: It seems I've hardly laid eyes on you all summer long. . . . (*Replacing wood in woodbox*) Well, when you get up there, you want to look up your Uncle Emerson and Aunt Lucy. Your Aunt Lucy took a great liking to

you when they were down here, and when
you're in a strange town it's mighty good sometimes to have someone you know. And say,
when you see your Uncle Emerson, you might
just tell him not to be surprised to see me any
time now. (*She nods pertly at him.*) I reckon
I can pick right up and light out the same as
the next fellow when I get ready. I'm not going to spend all my days slaving away for a lot
of boarders — it don't pay. If I can turn a
couple of trades here this fall, I just may start
out to see the world like I always intended to.
I was talking to Cash Rankin the other day
. . . he said, "Why, Mrs. Gant," he said, "if I
had your head for figures, I'd be a rich man
in . . ." (*Her talk drifts off.* EUGENE *stands
looking at her. There is another terrible silence between them. She points at him with
her finger, finally — her old loose masculine
gesture.*) Here's the thing I'm going to do.
You know that lot of mine on Sunset Terrace,
right above Dick Webster's place? Well, I
been thinking. If we started to build there
right away, we could be in our own house by
spring. I've been thinking about it a lot lately.
. . . (*There is another silence.*) I hate to see
you go, son.

EUGENE: Good-bye, Mama.

ELIZA: Try to be happy, child, try to be a little
more happy. . . .
          (*She turns and, with unsteady step,
          starts into the house.*)

EUGENE: MAMA! (*He drops the valise, takes*

the steps in a single bound, catching ELIZA's
*rough hands which she has held clasped across
her body, drawing them to his breast.*) GOOD-
BYE . . . GOOD-BYE . . . GOOD-BYE . . .
MAMA . . .

ELIZA (*Holding him*): Poor child . . . poor
child . . . poor child. (*Huskily, faintly*) We
must try to love one another.
> (*Finally,* EUGENE *moves from* ELIZA,
> *picks up the valise as the lights start
> dimming, holding a spot on her.* ELIZA
> *seems to recede in the distance as into
> his memory.*)

ELIZA: Now for Heaven's sake, spruce up, boy,
spruce up! Throw your shoulders back! And
smile, look pleasant! Let them know up there
that you *are* somebody!
> (ELIZA's *voice fades, The set is black.
> A spot holds on* EUGENE.)

EPILOGUE

BEN'S VOICE: So you're finally going, Gene?

EUGENE: Ben? Is that you, Ben?

BEN'S VOICE: Who do you think it was, you little idiot? Do you know why you're going, or
are you just taking a ride on a train?

EUGENE: I know. Of course I know why I'm going. There's nothing here for me. Ben, what
really happens? Everything is going. Everything changes and passes away. Can you remember some of the things I do? I've already
forgotten the old faces. I forget the names of
people I knew for years. I get their faces
mixed. I get their heads stuck on other people's bodies. I think one man has said what
another said. And I forget. There is something
I have lost and can't remember.

BEN'S VOICE: The things you have forgotten and
are trying to remember are the child that you
were. He's gone, Gene, as I am gone. And will
never return. No matter where you search for
him, in a million streets, in a thousand cities.

EUGENE: Then I'll search for an end to hunger, and the happy land!

BEN'S VOICE: Ah, there is no happy land. There is no end to hunger!

EUGENE: Ben, help me! You must have an answer. Help me, and I won't go searching for it.

BEN'S VOICE: You little fool, what do you want to find out there?

EUGENE: *I want to find the world. Where is the world?*

BEN'S VOICE (*Fading*):   The world is nowhere, Gene. . . .

EUGENE: Ben, wait! Answer me!

BEN'S VOICE: The world is nowhere, no one, Gene. *You* are your world.
          (*The train whistle sounds. Lights reveal Dixieland in dim silhouette.* EUGENE, *without looking back, exits.*)

Curtain

MARTY

by Paddy Chayefsky

Look Homeward, Angel and *All the Way Home* give stage directions for live theatrical performance. Because *Marty* was written expressly for television, it provides directions for the camera.

CHARACTERS

Marty
Clara
Angie
Mother
Aunt
Virginia
Thomas
Young man
Bartender
Critic
Twenty-year-old
Italian woman
Short girl
Girl

SYNOPSIS

The action takes place in New York City and covers a period of two days in the 1950's.

ACT I
That day

ACT II
That night

ACT III
The next day

ACT I

FADE IN: *A butcher shop in the Italian district of New York City. Actually, we fade in on a close-up of a butcher's saw being carefully worked through a side of beef, and we dolly back to show the butcher at work, and then the whole shop. The butcher is a mild-mannered, stout, short, balding young man of thirty-six. His charm lies in an almost indestructible good-natured amiability.*

The shop contains three women customers. One is a young mother with a baby carriage. She is chatting with a second woman of about forty at the door. The customer being waited on at the moment is a stout, elderly Italian woman who is standing on tiptoe, peering over the white display counter, checking the butcher as he saws away.

ITALIAN WOMAN: Your kid brother got married last Sunday, eh, Marty?

MARTY (*Absorbed in his work*):   That's right, Missus Fusari. It was a very nice affair.

ITALIAN WOMAN: That's the big tall one, the fellow with the mustache?

MARTY (*Sawing away*): No, that's my other brother Freddie. My other brother Freddie, he's been married four years already. He lives down on Quincy Street. The one who got married Sunday, that was my little brother Nickie.

ITALIAN WOMAN: I thought he was a big, tall, fat fellow. Didn't I meet him here one time? Big, tall, fat fellow, he tried to sell me life insurance?

MARTY (*Sets the cut of meat on the scale, watches its weight register*): No, that's my sister Margaret's husband, Frank. My sister Margaret, she's married to the insurance salesman. My sister Rose, she married a contractor. They moved to Detroit last year. And my other sister, Frances, she got married about two and a half years ago in Saint John's Church on Adams Boulevard. Oh, that was a big affair. Well, Missus Fusari, that'll be three dollars, ninety-four cents. How's that with you?

> (*The Italian woman produces an old leather change purse from her pocketbook and painfully extracts three single dollar bills and ninety-four cents to the penny and lays the money piece by piece on the counter.*)

YOUNG MOTHER (*Calling from the door*): Hey, Marty, I'm inna hurry.

MARTY (*Wrapping the meat, calls amiably back*): You're next right now, Missus Canduso.

(The old Italian lady has been regarding MARTY *with a baleful scowl.)*

ITALIAN WOMAN: Well, Marty, when you gonna get married? You should be ashamed. All your brothers and sisters, they all younger than you, and they married, and they got children. I just saw your mother inna fruit shop, and she says to me: "Hey, you know a nice girl for my boy Marty?" Watsa matter with you? That's no way. Watsa matter with you? Now, you get married, you hear me what I say?

MARTY *(Amiably)*: I hear you, Missus Fusari.
(The old lady takes her parcel of meat, but apparently feels she still hasn't quite made her point.)

ITALIAN WOMAN: My son Frank, he was married when he was nineteen years old. Watsa matter with you?

MARTY: Missus Fusari, Missus Canduso over there, she's inna big hurry, and . . .

ITALIAN WOMAN: You be ashamed of yourself.
(She takes her package of meat, turns, and shuffles to the door and exits. MARTY *gathers up the money on the counter, turns to the cash register behind him to ring up the sale.)*

YOUNG MOTHER: Marty, I want a nice big fat pullet, about four pounds. I hear your kid brother got married last Sunday.

MARTY: Yeah, it was a very nice affair, Missus Canduso.

YOUNG MOTHER: Marty, you oughtta be ashamed.
All your kid brothers and sisters, married and
have children. When you gonna get married?
(*Close-up:*   MARTY. *He sends a glance of
weary exasperation up to the ceiling.
With a gesture of mild irritation, he
pushes the plunger of the cash register.
It makes a sharp ping.*)

(*Dissolve to: Close-up of television set.
A baseball game is in progress. Camera
pulls back to show we are in a typical
neighborhood bar — red leatherette
booths — a jukebox, some phone booths.
About half the bar stools are occupied
by neighborhood folk.* MARTY *enters,
pads amiably to one of the booths where
a young man of about thirty-odd already
sits. This is* ANGIE. MARTY *slides into the
booth across from* ANGIE. ANGIE *is a little
wasp of a fellow. He has a newspaper
spread out before him to the sports
pages.* MARTY *reaches over and pulls one
of the pages over for himself to read.
For a moment the two friends sit across
from each other, reading the sports
pages. Then* ANGIE, *without looking up,
speaks.*)

ANGIE: Well, what do you feel like doing tonight?

MARTY: I don't know, Angie. What do you feel
like doing?

ANGIE: Well, we oughtta do something. It's Saturday night. I don't wanna go bowling like

last Saturday. How about calling up that big girl we picked up inna movies about a month ago in the RKO Chester?

MARTY (*Not very interested*):   Which one was that?

ANGIE: That big girl that was sitting in front of us with the skinny friend.

MARTY: Oh, yeah.

ANGIE: We took them home alla way out in Brooklyn. Her name was Mary Feeney. What do you say? You think I oughtta give her a ring? I'll take the skinny one.

MARTY: It's five o'clock already, Angie. She's probably got a date by now.

ANGIE: Well, let's call her up. What can we lose?

MARTY: I didn't like her, Angie. I don't feel like calling her up.

ANGIE: Well, what do you feel like doing to-night?

MARTY: I don't know. What do you feel like doing?

ANGIE: Well, we're back to that, huh? I say to you: "What do you feel like doing tonight?" And you say to me: "I don't know, what do you feel like doing?" And then we wind up sitting around your house with a couple of cans of beer, watching Sid Caesar on television. Well, I tell you what I feel like doing. I feel like calling up this Mary Feeney. She likes you. (MARTY *looks up quickly at this.*)

MARTY: What makes you say that?

ANGIE: I could see she likes you.

MARTY: Yeah, sure.

ANGIE (*Half rising in his seat*):   I'll call her up.

MARTY: You call her up for yourself, Angie. I
don't feel like calling her up.
> (ANGIE *sits down again. They both re-
> turn to reading the paper for a moment.
> Then* ANGIE *looks up again.*)

ANGIE: Boy, you're getting to be a real drag, you
know that?

MARTY: Angie, I'm thirty-six years old. I been
looking for a girl every Saturday night of my
life. I'm a little, short, fat fellow, and girls
don't go for me, that's all. I'm not like you.
I mean, you joke around, and they laugh at
you, and you get along fine. I just stand
around like a bug. What's the sense of kidding
myself? Everybody's always telling me to get
married. Get married. Get married. Don't you
think I wanna get married? I wanna get married. They drive me crazy. Now, I don't wanna
wreck your Saturday night for you, Angie. You
wanna go somewhere, you go ahead. I don't
wanna go.

ANGIE: Boy, they drive me crazy too. My old
lady, every word outta her mouth, when you
gonna get married?

MARTY: My mother, boy, she drives me crazy.
> (ANGIE *leans back in his seat, scowls at*

the paper-napkin container. MARTY *returns to the sports page. For a moment a silence hangs between them. Then . . .)*

ANGIE: So what do you feel like doing tonight?

MARTY (*Without looking up*): I don't know. What do you feel like doing?

(They both just sit, ANGIE *frowning at the napkin container,* MARTY *at the sports page.*

The camera slowly moves away from the booth, looks down the length of the bar, up the wall, past the clock — which reads ten to five — and over to the television screen, where the baseball game is still going on.)

(Dissolve slowly to: The television screen, now blank. The clock now reads a quarter to six.

Back in the booth, MARTY *now sits alone. In front of him are three empty beer bottles and a beer glass, half filled. He is sitting there, his face expressionless, but his eyes troubled. Then he pushes himself slowly out of the booth and shuffles to the phone booth; he goes inside, closing the booth door carefully after him. For a moment* MARTY *just sits squatly. Then with some exertion — due to the cramped quarters — he contrives to get a small address book out of his rear pants pocket. He slowly flips through it, finds the page he wants, and studies it, scowling; then he takes a dime from the change he has just received, plunks it into the proper slot, waits for a dial tone . . . then carefully dials a number. . . . He waits. He is beginning to sweat a bit in the hot little booth, and his chest begins to rise and fall deeply.*)

MARTY (*With a vague pretense at good diction*): Hello, is this Mary Feeney? . . . Could I please speak to Miss Mary Feeney? . . . Just tell her an old friend. . . . (*He waits again. With his free hand he wipes the gathering sweat from his brow.*) . . . Oh, hello there, is this Mary Feeney? Hello there, this is Marty Pilletti. I wonder if you recall me. . . . Well, I'm kind of a stocky guy. The last time we met was inna movies, the RKO Chester. You was with another girl, and I was with a friend of mine name Angie. This was about a month ago . . . (*The girl apparently doesn't remember him. A sort of panic begins to seize* MARTY. *His voice rises a little.*) The RKO Chester on Payne Boulevard. You was sitting in front of us, and we was annoying you, and you got mad, and . . . I'm the fellow who works inna butcher shop . . . come on, you know who I am! . . . That's right, we went to Howard Johnson's and we had hamburgers. You hadda milk shake. . . . Yeah, that's right. I'm the stocky one, the heavy-set fellow. . . . Well, I'm glad you recall me, because I hadda swell time that night, and I was just wondering how everything was with you. How's everything? . . . That's swell. . . . Yeah, well, I'll tell you why I called . . . I was figuring on taking in a movie tonight, and I was wondering if you and your friend would care to see a movie tonight with me and my friend. . . . (*His eyes are closed now.*) Yeah, tonight. I know it's pretty late to call for a date, but I didn't know myself till . . . Yeah, I know, well how about . . . Yeah, I know, well maybe next Saturday night. You free next Saturday night? . . . Well, how about the Saturday after that? . . . Yeah, I know. . . . Yeah . . . Yeah . . . Oh, I understand, I mean . . .

> (*He just sits now, his eyes closed, not really listening. After a moment he returns the receiver to its cradle and sits, his shoulders slack, his hands resting listlessly in the lap of his spotted white apron. . . . Then he opens his eyes, straightens himself, pushes the booth door open, and advances out into the bar. He perches on a stool across the bar from the bartender, who looks up from his magazine.*)

BARTENDER: I hear your kid brother got married last week, Marty.

MARTY (*Looking down at his hands on the bar*): Yeah, it was a very nice affair.

BARTENDER: Well, Marty, when you gonna get married?

> (MARTY *tenders the bartender a quick scowl, gets off his perch, and starts for the door — untying his apron as he goes.*)

MARTY: If my mother calls up, Lou, tell her I'm on my way home.

(Dissolve to: MARTY's *mother and a young couple sitting around the table in the dining room of* MARTY's *home. The young couple — we will soon find out — are* THOMAS, MARTY's *cousin, and his wife,* VIRGINIA. *They have apparently just been telling the mother some sad news, and the three are sitting around frowning. The dining room is a crowded room filled with chairs and lamps, pictures and little statues, perhaps even a small grotto of little vigil lamps. To the right of the dining room is the kitchen, old-fashioned, Italian, steaming, and overcrowded. To the left of the dining room is the living room, furnished in same fashion as the dining room. Just off the living room is a small bedroom, which is* MARTY's. *This bedroom and the living room have windows looking out on front. The dining room has windows looking out to a side alleyway. A stairway in the dining room leads to the second floor. The mother is a round, dark, effusive little woman.)*

MOTHER *(After a pause):*   Well, Thomas, I knew sooner or later this was gonna happen. I told Marty, I said: "Marty, you watch. There's gonna be real trouble over there in your cousin Thomas' house." Because your mother was here, Thomas, you know?

THOMAS: When was this, Aunt Theresa?

MOTHER: This was one, two, three days ago. Wednesday. Because I went to the fruit shop on Wednesday, and I came home. And I come arounna back, and there's your mother sitting onna steps onna porch. And I said: "Catherine, my sister, wadda you doing here?" And she look uppa me, and she beganna cry.

THOMAS (*To his wife*): Wednesday. That was the day you threw the milk bottle.

MOTHER: That's right. Because I said to her: "Catherine, watsa matter?" And she said to me: "Theresa, my daughter-in-law, Virginia, she just threw the milk bottle at me."

VIRGINIA: Well, you see what happen, Aunt Theresa . . .

MOTHER: I know, I know. . . .

VIRGINIA: She comes inna kitchen, and she begins poking her head over my shoulder here and poking her head over my shoulder there . . . .

MOTHER: I know, I know. . . .

VIRGINIA: And she begins complaining about this, and she begins complaining about that. And she got me so nervous, I spilled some milk I was making for the baby. You see, I was making some food for the baby, and . . .

MOTHER: So I said to her, "Catherine . . ."

VIRGINIA: So, she got me so nervous I spilled some milk. So she said: "You're spilling the milk," she says: "Milk costs twenny-four cents

a bottle. Wadda you, a banker?" So I said:
"Mamma, leave me alone, please. You're making me nervous. Go on in the other room and
turn on the television set." So then she began
telling me how I waste money, and how I can't
cook, and how I'm raising my baby all wrong,
and she kept talking about these couple of
drops of milk I split, and I got so mad, I said:
"Mamma, you wanna see me really spill some
milk?" So I took the bottle and threw it against
the door. I didn't throw it at her. That's just
something she made up. I didn't throw it any-
wheres near her. Well, of course, alla milk
went all over the floor. The whole twenny-four
cents. Well, I was sorry right away, you know,
but she ran outta the house.

(*Pause*)

MOTHER: Well, I don't know what you want me
to do, Virginia. If you want me, I'll go talk to
her tonight.

(THOMAS *and* VIRGINIA *suddenly frown
and look down at their hands as if of
one mind.*)

THOMAS: Well, I'll tell you, Aunt Theresa . . .

VIRGINIA: Lemme tell it, Tommy.

THOMAS: Okay.

VIRGINIA (*Leaning forward to the mother*): We
want you to do a very big favor for us, Aunt
Theresa.

MOTHER: Sure.

VIRGINIA: Aunt Theresa, you got this big house

here. You got four bedrooms upstairs. I mean, you got this big house just for you and Marty. All your other kids are married and got their own homes. And I thought maybe Tommy's mother could come here and live with you and Marty.

MOTHER: Well . . .

VIRGINIA: She's miserable living with Tommy and me, and you're the only one that gets along with her. Because I called up Tommy's brother, Joe, and I said: "Joe, she's driving me crazy. Why don't you take her for a couple of years?" And he said: "Oh, no!" I know I sound like a terrible woman. . . .

MOTHER: No, Virginia, I know how you feel. My husband, may God bless his memory, his mother, she lived with us for a long time, and I know how you feel.

VIRGINIA (*Practically on the verge of tears*): I just can't stand it no more! Every minute of the day! Do this! Do that! I don't have ten minutes alone with my husband! We can't even have a fight! We don't have no privacy! Everybody's miserable in our house!

THOMAS: All right, Ginnie, don't get so excited.

MOTHER: She's right. She's right. Young husband and wife, they should have their own home. And my sister, Catherine, she's my sister, but I gotta admit, she's an old goat. And plenny-a times in my life I feel like throwing the milk bottle at her myself. And I tell you now, as far as I'm concerned, if Catherine wantsa come live here with me and Marty, it's all right with me.

(VIRGINIA *promptly bursts into tears.*)

THOMAS (*Not far from tears himself, lowers his face*):   That's very nice-a you, Aunt Theresa.

MOTHER: We gotta ask Marty, of course, because this is his house too. But he's gonna come home any minute now.

VIRGINIA (*Having mastered her tears*):   That's very nice-a you, Aunt Theresa.

MOTHER (*Rising*):   Now, you just sit here. I'm just gonna turn onna small fire under the food. (*She exits into the kitchen.*)

VIRGINIA (*Calling after her*):   We gotta go right away because I promised the baby sitter we'd be home by six, and it's after six now. . . .
(*She kind of fades out. A moment of silence.* THOMAS *takes out a cigarette and lights it.*)

THOMAS (*Calling to his aunt in the kitchen*): How's Marty been lately, Aunt Theresa?

MOTHER (*Off in kitchen*):   Oh, he's fine. You know a nice girl he can marry? (*She comes back into the dining room, wiping her hands on a kitchen towel.*) I'm worried about him, you know? He's thirty-six years old, gonna be thirty-seven in January.

THOMAS: Oh, he'll get married, don't worry, Aunt Theresa.

MOTHER (*Sitting down again*): Well, I don't know. You know a place where he can go where he can find a bride?

THOMAS: The Waverly Ballroom. That's a good place to meet girls, Aunt Theresa. That's a kind of big dance hall, Aunt Theresa. Every Saturday night, it's just loaded with girls. It's a nice place to go. You pay seventy-seven cents. It used to be seventy-seven cents. It must be about a buck and a half now. And you go in and you ask some girl to dance. That's how I met Virginia. Nice, respectable place to meet girls. You tell Marty, Aunt Theresa, you tell him: "Go to the Waverly Ballroom. It's loaded with tomatoes."

MOTHER (*Committing the line to memory*): The Waverly Ballroom. It's loaded with tomatoes.

THOMAS: Right.

VIRGINIA: You tell him, go to the Waverly Ballroom.

> (*There is the sound of a door being un-latched off through the kitchen. The mother promptly rises.*)

MOTHER: He's here.

> (*She hurries into the kitchen. At the porch entrance to the kitchen, MARTY has just come in. He is closing the door behind him. He carries his butcher's apron in a bundle under his arm.*)

MARTY: Hello, Ma.

(*She comes up to him, lowers her voice
to a whisper.*)

MOTHER (*Whispers*): Marty, Thomas and Virginia are here. They had another big fight with
your Aunt Catherine. So they ask me, would it
be all right if Catherine come to live with us.
So I said, all right with me, but we have to
ask you. Marty, she's a lonely old lady. Nobody
wants her. Everybody's throwing her outta
their house. . . .

MARTY: Sure, Ma, it's okay with me.
(*The mother's face breaks into a fond
smile. She reaches up and pats his cheek
with genuine affection.*)

MOTHER: You gotta good heart. (*Turning and
leading the way back to the dining room.*
THOMAS *has risen.*) He says okay, it's all right
Catherine comes here.

THOMAS: Oh, Marty, thanks a lot. That really
takes a load offa my mind.

MARTY: Oh, we got plenny-a room here.

MOTHER: Sure! Sure! It's gonna be nice! It's
gonna be nice! I'll come over tonight to your
house, and I talk to Catherine, and you see,
everything is gonna work out all right.

THOMAS: I just wanna thank you people again
because the situation was just becoming impossible.

MOTHER: Siddown, Thomas, siddown. All right,
Marty, siddown. . . .

(She exits into the kitchen. MARTY has taken his seat at the head of the table and is waiting to be served. THOMAS takes a seat around the corner of the table from him and leans across to him.)

THOMAS: You see, Marty, the kinda thing that's been happening in our house is Virginia was inna kitchen making some food for the baby. Well, my mother comes in, and she gets Virginia so nervous, she spills a couple-a drops . . . .

VIRGINIA *(Tugging at her husband)*: Tommy, we gotta go. I promise the baby sitter six o'clock.

THOMAS *(Rising without interrupting his narrative)*: So she starts yelling at Virginia, wadda-ya spilling the milk for. So Virginia gets mad. . . . *(His wife is slowly pulling him to the kitchen door.)* She says, "You wanna really see me spill milk?" So Virginia takes the bottle and she throws it against the wall. She's got a real Italian temper, my wife, you know that. . . .

(He has been tugged to the kitchen by now.)

VIRGINIA: Marty, I don't have to tell you how much we appreciate what your mother and you are doing for us.

THOMAS: All right, Marty, I'll see you some other time. . . . I'll tell you all about it.

MARTY: I'll see you, Tommy.

(THOMAS *disappears into the kitchen
after his wife.*)

VIRGINIA (*Off, calling*):   Good-bye, Marty!
            (*Close in on* MARTY, *sitting at table.*)

MARTY: Good-bye, Virginia! See you soon!
            (*He folds his hands on the table before
            him and waits to be served. The mother
            enters from the kitchen. She sets the
            meat plate down in front of him and
            herself takes a chair around the corner
            of the table from him.* MARTY *without
            a word takes up his knife and fork and
            attacks the mountain of food in front of
            him. His mother sits quietly, her hands
            a little nervous on the table before her,
            watching him eat. Then . . .*)

MOTHER: So what are you gonna do tonight,
Marty?

MARTY: I don't know, Ma. I'm all knocked out.
I may just hang arounna house.
            (*The mother nods a couple of times.
            There is a moment of silence. Then . . .*)

MOTHER: Why don't you go to the Waverly Ballroom?
            (*This gives* MARTY *pause. He looks up.*)

MARTY: What?

MOTHER: I say, why don't you go to the Waverly
Ballroom? It's loaded with tomatoes.
            (MARTY *regards his mother for a mo-
            ment.*)

MARTY: It's loaded with what?

MOTHER: Tomatoes.

MARTY (*Snorts*): Ha! Who told you about the Waverly Ballroom?

MOTHER: Thomas, he told me it was a very nice place.

MARTY: Oh, Thomas. Ma, it's just a big dance hall, and that's all it is. I been there a hundred times. Loaded with tomatoes. Boy, you're funny, Ma.

MOTHER: Marty, I don't want you hang arrouna house tonight. I want you to go take a shave and go out and dance.

MARTY: Ma, when are you gonna give up? You gotta bachelor on your hands. I ain't never gonna get married.

MOTHER: You gonna get married.

MARTY: Sooner or later, there comes a point in a man's life when he gotta face some facts, and one fact I gotta face is that whatever it is that women like, I ain't got it. I chased enough girls in my life. I went to enough dances. I got hurt enough. I don't wanna get hurt no more. I just called a girl this afternoon, and I got a real brush-off, boy. I figured I was past the point of being hurt, but that hurt. Some stupid woman who I didn't even wanna call up. She gave me the brush. That's the history of my life. I don't wanna go to the Waverly Ballroom because all that ever happened to me there was girls made me feel like I was a bug. I got feelings, you know. I had enough pain. No, thank you.

MOTHER: Marty . . .

MARTY: Ma, I'm gonna stay home and watch Sid Caesar.

MOTHER: You gonna die without a son.

MARTY: So I'll die without a son.

MOTHER: Put on your blue suit. . . .

MARTY: Blue suit, gray suit, I'm still a fat little man. A fat little ugly man.

MOTHER: You not ugly.

MARTY (*His voice rising*): I'm ugly . . . I'm ugly! . . I'm UGLY!

MOTHER: Marty . . .

MARTY (*Crying aloud, more in anguish than in anger*):   Ma! Leave me alone! . . .
> (*He stands abruptly, his face pained and drawn. He makes half-formed gestures to his mother, but he can't find words at the moment. He turns and marches a few paces away, turns to his mother again.*)

MARTY: Ma, waddaya want from me?! Waddaya want from me?! I'm miserable enough as it is! Leave me alone! I'll go to the Waverly Ballroom! I'll put onna blue suit and I'll go! And you know what I'm gonna get for my trouble? Heartache! A big night of heartache!
> (*He sullenly marches back to his seat, sits down, picks up his fork, plunges it*)

*into the lasagna, and stuffs a mouthful
into his mouth; he chews vigorously for
a moment. It is impossible to remain
angry for long. After a while he is shaking his head and muttering.)*

MARTY: Loaded with tomatoes . . . boy, that's
rich . . . .
*(He plunges his fork in again. Camera
pulls slowly away from him and his
mother, who is seated — watching him.
Fade out.)*

ACT II

FADE IN: *Exterior, three-story building. Pan up to second floor . . . bright neon lights reading "Waverly Ballroom" . . . The large, dirty windows are open; and the sound of a fair-to-middling swing band whooping it up comes out.*

DISSOLVE TO: *Interior, Waverly Ballroom — large dance floor crowded with jitterbugging couples, eight-piece combination hitting a loud kick. Ballroom is vaguely dark, made so by papier-mâché over the chandeliers to create alleged romantic effect. The walls are lined with stags and waiting girls, singly and in small murmuring groups. Noise and mumble and drone.*

DISSOLVE TO: *Live shot — a row of stags along a wall. Camera is looking lengthwise down the row. Camera dollies slowly past each face, each staring out at the dance floor, watching in his own manner of hungry eagerness. Short, fat, tall, thin stags. Some pretend diffidence. Some exhibit patent hunger.*

Near the end of the line, we find MARTY *and* ANGIE, *freshly shaved and groomed. They are leaning against the wall, smoking, watching their more fortunate brethren out on the floor.*

ANGIE: Not a bad crowd tonight, you know?

MARTY: There was one nice-looking one there in a black dress and beads, but she was a little tall for me.

ANGIE (*Looking down past* MARTY *along the wall right into the camera*): There's a nice-looking little short one for you right now.

MARTY (*Following his gaze*): Where?

ANGIE: Down there. That little one there.
(*The camera cuts about eight faces down, to where the girls are now standing. Two are against the wall. One is facing them, with her back to the dance floor. This last is the one* ANGIE *has in mind. She is a cute little kid, about twenty, and she has a bright smile on — as if the other two girls are just amusing her to death.*)

MARTY: Yeah, she looks all right from here.

ANGIE: Well, go on over and ask her. You don't hurry up, somebody else'll grab her.
(MARTY *scowls, shrugs.*)

MARTY: Okay, let's go.
(*They slouch along past the eight stags, a picture of nonchalant unconcern. The three girls, aware of their approach, stiffen, and their chatter comes to a halt.* ANGIE *advances to one of the girls along the wall.*)

ANGIE: Waddaya say, you wanna dance?
(*The girl looks surprised — as if this*

*were an extraordinary invitation to re-
ceive in this place — looks confounded
at her two friends, shrugs, detaches herself from the group, moves to the outer
fringe of the pack of dancers, raises her
hands languidly to dancing position, and
awaits* ANGIE *with ineffable boredom.*
MARTY, *smiling shyly, addresses the short
girl.*)

MARTY: Excuse me, would you care for this
dance?

(*The short girl gives* MARTY *a quick
glance of appraisal, then looks quickly
at her remaining friend.*)

SHORT GIRL (*Not unpleasantly*): Sorry. I just
don't feel like dancing just yet.

MARTY: Sure.

(*He turns and moves back past the eight
stags, all of whom have covertly watched
his attempt. He finds his old niche by
the wall, leans there. A moment later he
looks guardedly down to where the short
girl and her friend are. A young, dapper
boy is approaching the short girl. He
asks her to dance. The short girl smiles,
excuses herself to her friend, and follows
the boy out onto the floor.* MARTY *turns
back to watching the dancers bleakly. A
moment later he is aware that someone
on his right is talking to him. . . . He
turns his head. It is a young man of
about twenty-eight.*)

MARTY: You say something to me?

YOUNG MAN: Yeah. I was just asking you if you was here stag or with a girl.

MARTY: I'm stag.

YOUNG MAN: Well, I'll tell you. I got stuck onna blind date with a dog, and I just picked up a nice chick, and I was wondering how I'm gonna get ridda the dog. Somebody to take her home, you know what I mean? I be glad to pay you five bucks if you take the dog home for me.

MARTY (*A little confused*):   What?

YOUNG MAN: I'll take you over, and I'll introduce you as an old army buddy of mine, and then I'll cut out. Because I got this chick waiting for me out by the hatcheck, and I'll pay you five bucks.

MARTY (*Stares at the young man*):   Are you kidding?

YOUNG MAN: No, I'm not kidding.

MARTY: You can't just walk off onna girl like that.

> (*The young man grimaces impatiently and moves down the line of stags. . . . * MARTY *watches him, still a little shocked at the proposition. About two stags down, the young man broaches his plan to another stag. This stag, frowning and pursing his lips, seems more receptive to the idea. . . . The young man takes out a wallet and gives the stag a five-dollar bill. The stag detaches himself from the*

wall and, a little ill at ease, follows the
young man back past MARTY *and into*
the lounge. MARTY *pauses a moment and*
then, concerned, walks to the archway
that separates the lounge from the ball-
room and looks in. The lounge is a nar-
row room with a bar and booths. In
contrast to the ballroom, it is brightly
lighted — causing MARTY *to squint. In*
the second booth from the archway sits
a girl, about twenty-eight. Despite the
careful grooming that she has put into
her cosmetics, she is blatantly plain. The
young man and the stag are standing,
talking to her. She is looking up at the
young man, her hands nervously grip-
ping her Coca-Cola glass. We cannot
hear what the young man is saying, but
it is apparent that he is introducing his
new-found army buddy and is going
through some cock-and-bull story about
being called away on an emergency.
The stag is presented as her escort-to-be,
who will see to it that she gets home
safely. The girl apparently is not taken
in at all by this, though she is trying
hard not to seem affected. She politely
rejects the stag's company and will get
home by herself, thanks for asking any-
way. The young man makes a few mild
protestations, and then he and the stag
leave the booth and come back to the
archway from where MARTY *has been*
watching the scene. As they pass MARTY,
we overhear a snatch of dialogue.)

YOUNG MAN: . . . In that case, as long as she's going home alone, give me the five bucks back . . . .

STAG: . . . Look, Mac, you paid me five bucks. I was willing. It's my five bucks. . . .

(*They pass on.* MARTY *returns his attention to the girl. She is still sitting as she was, gripping and ungripping the glass of Coca-Cola in front of her. Her eyes are closed. Then, with a little nervous shake of her head, she gets out of the booth and stands — momentarily at a loss for what to do next. The open fire doors leading out onto the large fire escape catch her eye. She crosses to the fire escape, nervous, frowning, and disappears outside.* MARTY *stares after her, then slowly shuffles to the open fire-escape doorway. It is a large fire escape, almost the size of a small balcony. The girl is standing by the railing, her back to the doorway, her head slunk down on her bosom. For a moment* MARTY *is unaware that she is crying. Then he notices the shivering tremors running through her body and the quivering shoulders. He moves a step onto the fire escape. He tries to think of something to say.*)

MARTY: Excuse me, Miss. Would you care to dance?

(*The girl slowly turns to him, her face streaked with tears, her lip trembling. Then, in one of those peculiar moments*

of simultaneous impluse, she lurches to
MARTY *with a sob, and* MARTY *takes her
to him. For a moment they stand in an
awkward embrace,* MARTY *a little embarrassed, looking out through the doors
to the lounge, wondering if anybody is
seeing them. Reaching back with one
hand, he closes the fire door, and then,
replacing the hand around her shoulder,
he stands stiffly, allowing her to cry on
his chest. Dissolve to: Exterior, apartment door. The mother standing, in a
black coat and a hat with a little feather,
waiting for her ring to be answered.
The door opens.* VIRGINIA *stands framed
in the doorway.*)

VIRGINIA: Hello, Aunt Theresa, come in.
(*The mother goes into the small foyer.*
VIRGINIA *closes the door.*)

MOTHER (*In a low voice, as she pulls her coat off*):
Is Catherine here?

VIRGINIA (*Helps her off with coat, nods — also in
a low voice*):   We didn't tell her nothing yet.
We thought we'd leave it to you. We thought
you'd put it like how you were lonely, and why
don't she come to live with you. Because that
way it looks like she's doing you a favor,
insteada we're throwing her out, and it won't
be so cruel on her. Thomas is downstairs with
the neighbors . . . I'll go call him.

MOTHER: You go downstairs to the neighbors
and stay there with Thomas.

VIRGINIA: Wouldn't it be better if we were here?

MOTHER: You go downstairs. I talk to Catherine alone. Otherwise, she's gonna start a fight with you.

> (*A shrill, imperious woman's voice from an off-stage room suddenly breaks into the muttered conference in the foyer.*)

AUNT (*Off*):   Who's there?! Who's there?!

> (*The mother heads up the foyer to the living room, followed by* VIRGINIA, *holding the mother's coat.*)

MOTHER (*Calls back*):   It's me, Catherine! How you feel?

> (*At the end of the foyer, the two sisters meet. The aunt is a spare, gaunt woman with a face carved out of granite. Tough, embittered, deeply hurt type face.*)

AUNT: Hey! What are you doing here?

MOTHER: I came to see you. (*The two sisters quickly embrace and release each other.*) How you feel?

AUNT: I gotta pain in my left side and my leg throbs like a drum.

MOTHER: I been getting pains in my shoulder.

AUNT: I got pains in my shoulder, too. I have a pain in my hip, and my right arm aches so much I can't sleep. It's a curse to be old. How do you feel?

MOTHER: I feel fine.

AUNT: That's nice.

> (*Now that the standard greetings are*

over, AUNT CATHERINE *abruptly turns
and goes back to her chair. It is obvi-
ously her chair. It is an old heavy oaken
chair with thick armrests. The rest of
the apartment is furnished in what is
known as "modern" — a piece from*
House Beautiful *here, a piece from* Better Homes and Gardens *there.* AUNT
CATHERINE *sits, erect and forbidding, in
her chair. The mother seats herself with
a sigh in a neighboring chair.* VIRGINIA,
*having hung the mother's coat, now
turns to the two older women. A pause.*)

VIRGINIA: I'm going downstairs to the Cappa-
cini's. I'll be up inna little while.
(AUNT CATHERINE *nods expressionlessly.*
VIRGINIA *looks at her for a moment, then
impulsively crosses to her mother-in-
law.*)

VIRGINIA: You feel all right?
(*The old lady looks up warily, sus-
picious of this sudden solicitude.*)

AUNT: I'm all right.
(*Virginia nods and goes off to the foyer.
The two old sisters sit, unmoving, wait-
ing for the door to close behind* VIR-
GINIA. *Then the mother addresses her-
self to* AUNT CATHERINE.)

MOTHER: We gotta post card from my son,
Nickie, and his bride this morning. They're in
Florida inna big hotel. Everything is very nice.

AUNT: That's nice.

MOTHER: Catherine, I want you come live with
me in my house with Marty and me. In my
house, you have your own room. You don't
have to sleep onna couch inna living room like
here. (*The aunt looks slowly and directly at the
mother.*) Catherine, your son is married. He
got his own home. Leave him in peace. He
wants to be alone with his wife. They don't
want no old lady sitting inna balcony. Come
and live with me. We will cook in the kitchen
and talk like when we were girls. You are dear
to me, and you are dear to Marty. We are
pleased for you to come.

AUNT: Did they come to see you?

MOTHER: Yes.

AUNT: Did my son Thomas come with her?

MOTHER: Your son Thomas was there.

AUNT: Did he also say he wishes to cast his
mother from his house?

MOTHER: Catherine, don't make an opera outta
this. The three-a you anna baby live in three
skinny rooms. You are an old goat, and she has
an Italian temper. She is a good girl, but you
drive her crazy. Leave them alone. They have
their own life.

> (*The old aunt turns her head slowly and
> looks her sister square in the face. Then
> she rises slowly from her chair.*)

AUNT (*Coldly*):   Get outta here. This is my son's
house. This is where I live. I am not to be cast
out inna street like a newspaper.

(*The mother likewise rises. The two old
women face each other directly*.)

MOTHER: Catherine, you are very dear to me.
We have cried many times together. When my
husband died, I would have gone insane if it
were not for you. I ask you to come to my
house because I can make you happy. Please
come to my house.

>   (*The two sisters regard each other. Then
>   AUNT CATHERINE sits again in her oaken
>   chair, and the mother returns to her
>   seat. The hardened muscles in the old
>   aunt's face suddenly slackens, and she
>   turns to her sister.*)

AUNT: Theresa, what shall become of me?

MOTHER: Catherine . . .

AUNT: It's gonna happen to you. Mark it well.
These terrible years. I'm afraida look inna
mirror. I'm afraid I'm gonna see an old lady
with white hair, like the old ladies inna park,
little bundles inna black shawl, waiting for the
coffin. I'm fifty-six years old. What am I to do
with myself? I have strength in my hands. I
wanna cook. I wanna clean. I wanna make dinner for my children. I wanna be of use to
somebody. Am I an old dog to lie in fronta the
fire till my eyes close? These are terrible years,
Theresa! Terrible years!

MOTHER: Catherine, my sister . . .
>   (*The old aunt stares distraught, at the
>   mother.*)

AUNT: It's gonna happen to you! It's gonna happen to you! What will you do if Marty gets married?! What will you cook?! What happen to alla children tumbling in alla rooms?! Where is the noise?! It is a curse to be a widow! A curse! What will you do if Marty gets married?! What will you do?!

(*She stares at the mother — her deep, gaunt eyes haggard and pained. The mother stares back for a moment, then her own eyes close. The aunt has hit home. The aunt sinks back into her chair, sitting stiffly, her arms on the thick armrests. The mother sits hunched a little forward, her hands nervously folded in her lap.*)

AUNT (*Quietly*): I will put my clothes inna bag and I will come to you tomorrow.

(*The camera slowly dollies back from the two somber sisters. Slow Fade-out.*)

(*Cut to: Close-up, intimate,* MARTY *and the girl dancing cheek to cheek. Occasionally the heads of other couples slowly waft across the camera view, temporarily blocking out view of* MARTY *and the girl. Camera stays with them as the slow dance carries them around the floor. Tender scene.*)

GIRL: . . . The last time I was here the same sort of thing happened.

MARTY: Yeah?

GIRL: Well, not exactly the same thing. The last

time I was up here was about four months ago.
Do you see that girl in the gray dress sitting
over there?

MARTY: Yeah.

GIRL: That's where I sat. I sat there for an hour
and a half without moving a muscle. Now and
then, some fellow would sort of walk up to me
and then change his mind. I just sat there, my
hands in my lap. Well, about ten o'clock, a
bunch of kids came in swaggering. They
weren't more than seventeen, eighteen years
old. Well, they swaggered down along the
wall, leering at all the girls. I thought they
were kind of cute . . . and as they passed me,
I smiled at them. One of the kids looked at
me and said: "Forget it, ugly, you ain't gotta
chance." I burst out crying. I'm a big crier, you
know.

MARTY: So am I.

GIRL: And another time when I was in college . . .

MARTY: I cry alla time. Any little thing. I can
recognize pain a mile away. My brothers, my
brother-in-laws, they're always telling me what
a goodhearted guy I am. Well, you don't get
goodhearted by accident. You get kicked
around long enough you get to be a real pro-
fessor of pain. I know exactly how you feel.
And I also want you to know I'm having a very
good time with you now and really enjoying
myself. So you see, you're not such a dog as you
think you are.

GIRL: I'm having a very good time too.

MARTY: So there you are. So I guess I'm not such a dog as I think I am.

GIRL: You're a very nice guy, and I don't know why some girl hasn't grabbed you off long ago.

MARTY: I don't know either. I think I'm a very nice guy. I also think I'm a pretty smart guy in my own way.

GIRL: I think you are.

MARTY: I'll tell you some of my wisdom which I thunk up on those nights when I got stood up, and nights like that, and you walk home thinking: "Watsa matter with me? I can't be that ugly." Well, I figure, two people get married, and they gonna live together forty, fifty years. So it's just gotta be more than whether they're good-looking or not. My father was a real ugly man, but my mother adored him. She told me that she used to get so miserable sometimes, like everybody, you know? And she says my father always tried to understand. I used to see them sometimes when I was a kid, sitting in the living room, talking and talking, and I used to adore my old man because he was so kind. That's one of the most beautiful things I have in my life, the way my father and my mother were. And my father was a real ugly man. So it don't matter if you look like a gorilla. So you see, dogs like us, we ain't such dogs as we think we are.

> (*They dance silently for a moment, cheeks pressed against each other. Close-ups of each face.*)

GIRL: I'm twenty-nine years old. How old are you?

MARTY: Thirty-six.
(*They dance silently, closely. Occasionally the heads of other couples sway in front of the camera, blocking our view of* MARTY *and the girl. Slow, sweet dissolve.*)

(*Dissolve to: Interior, kitchen,* MARTY's *home. Later that night. It is dark. Nobody is home. The rear porch door now opens, and the silhouettes of* MARTY *and the girl appear — blocking up the doorway.*)

MARTY: Wait a minute. Lemme find the light.
(*He finds the light. The kitchen is suddenly brightly lit. The two of them stand squinting to adjust to the sudden glare.*)

MARTY: I guess my mother ain't home yet. I figure my cousin Thomas and Virginia musta gone to the movies, so they won't get back till one o'clock, at least.
(*The girl has advanced into the kitchen, a little ill at ease, and is looking around.* MARTY *closes the porch door.*)

MARTY: This is the kitchen.

GIRL: Yes, I know.
(*Marty leads the way into the dining room.*)

MARTY: Come on inna dining room. (*He turns on the light in there as he goes. The girl fol-*

lows him in.) Siddown, take off your coat. You want something to eat? We gotta whole half a chicken left over from yesterday.

GIRL (*Perching tentatively on the edge of a chair*): No, thank you. I don't think I should stay very long.

MARTY: Sure. Just take off your coat a minute. (*He helps her off with her coat and stands for a moment behind her, looking down at her. Conscious of his scrutiny, she sits uncomfortably, her breasts rising and falling unevenly.* MARTY *takes her coat into the dark living room. The girl sits patiently, nervously.* MARTY *comes back, sits down on another chair. Awkward silence.*)

MARTY: So I was telling you, my kid brother Nickie got married last Sunday. . . . That was a very nice affair. And they had this statue of some woman, and they had whisky spouting outta her mouth. I never saw anything so grand in my life. (*The silence falls between them again.*) And watta meal. I'm a butcher, so I know a good hunka steak when I see one. That was choice filet, right off the toppa the chuck. A buck-eighty a pound. Of course, if you wanna cheaper cut, get rib steak. That gotta lotta waste on it, but it comes to about a buck and a quarter a pound, if it's trimmed. Listen, Clara, make yourself comfortable. You're all tense.

GIRL: Oh, I'm fine.

MARTY: You want me to take you home, I'll
take you home.

GIRL: Maybe that would be a good idea.
*(She stands. He stands, frowning, a little
angry — turns sullenly and goes back
into the living room for her coat. She
stands unhappily. He comes back and
wordlessly starts to help her into her
coat. He stands behind her, his hands
on her shoulders. He suddenly seizes
her, begins kissing her on the neck.
Camera comes up quickly to intensely
intimate close-up, nothing but the
heads. The dialogue drops to quick,
hushed whispers.)*

GIRL: No, Marty, please . . .

MARTY: I like you, I like you, I been telling you
all night I like you. . . .

GIRL: Marty . . .

MARTY: I just wanna kiss, that's all. . . .
*(He tries to turn her face to him. She
resists.)*

GIRL: No . . .

MARTY: Please . . .

GIRL: No . . .

MARTY: Please . . .

GIRL: Marty . . .
*(He suddenly releases her, turns away
violently.)*

MARTY (*Crying out*): All right! I'll take you
home! All right! (*He marches a few angry
paces away, deeply disturbed, and then turns
to her.*) All I wanted was a lousy kiss! What am
I, a leper or something?!

> (*He turns and goes off into the living
> room to hide the flush of hot tears
> threatening to fill his eyes. The girl
> stands, herself on the verge of tears.*)

GIRL (*Mutters, more to herself than to him*): I
just didn't feel like it, that's all.

> (*She moves slowly to the archway lead-
> ing to the living room.* MARTY *is sitting
> on the couch, hands in his lap, looking
> straight ahead. The room is dark except
> for the overcast of the diningroom light
> reaching in. The girl goes to the couch,
> perches on the edge beside him. He
> doesn't look at her.*)

MARTY: Well, that's the history of my life. I'm
a little, short, fat, ugly guy. Comes New Year's
Eve, everybody starts arranging parties, I'm
the guy they gotta dig up a date for. I'm old
enough to know better. Let me get a packa
cigarettes, and I'll take you home.

> (*He starts to rise, but doesn't . . . sinks
> back onto the couch, looking straight
> ahead. The girl looks at him, her face
> peculiarly soft and compassionate.*)

GIRL: I'd like to see you again, very much. The
reason I didn't let you kiss me was because I
just didn't know how to handle the situation.
You're the kindest man I ever met. The reason

I tell you this is because I want to see you
again very much. Maybe, I'm just so desperate
to fall in love that I'm trying too hard. But I
know that when you take me home, I'm going
to just lie on my bed and think about you. I
want very much to see you again.

> (MARTY *stares down at his hands in his
> lap.*)

MARTY (*Without looking at her*):   Waddaya doing tomorrow night?

GIRL: Nothing.

MARTY: I'll call you up tomorrow morning.
Maybe we'll go see a movie.

GIRL: I'd like that very much.

MARTY: The reason I can't be definite about it
now is my Aunt Catherine is probably coming
over tomorrow, and I may have to help out.

GIRL: I'll wait for your call.

MARTY: We better get started to your house because the buses only run about one an hour
now.

GIRL: All right.
> (*She stands.*)

MARTY: I'll just get a packa cigarettes.
> (*He goes into his bedroom. We can see
> him through the doorway, opening his
> bureau drawer and extracting a pack of
> cigarettes. He comes out again and looks
> at the girl for the first time. They start
> to walk to the dining room. In the arch-
> way,* MARTY *pauses, turns to the girl.*)

MARTY: Waddaya doing New Year's Eve?

GIRL: Nothing.
>   (*They quietly slip into each other's arms
>   and kiss. Slowly their faces part, and
>   MARTY's head sinks down upon her
>   shoulder. He is crying. His shoulders
>   shake slightly. The girl presses her cheek
>   against the back of his head. They
>   stand . . . there is the sound of the
>   rear porch door being unlatched. They
>   both start from their embrace. A mo-
>   ment later the mother's voice is heard
>   off in the kitchen.*)

MOTHER: Hallo! Hallo! Marty? (*She comes into
the dining room, stops at the sight of the girl.*)
Hallo, Marty, when you come home?

MARTY: We just got here about fifteen minutes
ago, Ma. Ma, I want you to meet Miss Clara
Davis. She's a graduate of New York University. She teaches history in Benjamin Franklin
High School.
>   (*This seems to impress the mother.*)

MOTHER: Siddown, siddown. You want some
chicken? We got some chicken in the icebox.

GIRL: No, Mrs. Pilletti, we were just going
home. Thank you very much anyway.

MOTHER: Well, siddown a minute. I just come
inna house. I'll take off my coat. Siddown a
minute.
>   (*She pulls her coat off.*)

MARTY: How'd you come home, Ma? Thomas give you a ride?
> (*The mother nods.*)

MOTHER: Oh, it's a sad business, a sad business. (*She sits down on a dining room chair, holding her coat in her lap. She turns to the girl, who likewise sits.*)

MOTHER: My sister Catherine, she don't get along with her daughter-in-law, so she's gonna come live with us.

MARTY: Oh, she's coming, eh, Ma?

MOTHER: Oh, sure. (*To the girl*) It's a very sad thing. A woman, fifty-six years old, all her life, she had her own home. Now, she's just an old lady, sleeping on her daughter-in-law's couch. It's a curse to be a mother, I tell you. Your children grow up and then what is left for you to do? What is a mother's life but her children? It is a very cruel thing when your son has no place for you in his home.

GIRL: Couldn't she find some sort of hobby to fill out her time?

MOTHER: Hobby! What can she do? She cooks and she cleans. You gotta have a house to clean. You gotta have children to cook for. These are the terrible years for a woman, the terrible years.

GIRL: You mustn't feel too harshly against her daughter-in-law. She also wants to have a house to clean and a family to cook for.
> (*The mother darts a quick, sharp look*

at the girl — then looks back to her hands, which are beginning to twist nervously.)

MOTHER: You don't think my sister Catherine should live in her daughter-in-law's house?

GIRL: Well, I don't know the people, of course, but, as a rule, I don't think a mother-in-law should live with a young couple.

MOTHER: Where do you think a mother-in-law should go?

GIRL: I don't think a mother should depend so much upon her children for her rewards in life.

MOTHER: That's what it says in the book in New York University. You wait till you are a mother. It don't work out that way.

GIRL: Well, its silly for me to argue about it. I don't know the people involved.

MARTY: Ma, I'm gonna take her home now. It's getting late, and the buses only run about one an hour.

MOTHER (*Standing*): Sure.
(*The girl stands.*)

GIRL: It was very nice meeting you, Mrs. Pilletti. I hope I'll see you again.

MOTHER: Sure.
(*Marty and the girl move to the kitchen.*)

MARTY: All right, Ma. I'll be back in about an hour.

MOTHER: Sure.

GIRL: Good night, Mrs. Pilletti.

MOTHER: Good night.
>   (MARTY *and the girl exit into the
>   kitchen. The mother stands, expression-
>   less, by her chair watching them go. She
>   remains standing rigidly even after the
>   porch door can be heard being opened
>   and shut. The camera moves up to a
>   close-up of the mother. Her eyes are
>   wide. She is staring straight ahead.
>   There is fear in her eyes. Fade out.)*

ACT III

FADE-IN: *Film — close-up of church bells clanging away. Pan down church to see typical Sunday morning, people going up the steps of a church and entering. It is a beautiful June morning.*

DISSOLVE TO: *Interior, MARTY's bedroom — sun fairly streaming through the curtains. Marty is standing in front of his bureau, slipping his arms into a clean white shirt. He is freshly shaved and groomed. Through the doorway of his bedroom we can see the mother in the dining room, in coat and hat, all set to go to Mass, taking the last breakfast plates away and carrying them into the kitchen. The camera moves across the living room into the dining room. The mother comes out of the kitchen with a paper napkin and begins crumbing the table.*

There is a knock on the rear porch door. The mother leaves her crumbing and goes into the kitchen. Camera goes with her. She opens the rear door to admit AUNT CATHERINE, holding a worn old European carpetbag. The aunt starts to go deeper into the kitchen, but the mother stays her with her hand.

MOTHER (*In low, conspiratorial voice*):   Hey, I
come home from your house last night, Marty
was here with a girl.

AUNT: Who?

MOTHER: Marty.

AUNT: Your son Marty?

MOTHER: Well, what Marty you think is gonna
be here in this house with a girl?

AUNT: Were the lights on?

MOTHER: Oh, sure. (*Frowns suddenly at her sister*) The girl is a college graduate.

AUNT: They're the worst. College girls are one
step from the streets. They smoke like men
inna soloon.
> (*The aunt puts her carpetbag down and
> sits on one of the wooden kitchen chairs.
> The mother sits on another.*)

MOTHER: That's the first time Marty ever
brought a girl to this house. She seems like a
nice girl. I think he has a feeling for this girl.
> (*At this moment a burst of spirited
> whistling emanates from* MARTY's *bed-
> room. Cut to:* MARTY's *bedroom —*
> MARTY *standing in front of his mirror,
> buttoning his shirt or adjusting his tie,
> whistling a gay tune. Cut back to: The
> two sisters, both their faces turned in
> the direction of the whistling. The whis-
> tling abruptly stops. The two sisters
> look at each other. The aunt shrugs.*)

MOTHER: He been whistling like that all morning.

> (*The aunt nods bleakly.*)

AUNT: He is bewitched. You will see. Today, tomorrow, inna week, he's gonna say to you: "Hey, Ma, it's no good being a single man. I'm tired running around." Then he's gonna say: "Hey, ma, wadda we need this old house? Why don't we sell this old house, move into a nicer parta town? A nice little apartment?"

MOTHER: I don't sell this house, I tell you that. This is my husband's house, and I had six children in this house.

AUNT: You will see. A couple-a months, you gonna be an old lady, sleeping onna couch in your daughter-in-law's house.

MOTHER: Catherine, you are a blanket of gloom. Wherever you go, the rain follows. Some day, you gonna smile, and we gonna declare a holiday.

> (*Another burst of spirited whistling comes from* MARTY, *off. It comes closer, and* MARTY *now enters in splendid spirits, whistling away. He is slipping into his jacket.*)

MARTY (*Ebulliently*):   Hello, Aunt Catherine! How are you? You going to Mass with us?

AUNT: I was at Mass two hours ago.

MARTY: Well, make yourself at home. The refrigerator is loaded with food. Go upstairs, take any room you want. It's beautiful outside, ain't it?

AUNT: There's a chill. Watch out, you catch a good cold and pneumonia.

MOTHER: My sister Catherine, she can't even admit it's a beautiful day.
   (MARTY — *now at the sink, getting himself a glass of water — is examining a piece of plaster that has fallen from the ceiling.*)

MARTY (*Examining the chunk of plaster in his palm*):   Boy, this place is really coming to pieces. (*Turns to mother*) You know, Ma, I think, sometime we oughtta sell this place. The plumbing is rusty — everything. I'm gonna have to replaster that whole ceiling now. I think we oughtta get a little apartment somewheres in a nicer parta town. . . . You all set, Ma?

MOTHER: I'm all set.
   (*She starts for the porch door. She slowly turns and looks at* MARTY, *and then at* AUNT CATHERINE — *who returns her look. Mother and* MARTY *exit. Dissolve to: Church. The mother comes out of the doors and down a few steps to where* MARTY *is standing, enjoying the clearness of the June morning.*)

MOTHER: In a couple-a minutes nine o'clock Mass is gonna start — in a couple-a minutes . . . (*To passers-by off*) hallo, hallo . . . (*To* MARTY) Well, that was a nice girl last night, Marty. That was a nice girl.

MARTY: Yeah.

MOTHER: She wasn't a very good-looking girl, but she looks like a nice girl. I said, she wasn't a very good-looking girl, not very pretty.

MARTY: I heard you, Ma.

MOTHER: She look a little old for you, about thirty-five, forty years old?

MARTY: She's only twenny-nine, Ma.

MOTHER: She's more than twenny-nine years old, Marty. That's what she tells you. She looks thirty-five, forty. She didn't look Italian to me. I said, is she an Italian girl?

MARTY: I don't know. I don't think so.

MOTHER: She don't look like Italian to me. What kinda family she come from? There was something about her I don't like. It seems funny, the first time you meet her she comes to your empty house alone. These college girls, they all one step from the streets.

(MARTY *turns, frowning, to his mother.*)

MARTY: What are you talkin' about? She's a nice girl.

MOTHER: I don't like her.

MARTY: You don't like her? You only met her for two minutes.

MOTHER: Don't bring her to the house no more.

MARTY: What didn't you like about her?

MOTHER: I don't know! She don't look like Italian to me, plenty nice Italian girls around.

MARTY: Well, let's not get into a fight about it,
Ma. I just met the girl. I probably won't see
her again.

> (MARTY *leaves frame.*)

MOTHER: Eh, I'm no better than my sister
Catherine.

> (*Dissolve to: Interior, the bar . . .
> about an hour latter. The after-Mass
> crowd is there, about six men ranging
> from twenty to forty. A couple of women
> in the booths. One woman is holding a
> glass of beer in one hand and is gently
> rocking a baby carriage with the other.
> Sitting in the booth of Act I are* ANGIE
> *and three other fellows, ages twenty,
> thirty-two, and forty. One of the fellows,
> aged thirty-two, is giving a critical
> résumé of a recent work of literature by
> Mickey Spillane.*)

CRITIC: . . . So the whole book winds up, Mike
Hammer, he's inna room there with this doll.
So he says: "You rat, you are the murderer."
So she begins to con him, you know? She tells
him how she loves him. And then Bam! he
shoots her in the stomach. So she's laying there,
gasping for breath, and she says: "How could
you do that?" And he says: "It was easy."

TWENTY-YEAR-OLD: Boy, that Mickey Spillane.
Boy, he can write.

ANGIE (*Leaning out of the booth and looking
down the length of the bar, says with some
irritation*):   What's keeping Marty?

CRITIC: What I like about Mickey Spillane is he knows how to handle women. In one book, he picks up a tomato who gets hit with a car, and she throws a pass at him. And then he meets two beautiful twins, and they throw passes at him. And then he meets some beautiful society leader, and she throws a pass at him, and . . .

TWENTY-YEAR-OLD: Boy, that Mickey Spillane, he sure can write . . . .

ANGIE (*Looking out, down the bar again*): I don't know watsa matter with Marty.

FORTY-YEAR-OLD: Boy, Angie, what would you do if Marty ever died? You'd die right with him. A couple-a old bachelors hanging to each other like barnacles. There's Marty now.
   (ANGIE *leans out of the booth.*)

ANGIE (*Calling out*): Hello, Marty, where you been?
       (*Cut to: Front end of the bar.* MARTY *has just come in. He waves back to* ANGIE, *acknowledges another hello from a man by the bar, goes over to the bar and gets the bartender's attention.*)

MARTY: Hello, Lou, gimme change of a half and put a dime in it for a telephone call.
       (*The bartender takes the half dollar, reaches into his apron pocket for the change.*)

BARTENDER: I hear you was at the Waverly Ballroom last night.

MARTY: Yeah. Angie tell you?

BARTENDER (*Picking out change from palm full of silver*):   Yeah, I hear you really got stuck with a dog.

> (MARTY *looks at him.*)

MARTY: She wasn't so bad.

BARTENDER (*Extending the change*):   Angie says she was a real scrawny-looking thing. Well, you can't have good luck alla time.

> (MARTY *takes the change slowly and frowns down at it. He moves down the bar and would make for the telephone booth, but* ANGIE *hails him from the booth.*)

ANGIE: Who you gonna call, Marty?

MARTY: I was gonna call that girl from last night, take her to a movie tonight.

ANGIE: Are you kidding?

MARTY: She was a nice girl. I kinda liked her.

ANGIE (*Indicating the spot in the booth vacated by the forty-year-old*):   Siddown. You can call her later.

> (MARTY *pauses, frowning, and then shuffles to the booth where* ANGIE *and the other two sit. The critic moves over for* MARTY. *There is an exchange of hellos.*)

TWENTY-YEAR-OLD: I gotta girl, she's always asking me to marry her. So I look at that face, and I say to myself: "Could I stand looking at that face for the resta my life?"

CRITIC: Hey, Marty, you ever read a book called *I, the Jury,* by Mickey Spillane?

MARTY: No.

ANGIE: Listen, Marty, I gotta good place for us to go tonight. The kid here, he says he was downna bazaar at Our Lady of Angels last night and . . .

MARTY: I don't feel like going to the bazaar, Angie. I thought I'd take this girl to a movie.

ANGIE: Boy, you really musta made out good last night.

MARTY: We just talked.

ANGIE: Boy, she must be some talker. She musta been about fifty years old.

CRITIC: I always figger a guy oughtta marry a girl who's twenny years younger than he is, so that when he's forty, his wife is a real nice-looking doll.

TWENTY-YEAR-OLD: That means he'd have to marry the girl when she was one year old.

CRITIC: I never thoughta that.

MARTY: I didn't think she was so bad-looking.

ANGIE: She musta kept you inna shadows all night.

CRITIC: Marty, you don't wanna hang around with dogs. It gives you a bad reputation.

ANGIE: Marty, let's go downna bazaar.

MARTY: I told this dog I was gonna call her today.

ANGIE: Brush her.
(MARTY *looks questioningly at* ANGIE.)

MARTY: You didn't like her at all?

ANGIE: A nothing. A real nothing.
(MARTY *looks down at the dime he has been nervously turning between two fingers and then, frowning, he slips it into his jacket pocket. He lowers his face and looks down, scowling at his thoughts. Around him, the voices clip along.*)

CRITIC: What's playing on Fordham Road? I think there's a good picture in the Loew's Paradise.

ANGIE: Let's go down to Forty-second Street and walk around. We're sure to wind up with something.
(*Slowly* MARTY *begins to look up again. He looks from face to face as each speaks.*)

CRITIC: I'll never forgive LaGuardia for cutting burlesque outta New York City.

TWENTY-YEAR-OLD: There's burlesque over in Union City. Let's go to Union City. . . .

ANGIE: Ah, they're always crowded on Sunday night.

CRITIC: So wadda you figure on doing tonight, Angie?

ANGIE: I don't know. Wadda you figure on doing?

CRITIC: I don't know. (*Turns to the twenty-year-old*) Wadda you figure on doing?

(*The twenty-year-old shrugs. Suddenly* MARTY *brings his fist down on the booth table with a crash. The others turn, startled, toward him.* MARTY *rises in his seat.*)

MARTY: "What are you doing tonight?" "I don't know, what are you doing?" Burlesque! Loew's Paradise! Miserable and lonely! Miserable and lonely and stupid! What am I, crazy or something?! I got something good! What am I hanging around with you guys for?!

(*He has said this in tones so loud that it attracts the attention of everyone in the bar. A little embarrassed,* MARTY *turns and moves quickly to the phone booth, pausing outside the door to find his dime again.* ANGIE *is out of his seat immediately and hurries after him.*)

ANGIE (*A little shocked at* MARTY's *outburst*): Watsa matter with you?

MARTY (*In a low, intense voice*):   You don't like her. My mother don't like her. She's a dog, and I'm a fat, ugly little man. All I know is I had a good time last night. I'm gonna have a good time tonight. If we have enough good times together, I'm going down on my knees and beg that girl to marry me. If we make a party again this New Year's, I gotta date for the party. You don't like her, that's too bad. (*He moves into the booth, sits, turns again to Angie, smiles.*) When you gonna get married, Angie? You're thirty-four years old. All your kid brothers are married. You oughtta be ashamed of yourself.

> (*Still smiling at his private joke, he puts the dime into the slot and then — with a determined finger — he begins to dial. Fade out.*)

ALL THE WAY HOME

By Tad Mosel

Based on the novel, *A Death in the Family,*
by James Agee.

CHARACTERS

Rufus
Boys
Jay Follet
Ralph Follet
Sally Follet
John Henry Follet
Jessie Follet
Jim-Wilson Follet
Aunt Sadie Follet
Great-Great Granmaw Follet
Catherine Lynch
Aunt Hannah Lynch
Joel Lynch
Andrew Lynch
Father Jackson

SYNOPSIS

The action takes place in and around Knoxville, Tennessee, and covers a period of four days in May of 1915.

ACT I

The first day

ACT II

The second day

ACT III

Two days later

THE SETTING OF THE PLAY

The FOLLETS *live in a mixed sort of neighborhood, fairly solidly lower middle class, with one or two juts apiece on either side of that. The houses correspond: middle-sized gracefully fretted wood houses built in the late nineties and early nineteen hundreds, with small front and side and more spacious back yards, and porches, and trees in the yards. These are soft-wooded trees, poplars, tulip trees, cottonwoods. There are fences around one or two of the houses, but mainly the yards run into each other with only now and then a low hedge that isn't doing very well.*

The stage itself is encircled by a high cyclorama of vertical grey clapboards, suggesting perhaps the walls of a house, the paling of a gigantic fence, or even the sky. It is a background for the action of the play, dim, indistinguishable at times, bright and sunny at others, but always unobtrusive.

The structure of the FOLLETS' *two story house fills most of the stage. The living room is stage*

199

left, with an upright piano against the cyclo-
rama, a Morris chair, and a davenport facing the
audience. The kitchen is stage center, with a ta-
ble and two chairs, a sink, an icebox, a small
cupboard, and a telephone. The stairs rise to the
second floor upstage, between the living room
and the kitchen. There are two bedrooms up-
stairs, the larger one belongs to MARY *and* JAY,
center stage, over the kitchen, and containing a
double bed and a bureau. RUFUS's *room is stage*
left, over the living room, with a small child's
bed, a rocking chair, and a decorated trunk.
Only the furniture mentioned is visible. Only
the most necessary properties are used.

There are no interior or exterior walls to the
house, and window shades suspended in mid-air
suggest windows. The characters move from
room to room, into the house or out of the
house, without regard to placement of doors. If
a character upstairs wishes to speak to a character
in the yard, he merely steps to the edge of the
second story and calls down to him. Sometimes
the characters cannot hear what is going on in
another room, and at other times the rooms
join together to become a single acting area.

The only solid wall on the stage is the up-
stage wall of the kitchen, behind which is an es-
cape area for the actors. From the kitchen, a
practical door in this wall leads to the bathroom.
At the foot of the stairs, another door opens into
a closet. By going around the other side of the
stairs, the characters presumably go into the oth-
er downstairs rooms of the house.

Stage right, between the structure of the house

and the cyclorama, there is an open area with an old-fashioned swing suspended from the flies. Sometimes this area is the FOLLETS' *yard, sometimes it is a streetcar stop (when the swing becomes the waiting bench), and one it is* GREAT-GREAT-GRANMAW's *yard. Below the house, running across the front of the stage, there is another shallow area which is sometimes part of the* FOLLETS' *yard, sometimes a sidewalk, and once it is a road.*

ACT I

AT RISE:

RUFUS, *aged six, in the yard. Four older boys wearing rakish, gaudy caps dance around him, jumping up and down with ferocious joy, shoving their fingers at his chest, his stomach, and face, screaming and chanting.* JAY *enters and watches, unseen by them.*

RUFUS (*As the curtain rises, one clear frantic call*): My name is Rufus!

BOYS (*Together*):   Nigger's name, nigger's name, nigger's name!

RUFUS: Rufus! Rufus!

FIRST BOY (*As the others chant "nigger's name!"*):
Nigger, nigger, black as tar,
Tried to ride a 'lectric car,
Car broke down and broke his back,
Poor nigger wanted his nickel back!

RUFUS: I'm Rufus!

BOYS (*Together*): Uh-Rufus, uh-Rastus, uh-Johnson, uh-Brown,

Uh-what ya gonna do when the rent comes 'roun'?

Uh-Rufus, uh-Rastus, uh-Johnson, uh-Brown, Uh-what ya gonna do when the rent comes 'roun'?

> (RUFUS *makes one desperate effort to escape, running straight into* JAY's *arms.*)

FIRST BOY: Nigger name! Hey, we're gonna catch hell!

> (*They scramble off, and* JAY *looks after them, glowering. Then he puts his hand on* RUFUS's *head and smiles down at him.*)

JAY: What in the world you doin', Google Eyes?

RUFUS: I wish my name was Google Eyes.

JAY: No you don't, because that's a funny name. You wouldn't want to be called by a funny name.

RUFUS: Rufus is a funny name.

JAY: No, honey, it ain't.

RUFUS: It's a nigger's name.

JAY (*Looking out over the valley*):   Look, we got a nice clear day for the outing, don't we. You can see all the way to North Knoxville. And if you squint your eyes you can see the North Pole. Squint your eyes (*They both squint for a moment.*) See the Pole? (RUFUS *nods, enchanted.*) And see that puff o' smoke comin' up over the hill? That means there'll be a train along the viaduct any minute. The one-oh-seven.

MARY (*Off*):   Rufus — ?

RUFUS: Mama's calling me.

JAY (*Taking his hand, in high good spirits*): Let's just watch that train go by! (*They both look out.*) You know, Rufus is a very fine old name, Rufus. Some colored people take it too, but that is perfectly all right and nothing for them to be ashamed of, or for white people to be ashamed of who take it. You were given that name because it was your Great-Grand-father Lynch's name, your mama's grandfather, and it's a name to be proud of. You're proud of it, ain't you?

RUFUS: Yes, sir.

JAY: Then you got to stand up for it. Can you spell brave?

RUFUS: B-r-a-v-e.

JAY: Now proud.

RUFUS: P-r-o-u-d.

JAY: That's the one. Just keep spellin' that.

RUFUS: P-r-o-u-d.

JAY: You know what I'm proud of?

RUFUS (*Guessing*):   Mama?

JAY: You, too. Why, you're only six years old,

and you can read and spell like I couldn't
when I was twicet your age.

RUFUS (*Looking off, after the boys*): I wish you
could be proud of me because I'm brave.

JAY: One of these days you'll get those boys to
shake you by the hand. When a man shakes
you by the hand, that means you've won him
over. (*He puts out his hand.* RUFUS *grabs it.*)
Hold on there, y'only got me by the ends of the
fingers. Push your thumb clear up against
mine, that's it! — then wrap your fingers as
far's you can around the palm of my hand,
right to the other side, if you can. Now
squeeze. Not too much, that's just braggin'.
Just enough to show you mean what you're
doin'. Now shake. (*They solemnly shake, and*
JAY *looks off excitedly.*) There she goes, right
on time! (*With a burst of good spirits, he begins to sing.*)

"Oh, I hear them train cars a-rumblin',
  And, they're mighty near at hand,
  I hear that train come a-rumblin',
  Come a-rumblin' through the land!"
    (*He lifts* RUFUS *to his shoulders.*)

"Git on board, little children,
  Git on board, little children,
  Git on board, little children,
There's room for many and more!"

    As he sings, the lights come up on the
    house. MARY FOLLET *is placing bowls of*
    flowers in the living room.)

"Oh, I look a way down yonder,
  And, uh-what do you reckon I see,

A band of shinin' angels
A-comin' after me!"
(MARY *gets a tray of glasses from the
kitchen table and joins them in the
yard, singing along with* JAY, *achieving
some pleasing harmonies.*)

JAY & MARY (*Singing*):
  "Git on board, little children,
  Git on board, little children,
  Git on board, little children,
  There's room for many and more!"
(*As they finish the song,* JAY *swings* RU-
FUS *lightly to the ground.*)

RUFUS: Here comes the one-oh-seven!
(*He chugs into the house like a train
and settles into the morris chair with
his coloring book.*)

MARY: Don't you go away, Rufus! Your daddy's
people will be here any minute! (*Turning to
Jay, as if with a very amusing confidence she
has been saving for him*) Ralph just called up
on the telephone!

JAY: Where from?

MARY: You know Ralph! He wasn't ten blocks
away, just downtown. But instead of coming
right on, he went to all the trouble of parking
the machine, going in some place, and calling
up to say they were *almost* here!
(*She laughs and places the tray on the
ground beside the swing.*)

JAY (*Laughing with her*):   Did you ever know
anyone to get such a kick outa telephones?

MARY: If you ask me, he was in a saloon. Probably didn't want to telephone at all, if you know what I mean, but used it as an excuse to Sally for stopping, and then once he was in there he felt he'd better *really* call us, because Sally'd find out from us if he didn't and then she'd know that wasn't why he stopped!

JAY (*Whistling*):   You sure can complicate a thought, Mama!

MARY: You know what I mean!

JAY (*Grinning*):   Did he say anything about knockin' Kaiser Wilhelm's block off?

MARY: No, thank goodness, he was *very pleasant*!

      (*She laughs.*)

JAY: Then I reckon we'll still have a nice day.

MARY (*Seriously*):   When they get here, Jay, you won't — I mean you won't let Ralph influence you?

JAY: Oh, I might hoist a few with him!

MARY (*Uncertainly*):   Jay — ?

JAY: Sure, you and the others go on to Great-Granmaw's! I figure Ralph and I'll stay here and have ourselves a bender! I'm just ripe for it!

MARY: Don't say that, even in fun!

JAY (*Laughing, putting his arms around her*):

Aw now, Mary, you don't ever worry about me any more, do you?

MARY: I just don't like jokes about that particular subject.

JAY: And you know what I don't like? Superintendents! No sir, I don't like people lookin' down on me, thinkin' they got to keep an eye on me.

MARY (*Shocked*): Was I looking down on you?

JAY: Why, you was about ten feet off the ground!

MARY (*Crushed*): Honestly, Jay?

JAY: Two feet.

MARY: Well, *shame* on me. And I *certainly* thank you for pointing it out.

JAY (*Impulsively holding her close, singing in her ear*): "I got a gal and a sugar babe, too — My honey, my baby . . ."

MARY: That awful song!
(*She laughs.*)

JAY: I guess I know how to get on the good side of you, don't I?

MARY: I guess you do! (*He kisses her. She steps back primly, really tremendously pleased.*) Well, I certainly hope the neighbors enjoyed that! (*And she turns briskly into the living room.*) Rufus, I had this room all straightened up for your daddy's *people*!

JAY (*Following*):   They won't be coming in here, Mary.

MARY: I want them to be able to if they want to, don't I?

JAY (*Scraping his pipe into the ash tray*):   Rufus'll clean up the mess he made, won't you, honey?

MARY: And will *you* clean up the mess *you're* making with that pipe? Honestly, Jay!

JAY (*Picking up the dirtied ash tray, looking around, not knowing what to do with it*):   Rufus, did you ever think of starting a collection of pipe scrapelings?

RUFUS (*At once interested*):   Scrapelings?

JAY: Sure, that's what they're called.

MARY: Really, Jay!

JAY: You wrap 'em up in a little piece of paper and you mark 'em with the date and whose pipe they come out of, then you put 'em away in some secret hiding place where no one'll ever find 'em.

MARY (*Laughing*):   All *right*, Jay!

RUFUS: Please, Mama, may I?

MARY: Of course you may, just don't spill them all over everything! And get your feet off your daddy's chair — !
> (*She stoops to pick up the coloring book.*)

JAY: Rufus, don't make your mama pick up after you —

MARY (*Straightening up quickly*): Oh — !

JAY: What is it, honey?

MARY: It just made me dizzy for a moment —

JAY: Here, you sit right down.

RUFUS: What's the matter, Mama?

JAY: Are you all right now?

MARY: Of course I am. It was just a thing of the minute. It's to be expected from now on.

RUFUS (*Demanding*): What's the *matter*?

MARY: Mama just stooped over very quickly, that's all, and it made the room go around.
   (RUFUS *stoops over very quickly and straightens up hopefully.*)

RUFUS: It's not going around.

MARY: Not for *you*, dear —

JAY: Why don't you tell him, Mary?

MARY: Oh Jay, please — !

RUFUS: Tell me what?

MARY: There, you *see*?

JAY: He has to find out some time.

MARY: But not *now* — !

RUFUS: Find out what, Mama?

JAY: Won't be long before he sees for himself that *some*thing's happening.

MARY (*Flaring*):   Not if you don't bring it to his attention!

JAY: I'd have told him weeks ago if you'd let me!

MARY: I wanted to talk to Father Jackson first.

JAY: You don't need any priest to tell you how to talk to your own boy.

MARY: Jay, I don't want him asking q-u-e-s-t-i-o-n-s!

JAY: That won't do y'any good, Mama, he can out-spell the both of us put together.
> (RUFUS *has been looking from one to the other during this. There is now a silence.*)

RUFUS: I can get dizzy on a swing! Or if I turn around in circles fast like this — ! (*He whirls.*) Look Mama, *I'm* gettin' dizzy! Look!

MARY: Rufus. (*He stops whirling.*) Come here to Mama. (*She takes him on her lap.*) Rufus — after a while you're going to have a wonderful surprise.

RUFUS: Like a present?

MARY: Something. Only very much nicer.

RUFUS: What's it going to *be*?

MARY: If I told you, it wouldn't be a surprise any more, would it?
> (JAY *begins to frown.*)

RUFUS: Will I get it today?

MARY: No dear, not for a long time yet.

RUFUS: When summer vacation starts?

MARY: Not till after summer vacation *ends,* and you've gone back to school. Not even till after you've cut out your pumpkin for Halloween.

RUFUS: Where is it now?

MARY: It's in heaven. Still up in heaven.

JAY: Tell him it's right here with us.

RUFUS: Right *here* —
(*He looks quickly under the davenport and under the piano.*)

JAY (*Stopping him*):   For the next few months, Rufus, you and I've got to take special care of Mama. (*He cups his hands as if holding a very fragile object.*) We've got to treat her like something that might just break.
(RUFUS *looks wonderingly into the cup of Jay's hands.*)

MARY: I think we've told him enough for the time being. He knows there's a surprise coming for us from heaven, and he has something to look forward to.

JAY: If we don't tell him all of it, honey, the older boys will in the streets. Would you like that?

RUFUS (*Astounded*):   What do *they* know?

MARY: Nothing dear, nothing at all!

RUFUS (*Excitedly*):   Is it a cap, Mama? Is the surprise a cap?

MARY (*Finding an outlet for her irritation*):   Rufus, I've told you again and again you can't *have* one of those cheap flashy caps! And I've told you to stay away from those rowdy boys!

JAY: What if *they* won't stay away from *him*?

MARY (*Hugging* RUFUS):   Now darling, will you do Mama a favor? There's a lunch hamper on the kitchen table, and I want you to take it out by the alley so it'll be all ready to put in Uncle Ralph's car. Will you do that?

RUFUS: Do I have to?

JAY: Do what your mamma says, Rufus.
        (*During the following,* RUFUS *struggles off with the hamper. There is an uncomfortable silence between* MARY *and* JAY.)

JAY: I think it'd make him feel more grown up if he had a cap like the older boys.

MARY: He's not grown up, Jay.

JAY: It's kind of hard for a fellow to know where he stands around here. You tell him to stay away from the older boys, and I tell him to win 'em over. You say the surprise is up in the sky some place, I say it's right here on earth. Yes sir, it sure is hard for a fellow to know what's going on.

MARY: He's just a *child*.

JAY: All that about priests and *heaven* — ! Sets
my teeth on edge.

MARY: Oh Jay, sometimes I pray —

JAY: That's your privilege.

MARY: Now I can't say what I was going to say.

JAY: I'm listening.

MARY: But you're keeping your distance. As you
always do when these things come up. There's
a space of about a hundred miles between us.

JAY: And you've got that pursed-*up* look. That
preachy pursed-up look.
           (*Another awkward silence. Neither one
           gives in. Finally she goes to him.*)

MARY: When the baby comes, it'll be time
enough for him to hear about it, Jay.
           (*She puts her arms around his waist and
           leans against him. He does not re-
           spond.*)

JAY: Sure, Mary.

MARY (*Stepping back, hurt, going to the kitchen*):
I thought we'd all have a glass of something
cold before we start. (*He bangs his pipe loudly
into the ashtray while she gets the lemonade
pitcher from the icebox. She stops in the middle of the kitchen and closes her eyes.*) Oh
Lord, in Thy mercy, Who can do all things,
close this gulf between us. Make us one in
Thee as we are in earthly wedlock. For Jesus'
sake, Amen.

(*She crosses herself.* JAY *has followed and heard. She turns and sees him looking at her. There is a sudden loud whooping, off, and* RUFUS *runs in.*)

RUFUS: They're here, they're here!
(*He tugs at his father to get him outside, then runs off again.*)

MARY: That's not Ralph's car!

JAY (*Laughing*): But that sure is Ralph gettin' out! (*He hurries excitedly to the yard to meet* RALPH FOLLET, *his brother.*) Hey there, Ralph!

RALPH: We made it, Jay, safe and sound!

JAY (*Eagerly*): Where'd you get the car?

RALPH: D'you like 'er?

JAY (*Impressed*): Chalmers, ain't it?

RALPH: Goes like sixty, Jay!

JAY (*Laughing*): What're you tryin' t'do, make me look like a piker?

RALPH (*Punching at him*): Well, y'are a piker, ya piker, with your ole Tin Lizzy! (*Dashing to* MARY *who has come out with the pitcher of lemonade*) How ya been, sweetheart!

MARY: I'm fine, Ralph!

RALPH (*Admiringly*): I gotta hug ya, just gotta hug ya! (*He grabs her.*) You can hug Sally if you want to, Jay! *Ever*'body hugs *my* wife!

MARY (*Pulls away from his whiskey breath*): I

thought we'd have a glass of something cold
before we start, Ralph!

RALPH: Did I do somethin' wrong, Mary?

MARY: Goodness sakes, *no*! Just tell the rest of
them to get out of the car before they suffo-
cate!

RALPH (*Yelling*):   Come on, ever'body, Mary's
got us a glass of somethin' cold! And isn't it
just like you, Mary! I was sayin' to them as we
were drivin' along, I'll bet Jay's wife thinks of
havin' somethin' cold waitin' —
          (RUFUS *runs in crying*.)

RUFUS: Daddy, Daddy — !

JAY: Why, what's the trouble honey? (*Squat-
ting to* RUFUS's *level*) What you cryin' about?
Wuzza matter, honey?
          (*He takes out his handkerchief*.)

RALPH: Oh, Jay, y'oughtn't ever to call a boy
"honey"!

JAY (*To* RUFUS):   Come on, blow. You know
your mama don't like you to swallah that stuff.

MARY: What is it, Rufus, what's happened?
          (RUFUS *hides from her*.)

JAY: I reckon it ain't fit for ladies' ears, Mary.
Maybe you better turn your back.

MARY (*Turning away*):   Oh, for goodness *sakes*!

JAY: Now *tell* Daddy. (RUFUS *whispers in his
ear*.)   Is that all? Why, is that all it is?

MARY: What is it, Jay?

JAY (*Standing, as* RUFUS *hides his face in shame*): It seems that Rufus, here, has had a little accident.

MARY: Accident — ?

RALPH: Did my Jim-Wilson hit him? Because if he did —

JAY: No Ralph, nothin' like that. You know, Mary. An accident.

MARY: Oh Rufus, you're too *old* for that! And I had you all dressed up for your daddy's people. Jay, you'll have to help him change.

JAY: He's old enough to manage by himself.

RALPH (*With a whoop of delight*): *That* kind of an accident?

JAY: Musta been the excitement of the day.

RALPH: Oh that's rich, that is! (*In a sing-song*): Rufus is a baby, Rufus is a baby!
(RUFUS *runs into the house.*)

JAY: That'll do, Ralph!

RALPH (*Laughing happily as* SALLY, JIM-WILSON, JESSIE, *and* JOHN HENRY *come in from the car.* JESSIE *carries a small rubber inner tube.*): Did y'hear that ever'body? Rufus had an accident! That's how my Chalmers affects people, they take one look at it and wet their britches!

SALLY: Ralph!

RALPH: Pee their pants!
(*There is sudden loud activity as every-body greets one another.*)

SALLY (*To* MARY):   I think I'll take him right in-side, Mary, and get it over with —
(SALLY, RALPH'*s wife, and* JIM-WILSON, *their son, start for the house.*)

MARY: You'll find everything ready for you, Sally, make yourself at home — Mama Follet, how good to see you!

RALPH (*Simultaneously with above*):   Find a chair for Paw to sit down, Jay, he shouldn't stand around too much — this is what I like, all the Follets in one yard — where you goin', Sally?

JESSIE (*To* MARY, *simultaneously with above*): I reckon I'll just never get used to ridin' in au-tomobiles, Mary, m'ear's all plugged up — not that Ralph ain't a good driver —

JAY (*Simultaneously with above*):   You sit down right over here, Paw, and rest yourself —

RALPH (*Shouting*):   Sally! (*All talking, greeting, and movement stop.*) I asked you where you were goin'!

SALLY: I'm taking Jim-Wilson to the bathroom before we have any more accidents.

RALPH: Oh. Well, I just like you to answer me when I ask you a question! (SALLY *and* JIM-WILSON *continue on with* RALPH *following as far as the kitchen.*) Did you hear me, Sally? I just like you to answer when I ask you a question!

> (*She is gone, and as the others talk in the yard,* RALPH *takes out a pint from his pocket and has a swallow.*)

JESSIE: Here Paw, you better sit on your tube. (*She helps him to rise halfway and puts the inner tube underneath him.*)

MARY: Will you have something cold to drink, Mama Follet?

JESSIE: Wait on Paw first, if you will, Mary dear. I know how parched he gets. How's your breath, Paw?

JOHN HENRY: Pretty fair.

JAY: You haven't had any more of your attacks, have you, Paw?

JOHN HENRY: Not since that time last fall, Jay. (*He and* JESSIE *knock on the wood of their chairs.*)

JAY (*Grinning*): Maw sure does spoil you then.

JESSIE: When you come close to losing someone, that's the way you do.

JAY: Some easy life, I'll say!

JESSIE: I'm sure Mary spoils you enough.

MARY (*Serving*): Oh no, I think Jay spoils me!

JESSIE: So he should with another baby on the way. (*Eyeing her appraisingly*) It don't show yet, do it, Mary. (MARY *laughs, embarrassed, and smooths her dress.*) Well, some show early, some show late. Ralph showed almost afore I knew he was there. Jay, you was a kicker. You all right, Paw?

JOHN HENRY: Pretty good.

MARY (*Calling, as she returns to the tray of glasses*):   Ralph, are you in there?

RALPH (*In the kitchen, quickly putting the bottle into his pocket*):   Be right with yuh, Mary!

MARY: Do you want some lemonade?

RALPH (*Bustling out*):   Thank yuh, Mary, I'm dry's a bone.
          (MARY *serves them lemonade.*)

JAY: Things must be pretty good for you, Ralph, if you can afford to go out and buy a new Chalmers.

RALPH: Oh yes, Jay, considerin' the state of the world 'n' all, Ralph Follet's doin' fine, just fine!

JESSIE (*Shaking her head*):   Tst, tst.

RALPH: Aw right, Maw, so I borrowed the money, but in this day and age you got to be in a sound financial situation to borrow money! (*Turning to* JAY *enthusiastically*) Why Jay, I walked into Ed Briggs' office at the bank in LaFollette, and he says "You want to buy a car, Ralph? Take whatever you need!" That's how highly thought of I am in *that* bank!

JAY: I'm surprised he didn't give you the keys to the safe, Ralph.

RALPH (*To his parents, gratified*): You hear what Jay said?

JOHN HENRY: I reckon Ed Briggs knew what he was doin'. An undertaker's always a good risk.

RALPH: It wasn't that, Paw!

JOHN HENRY (*Bewildered*): I'm tryin' to give you a compliment, son.

JESSIE: Paw's right. Only thing you can be sure of in life is, people go on dyin'.

MARY: Oh Mama Follet, I'd rather say they go on being born.

JESSIE (*Nodding*): That too, Mary, they got to be born afore they can die.

RALPH: Ed Briggs give me that money because it was *me* askin' for it! Why there's other undertakers in LaFollette he wouldn't give the time o' day to!

JESSIE: Just the same, your paw never owed a cent in his life, Ralph, did you, Paw?
    (SALLY *comes out of the house.*)

JOHN HENRY: I'm even thinkin' maybe the farm'll be free and clear afore I die, Jay.

JAY: You worked hard for it, Paw.

JOHN HENRY (*Vaguely*): You owe any money, Jay?

RALPH (*Before* JAY *can answer*): What if he
don't, *I* happen to want to give *Sally* some of
life's refinements! I don't like the idea *my*
wife ridin' around town in some old Tin
Lizzy!

MARY (*Laughing*): Why, Ralph, I just love our
Ford!

SALLY: I never get to ride around town in *any*-
thing! *He's* always off some place! He only
bought that new car because of you, Jay, so
he'd have a better one than yours, and don't
let him tell you different!

MARY: I'm certainly anxious to *ride* in it!
Aren't you, Jay?

JAY (*Grinning at her*): Just can't wait!

RALPH (*Angrily to* SALLY): And what're *you*
doin' at home while I'm out in the car on
business, just tell me that!

MARY: Why don't we get started! (*Calling*) Rufus — ?

RALPH: The trouble with my wife is she don't
appreciate how I try to please her! (*To* SALLY)
You ask Maw the things she's had to do without all her life and see how lucky y'are!

JESSIE: Now I know one thing I *can* do without, and that's any more of this talk.

JAY: Sure Ralph, come on! We've all been
lookin' forward to a good time today!

RALPH (*Sulking*): I'm *havin'* a good time. (*As*

JIM-WILSON *comes out; snapping at him)* Get out here, Jim-Wilson, and start enjoyin' yourself.

SALLY (*To* JIM-WILSON): Would you like some lemonade, dear?

RALPH: My God, she just gets him all drained out and she fills him up again!

MARY: Did you see Rufus in there, Jim-Wilson?

RALPH (*Sing-song)*:   Rufus is a baby, Rufus is a baby!

MARY: Please Ralph, that's enough of that.

RALPH: Rufus is a ba-by!

MARY: Ralph, you're to stop!

RALPH: Just teasin', Mary!

MARY: Well, you're to stop it, what*ever* it is! The child had a perfectly normal accident!

RALPH: Why, Jim-Wilson hasn't had an accident like that in years, and he's younger'n Rufus by 'leven months!

MARY (*Angrily*):   I don't care what Jim-Wilson does! (*Catching herself*) I didn't mean that, of course, Sally. (*Stooping quickly to hug* JIM-WILSON) Aunt Mary cares the *world* about Jim-Wilson!

RALPH (*Laughing*):   Goddamn it, why is it ever'-thin' I say today gets me into trouble!

MARY (*Flaring again*):   And I'll thank you not to take the Lord's name in vain!

RALPH (*Exploding*): This family ain't Catholics and I'll take the Lord's name any way that comes to mind!
> (*There is a shocked silence.*)

JESSIE: Tst, tst.

JAY: You sure like to hit all bases, don't you, Ralph.

RALPH: I'm sorry for what I said, Jay. (*Crossing shyly, apologetically to* MARY) Mary, Jim-Wilson does pee his pants ever' day without fail.

JAY: Then I think you oughta get Rufus out here and apologize to him for making fun of him.

RALPH: Sure, Jay, of course. (*Calling*) Rufus? Come on out here, Rufus! (RUFUS *steals down the stairs from his room.*) This is your Uncle Ralph callin' to you. I promise not t'tease y'-any more. D'you hear me, Rufus? (RUFUS *comes out of the house.*) There he is! Looky here. (*He digs into his pocket and pulls out a business card.*) I got somethin' for you. Take it. (RUFUS *takes the card and looks at it.* RALPH *reads it for him.*) "Ralph Follet, Mortician." We friends again? (RUFUS *looks to* JAY *who pantomimes shaking hands.* RUFUS *puts out his hand and* RALPH *takes it. They shake.* RALPH *sinks to his knees, pretending to writhe in the strength of* RUFUS's *grip.*) Oh-o-o-ooh — ! (RUFUS *laughs and squeezes harder.* RALPH *howls in mock pain.* JAY *laughs and* MARY *laughs.* RALPH *leaps to his feet with an exuberant whoop.*) That's what I like, ever'body

friends again! All the Follets is friends, ain't
we, Mary?

MARY: Of course we are, Ralph!

JESSIE (*Rising, helping* JOHN HENRY *up*): If
we're goin' t'get there this afternoon, we'd best
get started.

RALPH: Maw's right! Come on ever'body, pile
in the Chalmers! Jay, you and Mary sit up
front with me and Rufus! (*He lifts* RUFUS
high in the air.) You can sit on my lap, Rufus,
and maybe I'll even let you steer!

SALLY: I think Jay ought to drive.
          (*It rings through the happy activity, and
          all movement stops as everybody looks
          to* RALPH.)

RALPH (*Incredulous, dropping* RUFUS *to the
ground*):   Drive *my* car?

SALLY: You're in no fit condition to drive it.

RALPH: Well, nobody else is goin' to drive it,
I'll tell you that! Not *my* car!

SALLY: Can we go in your car, Jay?

RALPH: His old Tin Lizzy? We couldn't even all
get in it!

SALLY: I'd rather be a little crowded and have
Jay drive.

RALPH: Jay this an' Jay that, ever'body always
lookin' up to Jay, askin' *Jay's* advice, lettin'
Jay do the drivin'! Well, let me tell you,

there's been times when you wouldn't ride
with him neither! *He's* been hauled outa the
gutter more times'n you can count *and* put in
jail *and* worse!

SALLY: You go ahead in the Chalmers, Ralph,
and the rest of us'll follow with Jay in his car.

RALPH (*Beside himself*):   And you'll be sittin' up
there next to him, I suppose, rubbin' legs with
him! So it's *Jay* you're after now!

JAY: That thought never once came into Sally's
head and you know it. So dry up!

RALPH: Don't think you're the only one she's
after, either! Don't get no swelled head it's just
you! It's any man with a flat belly, that's who it
is! Any man at all, so long as his belly don't
get in the way! (JAY *attempts to take his arm,
but* RALPH *swings wildly at him.*) Goddamn
your flat belly! (*He stumbles towards the
house, turning back for only a moment.*) I've
a good mind to'go over there an' punch that
Kaiser Wilhelm in the nose! Then maybe the
lotta y'll treat me with a little respect!

>(*He goes into the kitchen and a deep
>sigh seems to pass among the people in
>the yard. He takes out his pint and has
>a swallow.*)

JESSIE: Better let me make you comfortable
again, Paw.

>(*She puts the inner tube under him.*)

SALLY: Every time he sets out to enjoy himself
he — gets so unhappy.

MARY: I'll look after him, Jay.
          (*She starts for the house.*)

JAY (*Stopping her*):   I reckon you've had to do
   enough of that kinda lookin' after people —
   for your time.
          (*He goes into the kitchen to find* RALPH
          staring fixedly at his hands. MARY *cross-
          es to the swing with* RUFUS. *Then she
          joins* SALLY *on the swing.* RUFUS *and*
          JIM-WILSON *go to play in the yard be-
          hind them.*)

RALPH: Smell my hands, Jay, go ahead, smell
   'em.

JAY: Now there's nothin' on your hands,
   Ralph.

RALPH: Yes there is, Jay, it's that f'maldehyde.
   I can't smell it but ever'body else can. I scrub
   'em and scrub 'em, and I can't ever get rid of
   that smell. Why last night I went to the picture show, and I was sittin' there next t'this
   girl and she got up and moved. It was that
   smell, Jay, don't you think?

JAY: Go on, Ralph, you're the worst tail chaser
   in LaFollette!

RALPH (*Angrily*):   It was 'at smell made her
   move, I tell yuh! It's terrible t'work with it
   ever' day of your life, and then even when
   you go out for a good time t'have it go along
   with yuh. The picture show was good though.
   Charlie. You like Charlie?

JAY: Sure do.

RALPH: Last night he put a bag of eggs in the seat of his pants and then forgot and sat on 'em.

> (*He pantomimes this and sits in chair at the table.*)

JAY (*Laughing*):   Rufus and I seen that one.

RALPH (*Laughing with him*):   You 'n' I like lotsa the same things, Jay, maybe we're more brothers than we seem.

JAY: I reckon people'd know we was brothers.

RALPH: Thank yuh for that. (*Taking up the bottle*) Well, outside they're thinkin' he's been in there long enough for two drinks, and I've only had one. If that's what they're goin' to think, I might's well *have* two!

> (*He drinks.*)

JAY: You sure can hold it, Ralph.

RALPH (*Pushing the bottle across the table to him*):   He'p yourself.

JAY: Ever'body's waitin' on us, Ralph!

RALPH: Go on, Jay, Mary can't see. I tell you what, I'll keep watch for yuh!

JAY: It ain't that.

> (*He shoves the bottle at* RALPH *who grabs it from him.*)

RALPH: So Goddamned reformed, ain't you!

JAY: I'm just thinkin' of you. If you keep pullin' away at that bottle, it ain't goin' to last you through the day. And I know that feelin' when the bottle's empty and you ain't full.

RALPH (*Close to tears*):   I want it to be empty,
Jay. I'm no good when I'm like this. No good
at all. I'm mean and I'm reckless. I'm not even
real. *I wish this bottle was empty!*
> (*After a short silence,* JAY *grabs the
> bottle from him, drinks the last of the
> whiskey, and drops the bottle loudly
> into the trash can.*)

JAY: Empty. Now are you ready to go?

RALPH: How's it make you feel, Jay?

JAY: That little bit don't make me feel anything.

RALPH: If you had a lot?

JAY: Come on, Ralph, it's gettin' late. If we're
going to get to Great-Granmaw's and back before dark, we got to start.

RALPH: I ain't movin' from this spot till you tell
me how it makes you feel!

JAY: Well, if I had as much as you, Ralph, I'd
go quiet. So quiet, I could hear the tickin' of
the earth. And I'd be young as ever I could remember, and nothin' bad had ever happened
to me or ever would. I wouldn't dare talk to
no one, of course, for fear they'd show me the
lie. And after a while it'd get lonesome in there
all by myself, and I'd go off like a fire-cracker.
If you happened to be standin' by, you'd get a
few powder burns, let me tell you.

RALPH: What made you change, Jay? Was it
Mary's religion?

RAY: Mary's religion is her own.

RALPH: How'd you do it, then?

JAY: I made a vow to myself. I said if I ever
get drunk again, I'll kill myself.

RALPH: Oh Jay. That's a strong vow.

JAY: Couldn't afford to leave myself any loop-
holes.

RALPH: Don't y'ever get thirsty?

JAY: There's too many reasons why I don't
want to kill myself.

RALPH: What reasons?

JAY: There's two of 'em right out in the yard.
(*Grinning*) As a matter of fact, two'n a half.

RUFUS (*Outside*):   Daddy!

JAY (*His patience beginning to go*):   Now come
on, Ralph, I promised them an outing today!
They been lookin' forward to it for weeks, and
I'm not goin' to disappoint them!

RALPH: I got reasons out in the yard too, don't
I, Jay?

JAY (*Giving him a towel, briskly*):   Now wipe
off your face. You worked yourself into a
sweat.

　　　　(RALPH *wipes his face.*)

RALPH: I could take that vow of yours, couldn't
I, Jay?

JAY: Nobody's goin' to try and stop you!

RALPH: I'm takin' that vow this minute! Stand back! (*He stands up and straightens himself.*) Or Jay, maybe I could just take a vow that if ever I get drunk again I'll take your vow.

JAY: You better think on it, Ralph, that's a pretty serious step!

RALPH (*Enthusiastically*):   All right, Jay, I tell you what! I hereby take a vow — to think on it!

JAY: Good for you! (*They come outside.*) All set everybody?

SALLY: Which car are we going in?

JAY: Why, the Chalmers, of course. I wouldn't pass up a chance to ride in a Chalmers!

RALPH: But I've asked Jay to do the drivin'! I'm going to ride on the running board!

SALLY: Oh, Ralph!

RALPH: I got to point out the route to Jay, because I'm the only one remembers how to get there!

> (*They begin to arrange themselves on two benches which vaguely represent the* CHALMERS. SALLY *is on the upstage end of the rear bench,* JESSIE *next to her,* JOHN HENRY *downstage holding* RUFUS *on his lap.* JAY *is on the downstage end of the front bench with* MARY *beside him, holding* JIM-WILSON *in her lap.* RALPH *stands above them on the "running board.")*

JESSIE: Be sure you do remember, Ralph. We
don't want to get lost in those mountains.

JOHN HENRY: There used to be cats back in
those mountains. We called 'em painters then,
Rufus. That's the same as a panther.

JAY: They was around here when I was a boy,
Paw. And there still is bear, they claim. (JIM-
WILSON *whimpers*.) Don't you fret, Jim-Wilson,
we ain't likely to see any.

MARY: When was the last time all of you saw
Great-Granmaw?

RALPH: I was the last to see her! I come out one
day about twenty years ago!

MARY: Twenty years! Why for goodness sake,
Ralph, you certainly have a wonderful memory to find the way!

RALPH (*Pleased*):   I've always had a pretty good
memory.

MARY: Why, that's *remarkable*! How long since
you came out here, Jay?

JAY: I'm a-studyin' it. Nearly thirteen years.
The last time was just before I went to Panama.

MARY: Then *you* were the last one to see her!

RALPH: Wait a minute, seems to me I seen her
since then!

JOHN HENRY: Are you sure that's the place,
Ralph? That don't look like I remember it.

RALPH: Oh that's it all right! Why sure! Only we come up on it from behind!

MARY: She doesn't live there alone, does she?

JOHN HENRY: My sister Sadie give her life to her. She wouldn't come and live with any of us. I raised my family in this cabin, she said, I lived all my life from fourteen years on and I aim to die here. That must have been a good thirty-five, most, a good forty years ago, Grampaw died.
>   (SADIE *has begun slowly to push Great-Granmaw in a home-made wheelchair from upstage right to down right apron.*)

MARY: Goodness' sakes, and she was an old woman then!

JAY: She's a hundred and three years old. Hundred and three or hundred and four, she never could remember for sure which. But she knows she wasn't born later than eighteen twelve. And she always reckoned it might of been eighteen eleven.

MARY: Do you know what she is, Rufus? She's Grampa Follet's grandmother!

JOHN HENRY: That's a fact, Rufus. Woulda never believed you'd hear *me* call nobody Granmaw, now would you?

RUFUS: No sir.

JOHN HENRY: Well, you're gonna!

RALPH (*Picking* JIM-WILSON *up from* MARY'S *lap*): Are you listenin' to all this, Jim-Wilson?

JAY: She's an old, old lady.

RALPH (*An echo, awed*): Old.
(AUNT SADIE *comes to meet them, they all stand.*)

SADIE: Lord God. (*She looks from one to the other.*) Lord God.

JOHN HENRY: Howdy, Sadie.

SADIE: Howdy, John Henry.

JOHN HENRY: Thought maybe you wouldn'ta knowed us.

SADIE: I know'd you all the minute I laid eyes on you. Just couldn't believe it. Howdy, Jessie.

JESSIE: It's good to see you, Sadie.

JAY: Howdy, Aunt Sadie.

SADIE: Howdy, Jay. You Jay's brother?

RALPH: I'm Ralph, Aunt Sadie.

SADIE: Howdy, Ralph.

RALPH: That's my machine we come in. And this is my bride Sally. (*Glancing shyly at* SALLY) That's how I thinka her.

SADIE (*Looking at* SALLY): Pretty.

JAY: And this is Mary, Aunt Sadie. Mary, this is Aunt Sadie.

SADIE: I'm proud to know you. I figured it must be you. And Rufus.

MARY (*To* RUFUS): Say hello to Aunt Sadie.

RUFUS: Hello, Aunt Sadie.

RALPH: Jim-Wilson? Step up and kiss your Aunt Sadie and give her a hug. *This* is *my* boy, Aunt Sadie.

> (SADIE *snorts and grabs* JIM-WILSON's *hand, scaring him back to* SALLY's *skirts. Then she stands back.*)

SADIE: Lord God.

JAY: How's Granmaw?

SADIE: Good's we got any right to expect. But don't feel put out if she don't know none-a-yews. She mought and she mought not. Half the time she don't even know me.

RALPH: Poor old soul.

SADIE: So if I was you-all, I'd come up on her kind of easy. Bin a coon's age since she seen so many folks at oncet. Me either. Mought skeer her if you all come a-whoopin' up on her in a flock.

JAY: Whyn't you go see her the first, Paw? You're the eldest.

JOHN HENRY: 'Tain't me she wants to see. Hit's the younguns'd tickle her most.

SADIE: Reckon that's true, if she can take notice. (*To* JAY) She shore like to cracked her

heels when she heard *yore* boy was borned.
Proud as Lucifer. 'Cause that was the first.

MARY: I know. Fifth generation that made.

RALPH: Sally and I lost a baby the year *before*
Rufus was born. That *woulda* been the first.

SADIE (*To* JAY):   She always seemed to take a
shine to you.

JAY: I always did take a shine to her.

SADIE: Did you get her postcard?

JAY: What postcard?

SADIE: When yore boy was borned.

MARY   Why, no!

SADIE: She told me what to write on one a them
postcards and put hit in the mail to both a
yews and I done it. Didn't you never git it?

JAY: First I've heard tell of it.

MARY: What street did you send it to, Aunt
Sadie? Because we moved just before Rufus
was born —

SADIE: Never sent it to no street. Never knowed
I needed to, Jay working for the post office.

JAY: Why, I quit working for the post office a
long time back, Aunt Sadie. I'm in law now,
for Mary's paw.

SADIE: Well I reckon that's how come then.
'Cause I just sent it to "Post Office, Cristobal,

Canal Zone, Panama." And I spelt it right, too. C-r-i —

MARY: Oh.

JAY: Aw — why Aunt Sadie, I thought you'd a known. I been living in Knoxvul since before I was married even.

SADIE (*Looking at him keenly, almost angrily, then nodding several times*): Well, they might just as well put me out to grass. Let me lay down and give me both barls threw the head.

MARY: Why, Aunt Sadie.

SADIE: I knowed that like I knowed my own name and it plumb slipped my mind.

MARY: Oh, what a shame.

SADIE: If I git like that, too, then who's a-goana look out for *her*?

RALPH: What did she say on the postcard, Aunt Sadie?

SADIE: Lemme figger. Bin so long ago. (*She thinks for a moment.*) "I bin borned again," she says. "Love, Great-Granmaw."

MARY: Born again. Why that's beautiful.

SADIE: Mebbe. I always figgered bein' borned oncet was enough. (*She goes to* GREAT-GRAN-MAW.) Granmaw, ya got company. (*The old woman does not move.* SADIE *speaks loudly but does not shout.*) It's Jay and his wife and the others come up from Knoxvul to see you. (*The hands crawl in the lap and the face turns toward the younger woman. A thin, dry cackling, but no words.*) She knows ye. Come on over, Jay. (JAY, MARY, *and* RUFUS *advance slowly, shyly.*) I'll tell her about the resta yuns in a minute.

RALPH (*Herding the others back further*): Aunt Sadie'll tell her about us in a minute.

SADIE: Don't holler. It only skeers her. Just talk loud and plain right up next her ear.

MARY: I know. My mother is deaf.

JAY (*Bending close to* GRANMAW's *ear*): Granmaw? (*He draws away a little where she can see him.* GREAT-GRANMAW *looks straight into his eyes and her eyes and face never change.* JAY *leans forward again and gently kisses her on the mouth. Then he draws back again, smiling a little anxiously. He speaks into her ear.*) I'm Jay. John Henry's boy.

      (*The old lady's hands crawl on her skirt. Her mouth opens and shuts, emitting the low dry croaking. But her eyes do not change.*)

SADIE (*Quietly*): I figure she knows you.

JAY: She can't talk any more, can she?

SADIE: Times she can. Times she can't. Ain't only so seldom call for talk, reckon she loses the hang of it. But I figger she knows ye and I'm tickled she does.

JAY: Come here, Rufus.

MARY: Go to him.
(*She gives* RUFUS *a gentle push toward* JAY.)

JAY: Just call her Granmaw. Get right up to her ear like you do to Granmaw Lynch and say, "Granmaw, I'm Rufus."
(RUFUS *walks over to* GRANMAW *as quietly as if she is asleep. He stands on tiptoe and puts his mouth to her ear.*)

RUFUS: Granmaw, I'm Rufus.

JAY: Come out where she can see you.
(RUFUS *draws back and stands still further on tiptoe, leaning across where she can see him.*)

RUFUS: I'm Rufus.
(*Suddenly the old eyes dart a little and look straight into his, not changing expression.*)

JAY: Tell her "I'm Jay's boy Rufus."

RUFUS: I'm Jay's boy Rufus.

JAY: Now kiss her.
(RUFUS *kisses her. Suddenly the old woman's hands grip his arms and shoulders, drawing him closer, looking at him, almost glaring and suddenly she is smiling so hard that her chin and nose almost touch, and her eyes fill with light and almost giggle with joy. And again the croaking gurgle, making shapes that are surely words but in-*

comprehensible words, and she holds
him even more tightly and cocks her
head to one side. With sudden love,
RUFUS *kisses her again.*)

MARY (*Whispering, frightened*): Jay — !

JAY: Let them be.
(*After a moment,* SADIE *gently disen-*
gages GRANMAW's *hands from* RUFUS's
arms. RUFUS *steps back with his parents,*
and the three of them edge away to-
ward the others. They are now a good
distance from GRANMAW, *watching in-*
tently as SADIE *bends over her.* GRAN-
MAW's *face settles back into its former*
expression, as if nothing has taken
place.)

MARY (*Hushed*): Is she all right?

SADIE: All she knows is somethin's been took
from her.
(*A silence, and in the silence, the lights*
dim on GRANMAW, *leaving the family*
gazing at empty space.)

JOHN HENRY: We won't none of us ever see
Granmaw again.

JAY: I wouldn't be surprised, Paw.
(*He goes into the house and up to* RU-
FUS's *room.*)

JOHN HENRY: The hand of death is comin' close
to this family.
(JIM-WILSON *whimpers.*)

RALPH (*Reverently*): Well — when her time comes, I'll be — *honored* to 'ficiate. Free of charge.

>   (RALPH, SALLY, *and* JIM-WILSON *go off.*)

RUFUS: Mama? Do you know what happened?

MARY: What, dear?

RUFUS: Great-great-granmaw had an accident. (MARY *looks down at him.*) When I kissed her. (MARY *looks away, close to tears.*) Isn't she too old for that? (MARY *takes his hand and leads him off.*) Isn't she, Mama?

JESSIE: How's your breath, Paw?

JOHN HENRY: Pretty fair.

>   (*They exit and the lights dim.* JAY *has been singing softly; now the lights come up on him as he stands by* RUFUS's *bed singing him to sleep. He holds a tattered cloth dog in his hands.*)

JAY (*Singing*):
Every time the sun goes down,
'Nother dollar made for Betsy Brown.
Sugar Babe.
There's a good old saying, Lord, everybody know
You can't track a rabbit when there ain't no snow.
Sugar Babe.

>   (MARY *comes out of the bath room in her nightgown. As she goes upstairs, her voice joins his in clear, graceful har-*

*monies. The lights come up on their
bedroom. She pulls the shade, brushes
her hair, turns down the bed, and sits
on it to braid her hair.*)

Now it ain't going to rain and it ain't going
to snow.

The sun's going to shine and the wind's going
to blow.

Sugar Babe.

(*He looks down at* RUFUS's *bed and
speaks softly.*)

'Sleep now, Google-Eyes? (*There is no answer.
He quietly leaves the room. The light fades
there. He joins* MARY.) Look what I found.

MARY: What, dear?

JAY: His ole dog Jackie.

MARY (*Taking it*): Goodness sakes, where was
it?

JAY: Back in a corner under the crib. I was
scarin' the Boogee Man outa there.

MARY: The *crib*! Shame on *me*!

JAY: Poor ole Jackie.

MARY: Is Rufus asleep?

JAY: Yeah, he's asleep.

MARY: What was the matter with him?

JAY: Bad dream, I reckon. (*He starts to undo
his necktie.*) Pore little ole Jackie, so lonesome
and thrown away. Remember when I got him?

MARY: Of course I do. You took such pleasure
in picking him out.

JAY: Little ole Jackie was bigger'n Rufus. And I had to explain. "It's a dog," I had to say. Only "dog" was too big a word in those days. I gave you too soon, Jackie. And here it is too late. Left behind with the baby crib.
> (*He picks up the toy from the bed.*)

MARY: I'm certainly glad we kept that crib. It'll save buying a new one.

JAY (*Tossing the toy to the floor*): Back to the corner with you, Jackie.

MARY: Don't leave it there, darling. (*He retrieves the dog.*) What is it, Jay?

JAY: Nothin'. (*He stands in the middle of the room, the dog in his hands. She waits.*) I reckon it's just seein' Great-Granmaw again and rememberin' the summers I had out there. And it's seein' Paw begin to shrink up, and watchin' Ralph. And it's feelin' Rufus growin' bigger, and singin' those sad ole songs. And findin' Jackie. It's just the day, Mary.

MARY: It's been a long one.
> (JAY *pulls at the dog and a piece comes off in his hand.*)

JAY: Jackie's ear come off. It's enough to make a man thirsty. (*Abruptly, grimly, he dashes Jackie to the floor and runs downstairs where he takes a whiskey bottle from the hall closet.* MARY *picks up her robe and hurries down to find him standing in the living room, staring at the bottle. He goes into the kitchen.*) How far we all come, Mary. How far we all come away from ourselves. So far, so much between,

you can't even remember where you started or
what you had in mind or where you thought
you were goin'. All you know is you were head-
in' *some* place. (*He hefts the bottle, as if test-
ing its weight.*) One way you do remember.
(*He puts the bottle on the kitchen table.*) You
have a boy or a girl of your own, and now and
then you sing to them or hold them, and you
know how they feel, and it's almost the same as
if you were your own self again. Just think,
Mary, my paw used to sing to me. And before
my time, even before I was dreamed of in this
world, his daddy or his mother used to sing to
him, and away on back through the mountains, back past Great-Granmaw, away on back
through the years, right on back to Adam, only
nobody ever sang to Adam.

MARY: God did.

JAY: Maybe God did.

MARY: We're supposed to come away from ourselves, Jay. That's the whole point. We're supposed to come away to —
    (*She stops herself.*)

JAY: I know. To God.
    (*She nods.*)

MARY: I don't see how you can *feel* the way
you do and not believe in Him.

JAY: We come from people, Mary, and in time
they fall away from us, like Great-Granmaw.
We give birth to others, and in time they *grow*
away from us, like Rufus will. (*He picks up
the bottle.*) When we're about eighty years old,

you'n me, all we'll have left is us. And that's
what I believe in. (*He puts the bottle back in
the closet.*) Maybe that's it. Maybe that's where
we're heading — to each other. And the sad
thing all our lives is the distance between us.
But maybe if we keep goin' in the direction we
think is right, maybe we can't ever get all the
way there, but at least we can make that distance less'n it was. (*She goes to him and they
embrace.*) You'll catch cole down here like
that. Now wait'll I warm up the bed for you.
(*He runs upstairs and rubs his hand swiftly between the sheets. She follows him and sits on
the bed. He kneels before her, removes her
slippers, and warms her feet in his hands.*)
When I was a youngster on the farm, on cold
nights we all used to pile into one bed together. Finally I was too big for that, but I
wasn't too big to cry at bein' left alone in a
big cold bed all by myself. An' my maw, she
brought me her own pillah and she put it under the covers next to me. And she said to pretend it was one o' *them* keepin' me warm
through the night and watchin' over me. Pore
Maw. She slep' without a pillah for a coupla
months there. (*He takes her in his arms and
kisses her.*) Now *your* job is to get the *other*
side o' the bed warm for *me*! (*Under the
covers,* MARY *runs her hands on* JAY's *side of
the bed and warms it. There is the sudden
sharp ring of the telephone downstairs. All
sound, all movement stops for a moment. The
ring is repeated.* MARY *sits up in bed and* JAY
goes out grumbling.) Now who could that be
this time o' night? (*He goes down to the kitch-*

en and answers the telephone.) Hello — ?
Yeah, Central, this is Jay Follet — put 'im
through. Hello, Ralph? What's the trouble?
Ralph? Sure I can hear you, what's the matter? Are you cryin', Ralph? (*Impatiently*)
Paw? Listen, Ralph, I 'preciate your calling
and you're *not* putting me out — now tell me
about Paw. (*He listens.*) I should come up,
huh? (*Suddenly angry*) Hold on, Ralph, you
hold on there! I'm glad I'm not where I
could hit you — ! If Paw's that bad you know
damn well I'm comin' so don't give me none
o' that! Will you stop *cryin'*! Now listen to
me, Ralph, I want you to get it straight I'm not
tryin' to jump on you, but sometimes you're
likely to exaggerate and — no, I don't think
you're alyin' to me — and no, I don't think
you're drunk! I just want you to think for a
minute! *Just how sick is he really,* Ralph? (*In
a fury*) *Think,* Goddamn it! (MARY *has followed him downstairs, turned on the kitchen
light, lighted the stove, put a few fresh grounds
into the coffee pot and placed it on the flame.
She is now sitting in the chair left of the table,
listening.*) Listen, Ralph, I know you would-
n'ta phoned if you didn't think it was serious.

MARY (*Whispering*):   Is Sally there?

JAY: Is Sally out to the farm? And 'course
Maw's there.

MARY: Doctor?

JAY: And the doctor? What's he say? — From
the way you tell me that, I suspect the doctor
said a *good* chance. (*Now anxious to hang up*)

Look here, Ralph, I'm talkin' too much. I'm startin' right on up. I ought to be there by — what time is it now?

MARY (*Looking at living room clock*): It's eleven-thirty.

JAY: It's eleven-thirty, Ralph. I ought to be there by two, two-thirty. Well, I'm afraid that's the best my ole Tin Lizzy can make it, Ralph. You tell Maw I'm comin' right on up quick's I can.

MARY: Is he conscious?

JAY: Is he conscious? Well, if he gets conscious, just let him know I'm comin'! That's all right, Ralph. Don't mention it — Mary understands. . . . Good-bye, Ralph. That's all right . . . Thanks for calling. *Good-bye, Ralph!* (*He hangs up.*) My God, talkin' to him's like tryin' to put socks on an octopus.

MARY: Is it very grave?

JAY: Lord knows. I can't be sure of anything with Ralph, but I can't afford to take the risk.

MARY (*To table with cup and saucer*): Of course not.

JAY: What're *you* up to?

MARY: I'm fixing you something to eat.

JAY: Aw, honey, I'll get a bite on the way if I want to.

MARY: In one of those all-night lunchrooms? Sakes alive!

JAY: It'll be quicker, honest it will.
             (*He goes upstairs.*)

MARY: I don't want your mother to think I
don't feed you.
             (*She checks the coffee, runs into the
             living room, selects a pipe from the
             rack on the piano, picks up* JAY's *to-
             bacco pouch, and returns to the kitchen,
             putting them on the table by the cup
             and saucer. She returns to the stove to
             tend the coffee. During this,* JAY *has
             been putting on his vest and coat in
             their bedroom. He is about to go out of
             the room when he sees the rumpled
             bed. He smooths out the covers, pulling
             them high to keep in the warmth.
             Then, on a sudden thought, he puts his
             pillow well down under the covers
             where he would normally sleep. He
             leaves the room, looks in briefly on*
             RUFUS, *then goes down into the living
             room. He selects a pipe, searches vainly
             for his tobacco pouch and enters the
             kitchen.*)

JAY: Have you seen my tobacco — aw, you had
it all ready for me.

MARY: I had to guess which pipe you wanted
to take.

JAY (*Picking up her choice, slipping his own
into his pocket*):   Just the one I was looking
for.

MARY (*Pleased*):   It's the one I gave you. (*Pulling back a chair at the table*) At least you have

time for a cup of coffee. (*As he hesitates*) It's the way you like it. (*He grins and sits. She pours the coffee.*) The pot's choked *full* of old grounds, and I added some new.

JAY (*Sipping*):   Now that's *coffee*.

MARY: I'd as soon watch you drink sulfuric acid.

JAY: The outing musta been too much for him. Paw just sits there so quiet anymore we don't always know what's going on underneath. He got home and just collapsed.

MARY: Isn't it funny, Jay. This afternoon he was saying we'd be losing your great-grandmother soon. And now it turns out your father's the one in danger.

JAY: I guess we never know who's in danger. (*She fills his cup again.*) You got a birthday coming up. What would you like to do?

MARY: Why Jay. Why — you nice thing. Why —

JAY: You think it over. Whatever you'd like best. Within reason, of course. I'll see we manage it. (*Then as they both remember*) That is, of course, if everything goes the way we hope it will, up home.

> (*He goes into living room where he scrapes out his pipe. She follows him.*)

MARY: It's time, isn't it? You're almost looking forward to it, aren't you, Jay? The all-night lunchroom. Driving through the night when everybody else is asleep, going fast.

JAY: I just know I have to go, Mary. So I'm
   anxious to get started.

MARY (*Giving him a hug*):   Don't drive too fast.

JAY (*Pointing to the ashtray*):   Scrapelings for
   him to find in the morning. For his collection.

MARY: I wonder if we should wake him up. I'm
   afraid he's going to be disappointed you didn't
   tell him good-bye.

JAY: I've looked in on him. Tell you what. Tell
   him, don't promise him or anything, of course,
   but tell him I'm practically sure to be back before he's asleep tomorrow night. Tell him I'll
   do my best.

MARY: All right, Jay. Give my love to your
   mother. Tell her they're both in my thoughts
   and wishes constantly. And your father, of
   course, if he's — well enough to talk.
      (*By now they are at the back door.*)

JAY: Don't you come any further.

MARY (*Feeling a chill*):   It was so warm this
   afternoon. (*He kisses her.*) I wish I could go
   with you, Jay. In whatever happens.

JAY: Why'd you add that?

MARY: It's the way I feel.
      (*He kisses her again.*)

JAY: I'll let you know quick's I can, if it's serious. (*He goes across the yard rapidly. She
   stands in the door. He stops, halfway.*) Hey,
   how's your money?

MARY (*Thinking quickly*):   All right, thank you.

JAY: Tell *him* I'll even try to make it for supper!

MARY: All right, dear.

JAY: Goodnight.

MARY: Goodnight.
>   (*He goes to the edge of the stage and turns back once more.*)

JAY (*In a loud whisper*):   I keep forgettin' to tell you! I want this next one to be a girl!
>   (*He goes. She stands waiting in the door, but is chilled again and goes inside, turns off stove and kitchen light, goes upstairs. She sees the lump on the bed, pulls back the covers wonderingly, then she smiles.*)

MARY: The dear. Why, the dear.
>   (*She gets into bed and hugs the pillow as . . . The Curtain Falls*)

ACT II

AT RISE:

CATHERINE, MARY's *mother, is sitting in chair left of kitchen table.* MARY *is measuring a slipcover which she is making for the living room davenport.*

CATHERINE: Father Jackson and I have had the loveliest afternoon planning aid to war-stricken Europe. And since we were all to come here for supper, I saw no reason for going home, only to come out again. So I thought I'd stop by early, Mary dear, and we could have a nice quiet chat.

MARY: Lovely, Mama.

CATHERINE (*Lifting her ear trumpet*): Beg pardon?

MARY (*Loudly into trumpet*): We can have a nice quiet chat!

CATHERINE: Lovely. Of course when your papa finds out I've been with Father Jackson, there's no telling what he'll say. (*Dropping her ear trumpet firmly to her lap*) Well, I simply shan't listen. (*The telephone rings and* MARY *starts for the kitchen.*) Bathroom?

MARY: Telephone!! (*She answers.*) Hello? Yes, Central, go ahead — Jay? Jay darling, I've been so anxious all day. How's your father? Oh dear, then you went all that way for nothing. Now there's no sense in getting angry about it, darling, you know Ralph — just be thankful your father's all right. (RUFUS *runs down the stairs and starts to tiptoe out.*) Rufus, come say hello to Grandma Lynch. (*He puts out his hand to* CATHERINE *who hugs him.*) Where's your hat?

RUFUS: I forgot.

MARY: Well, *get* it, darling.
(RUFUS *goes into the living room where he pulls his hat out from under his jacket where he has hidden it.*)

MARY: What's that, dear? Oh then you'll definitely be here for supper — the family's coming up —

CATHERINE (*Overlapping*): If that's Jay, give him my love.

MARY: Yes, Mama's here already and she sends her love. The others are coming up later and Andrew has a present for me that they're all being very mysterious about, so do try to make it, Jay. Well, don't hurry, not if it means driving fast, because I can hold supper — I'd rather hold it than have you race — all right, darling, we'll see you very soon then — thank you for calling — good-bye. (*She hangs up and speaks into* CATHERINE's *ear trumpet.*) Excuse me! (*She goes into the living room.*) Rufus, what are you doing under there — ? You're supposed to be at the street car stop.

RUFUS (*Climbing out from under the piano bench where he has been searching for something*):   I was looking for the surprise.

MARY: The surprise?

RUFUS: Daddy said it was in here some place.

MARY: Oh Rufus, oh darling — !

RUFUS: He said so, didn't he?

MARY (*Adjusting his hat*):   Now don't ask questions, darling, you *can't* keep Aunt Hannah waiting. That was Daddy on the telephone and Grampa Follet's going to be all right! Isn't that wonderful? And Daddy said he'd be home in time for supper — think of that, Rufus! You'll see him before you go to bed! (*Stepping back to survey his appearance*) Now — what are you going to say to Aunt Hannah?

RUFUS (*As if reciting a piece in school*):   I am glad to go shopping with you —

MARY: *So* glad.

RUFUS: I am so glad to go shopping with you, Aunt Hannah, and thank you for —

MARY: Thank you *very much*.

RUFUS: And thank you very much for thinking of me.

MARYS Now say it all together.

RUFUS: I - am - so - glad - to - go - shopping - with - you - Aunt - Hannah - and - thank - you - very - much - for - thinking - of - me!

MARY (*Laughs and kisses him*):   And be sure to help with her parcels.

>   (RUFUS *goes out to the yard.*)

CATHERINE: You always dress him so well, Mary dear.

>   (*She and* MARY *go into the back part of the house. Alone,* RUFUS *takes off his hat and stuffs it contemptuously under his jacket. The lights dim in the house.*)

RUFUS (*Placing one foot ahead of the other, balances, and sings softly*):
I'm a little busy bee, busy bee, busy bee,
I'm a little busy bee, singing in the clover!

>   (*The older boys enter, pushing a home-made cart with an elaborate, mastlike steering rod.*)

FIRST BOY: Hey Busy bee —

SECOND BOY: Bzz-bzz-bzz!

FIRST BOY: What's your name?

RUFUS: You know.

FIRST BOY: No I don't. Tell me.

SECOND BOY: Bzzzzzzzzzzzz — !

RUFUS: I told you yesterday.

FIRST BOY: No, honest! I don't know your name!

THIRD BOY: He wouldn't ast you if he knowed it already, would he?

RUFUS: You're just trying to tease me.

SECOND BOY: I don't think he's got a name at all! He's a no-name nothin'!

THIRD BOY: No-name nothin'!

FIRST BOY: Leave 'im alone! Stop pickin' on 'im! What d'you mean, pickin' on a little kid like that! Pick on someone your own size!

THIRD BOY (*The picture of innocence*): I didn't mean nothin'!

FIRST BOY (*To Rufus*): Don't pay no 'tention to them! (RUFUS *looks longingly at the cart.*) Yeah, get on up. (RUFUS *climbs on eagerly, tests the steering rod, then puts out his hand gratefully.*) What you puttin' your hand out for?

RUFUS: So you can shake it.
       (*The boys giggle, but the first boy shushes them up.*)

FIRST BOY: I'll tell you what — I'll shake your hand if you'll tell me your name.

RUFUS (*Suddenly bold*): I'll tell you my name if you'll answer a question!

FIRST BOY: What question?

RUFUS: You've got to promise to answer it first.

FIRST BOY: Cross my heart and body! Now what's your name?
> (RUFUS *looks from one to the other. They wait, respectful and interested.*)

RUFUS: It's Rufus.
> (*The minute it is out of his mouth, the boys scream and jeer.*)

THE BOYS: Nigger name! Nigger name! Nigger name!

RUFUS: It is not either! I got it from my Great-Grampa Lynch!

THIRD BOY: Then your grampa's a nigger too!
> (*They run through all their chants, adding "Rufus's Grampa's a nigger!"*)

RUFUS: It's my *great*-grampa and he is *not*!

THE BOYS: He's a ning-ger! He's a ning-ger!
> (HANNAH LYNCH *is suddenly in their midst.*)

HANNAH (*Peering near-sightedly*): Now what's all *this*!
> (*The boys, at once subdued, murmur "Afternoon, ma'am!" and "We gotta go!" and "Yeah, it's time!" backing away and suddenly running off.*)

RUFUS (*Yelling after them*): You didn't answer my question — !

HANNAH (*Observing his distraught state*):   Never mind, Rufus, see what I've brought you.
(*She gives him a small bag. He looks inside.
She waits for ehim to be pleased. But he turns
to look after the departed boys.*) Well — ?

RUFUS: They didn't play fair.

HANNAH: There are chocolate drops in there,
Rufus, and speckled pennies and I don't know
what all. I was almost *late* picking them out.

RUFUS (*Clutching the bag*):   Thank you, Aunt
Hannah.

HANNAH: Don't you think it would be polite to
offer me one?

RUFUS: Will you have a piece of my candy,
Aunt Hannah?

HANNAH: Why, thank you, Rufus, for thinking
of me. I'd like a chocolate drop, if you'll pick
it out for me. My eyes, you know. (*He digs for
the candy. She looks up the street.*) How
many street cars have we missed?

RUFUS: I don't know.

HANNAH: What was the question you wanted
to ask those boys? Perhaps I can help you.

RUFUS: Mama says we've got a surprise coming
to our house.

HANNAH: Why were you going to ask those boys
about it?

RUFUS: Because Daddy said if Mama didn't tell

me about it, I'd find out from the older boys in the street.

HANNAH: And she didn't tell you?

RUFUS: She and Daddy had a fight about it, and now Mama won't let me ask questions at all.

HANNAH: I see. (*She considers this for a moment.*) Rufus, aren't you going to eat your candy?

RUFUS: The teacher says we should send things to the Belgian orphans.

HANNAH: Well, that's very generous of you, but I bought the candy for *you,* in case you grow tired of traipsing from store to store, for we have a great deal of shopping to do this afternoon. A scarf for your mother's birthday — you mustn't tell her! — and something called *A Grammar of Ornament* for your Uncle Andrew, and bunion pads for me, and hooks and eyes —

RUFUS (*Eagerly*):   Can I watch you pare your bunions?

HANNAH: We'll see. But for the time being, I'm sure the Belgian orphans wouldn't mind if you had one piece of their candy.

RUFUS: Would *you* like another piece of my candy, Aunt Hannah?

HANNAH: Thank you, Rufus, a speckled penny this time I think.
          (*He gives her one.*)

RUFUS: What do those boys know about a surprise that's coming to our house, Aunt Hannah? Did Daddy tell them?

HANNAH: Of course not. They don't know a thing.

RUFUS: Daddy said they did.

HANNAH: He didn't mean they *knew* exactly, he just meant they — (*She stops, at a loss, and takes her glasses off, holding them up to the light.*) Rufus, I'm sure your mother saw to it that you had a clean handkerchief before you came out of the house.

RUFUS (*Excitedly*): Can I clean your glasses, Aunt Hannah?

HANNAH: If you'll promise to be *very* careful.

RUFUS: I promise!

HANNAH (*Handing him the glasses*): I'll hold the candy for you. (*He gives her the bag of candy and she munches absentmindedly during the following.*) Rufus, I know about the surprise.

RUFUS (*Astonished*): You *do*?

HANNAH: Oh yes, And I could tell you about it. But there are certain things that should only be told by certain people. For instance, your teacher should be the one to tell you about arithmetic, because she knows about it. And a priest, or a minister, should be the one to tell you about God because he's a *man* of God.

And your mama and daddy are the only ones
to tell you about this particular surprise. Oh,
there are others who'd be *willing* to tell you
about it, if you ask them. But you mustn't ask
them.

RUFUS: Why not, Aunt Hannah?

HANNAH: Because they wouldn't tell it right.

RUFUS: Wouldn't *you* tell it right?

HANNAH (*After a moment*):   Breathe on the
lenses, child. That's right. (*She holds out her
hand and he gives her the glasses.*) You wait
for your mama to explain. You'll be glad later
on. (*Her glasses are on now and she leans
close to peer at him.*) *There* you are! (*He
laughs, delighted.*) What's that bunchy place
under your jacket?

RUFUS (*Guilty*):   My hat.

HANNAH: Well, let's put it on. (*She pulls out
and smooths the rumpled hat, examining it
distastefully.*) Where *does* your mother buy
your clothes? (*She looks at the label inside his
jacket collar.*) Millers? (*He nods. She plunks
the hat on his head.*) Hmp. *Women's clothes*
cut to fit little boys. After we've done our
shopping on Gay Street, I think we'll go
around to Market Street.

RUFUS (*Intrigued*):   Mama won't *go* on Market
Street.

HANNAH: We're going into Harbison's there.
(*With satisfaction*) I hear they're *very* sporty.

And I'm going to buy you a cap. (*He is speech-less.*) Or is there something else you'd rather have?

RUFUS (*Passionately*):   Oh no — no!

HANNAH (*Pleased*):   We'll see what we can do about it. (*Taking her change purse from her bag*) Now, Rufus, when a gentleman takes a lady out for an afternoon of shopping *he's* the one to pay for everything. So I'm going to let you carry my money. First of all, you'll need street car fares — (*She puts two coins into the palm of his hand.*) Five cents for you and five cents for me. Or would you rather walk? Then you can keep the street car fares for yourself.

RUFUS (*In seventh heaven*):   Oh-Aunt-Hannah-I'm - so - glad - to - go - shopping - with - you - and - thank - you - very - much - for - think-ing - of - me!

HANNAH: Your mother told you to say that, didn't she?

RUFUS (*Tugging her hand*):   I forgot.

HANNAH (*As they start off*):   I know direct quo-tation when I hear it.
> (*The lights dim. A small light comes up on* MARY, *sitting by* RUFUS's *bed, singing him to sleep.*)

MARY (*Singing*):
"Go tell Aunt Rhoda, go tell Aunt Rhoda,
Go tell Aunt Rhoda that the old grey goose is
     dead.
One she's been savin', the one she's been savin',

Yes, the one she's been savin' to make a feather
    bed.
Old gander's weepin', the old gander's weepin',
Oh, the old gander's weepin' because his wife is
    dead.
The goslins are mournin', the goslins are
    mournin',
The goslins are mournin' because their
    mother's dead.
She died in the mill-pond, she died in the mill-
    pond,
She died in the mill-pond from standin' on her
    head.
Go tell Aunt Rhoda, oh go tell Aunt Rhoda,
Oh, go tell Aunt Rhoda the old grey goose is
    dead."

> (*The lights have come up on the living
> room where* CATHERINE *sits at the piano
> running her fingers over the keys but
> playing no music.* JOEL LYNCH, MARY's
> father, comes into the room and watch-
> es her.* ANDREW LYNCH, MARY's brother,
> comes into the yard by the swing and
> spreads a quilt on the ground. During
> the following,* HANNAH *enters the kitch-
> en from the unseen dining room, the
> last of the supper dishes in her hands.*)

CATHERINE: I wish you wouldn't stand there,
Joel. I can't do my best when I'm being
watched.

JOEL (*Loudly*):   What the devil do you think
you're playing?

CATHERINE: "The Burning Of Rome."

JOEL: Well, let's hear it, then!

CATHERINE *(Impatiently)*:   Rufus is asleep!
          *(She turns a page and goes on "play-
          ing.")*

JOEL: Good God!
          (He crosses out to the yard.)

ANDREW: You know, Papa, we've got to face
the possibility, you and I, that Jay is drunk
somewhere and be ready for it!

JOEL: Rot!

ANDREW: Mary's thinking it though — ever
since supper — and she's worried, I can tell,
Papa — she's got what Jay calls that pursed-up
look. Shall I go look for him?

JOEL: Where would you look?

ANDREW: He used to like those places down off
Market Square. It's lively down there at night,
Papa, with the farmers rolling into town and
the smell of salt and leather and fresh vege-
tables and whiskey!

JOEL: If that's where he is, let the man come
home on his own. It will be hard enough for
him when he gets here. You might as well
learn, Andrew, it's the way of our women to
try to break their men with piety.

ANDREW: Or is it the way of our men, Papa, to
try to break their women with impiety. (JOEL
snorts.) I'm just asking. I've never been able
to decide who I am, your son or Mama's.

JOEL: Not everyone has such a wide choice.

(MARY *has stopped singing, come down the stairs, and now passes through the kitchen.*)

MARY: Rufus is finally asleep. He was terribly disappointed that Jay hadn't come home.

HANNAH: He'll be along soon.

(MARY *crosses out to yard.*)

MARY (*She sits beside* JOEL *on the swing.*):   Do you think I've been deserted, Papa? Do you think my husband's gone away, never to return? Will you take care of me again, Papa, if I'm deserted? Will you let me come home again and sit on your lap and cry for my lost love?

JOEL: No, daughter.

MARY: Why not, Papa?

JOEL: Because you'll never be deserted.

MARY: You always defend Jay, don't you, Papa?

JOEL: I always thought highly of him. From the first.

MARY: You'd praise Jay to the skies on the one hand, and on the other, why practically in the same breath, you'd be telling me one reason after another why it would be plain foolhardy to marry him.

JOEL: Isn't it possible that I meant both things?

MARY: I don't see how.

JOEL: You learned how yourself, Mary.

MARY: Is that what I've learned?

JOEL: I've taken Jay into the office. That shows confidence.

MARY: And he's teaching himself law! Your confidence is justified!

JOEL (*Laughing*): That's what I wanted. To hear you defend him!

MARY: Me defend him — ? Why, Papa, why — I couldn't ever defend Jay enough! Oh Papa, in these past few months we've come to a — a kind of harmoniousness that is so beautiful I've no business talking about it. It's only the gulfs between us. If I could fill them in, it would all be perfect. I want life to be perfect, Papa. (*Looking off*) Why doesn't he come home? (*Turning back to them*) Andrew, I'm ready to see that present now!

ANDREW (*Going into the living room as the others follow.* HANNAH *joins them from the kitchen.*): I should make you wait for your birthday, Mary, it was meant to be a birthday present.

MARY: What is it, a new picture you've done?

JOEL: I think you'll like it, Mary.

HANNAH: Yes, Mary!

MARY: Oh, you've all seen it!
(*They agree with "Oh yes!" and "Andrew showed it to us at breakfast!" and* MARY *says "That's no fair!" There is a*

festive, family air. CATHERINE *turns to face the group, putting her trumpet to her ear.*)

ANDREW: Mama, will you give us a nice fanfare for the unveiling?

JOEL: She didn't hear you, Andrew.

MARY (*Into* CATHERINE'S *trumpet*):   Mama, Andrew wonders if you'd play us a fanfare! (CATHERINE *does so.* ANDREW *removes the wrapping from the picture, which turns out to be a painting of* JAY. *There is silence. They all look at* MARY'S *reaction.*) Oh, Andrew. It's Jay.

ANDREW: Do you like it?

MARY: It *is* Jay!

HANNAH: I think Andrew caught a very good likeness.

JOEL: Especially around the mouth and chin.

MARY: Yes, right in through there, especially!

ANDREW: The eyes were the hardest. They always are unless the subject sits for you, and I didn't want Jay to do that because then you'd both have known. I've been making sketches for months.

MARY: He wouldn't have done it anyhow. Imagine Jay sitting still for an artist!

HANNAH: The picture has great dignity.

JOEL: So has Jay.

MARY (*Hugging* ANDREW):   Oh, Andrew, I just
love it! Thank you!
>   (RUFUS *runs down the stairs calling.*)

RUFUS: Daddy! Daddy!

MARY: Oh dear!

HANNAH: I guess we *were* making a racket.
>   (RUFUS *runs into the room, wearing his
>   night shirt and a thunderous fleecy
>   check cap in jade green, canary yellow,
>   black and white, which sticks out inches
>   to either side above his ears and has a
>   great scoop of a visor beneath which his
>   face is all but lost.*)

CATHERINE: There's little Rufus!

RUFUS: Did Daddy come home yet?

MARY: No dear, what made you think so?

RUFUS: I woke up. I wanted to show him my
cap!

MARY: Rufus, I told you not to wear that cap to
bed! (*Exasperated*) Aunt Hannah! I'll never
forgive you.
>   (HANNAH *smiles rather secretly and
>   shrugs.*)

CATHERINE: Rufus, come give Grandma a good
hug! (RUFUS *goes to her and hugs her. She
vigorously slaps his back.*) Mmm-mm. Nice
little boy! (*Over his shoulder to* MARY, *gently
reproving*) Mary dear, do you think he ought
to wear his cap to *bed*?
>   (*They all laugh. The telephone rings.*)

MARY: Maybe that's Jay.
         (*She goes quickly to the kitchen.*)

CATHERINE (*Discreetly to* HANNAH):   Bathroom?

RUFUS (*Loudly*):   Telephone!
         (CATHERINE *nods and smiles.*)

MARY (*At telephone*):   Hello — ?

CATHERINE (*Taking* RUFUS's *hand*):   Come along,
   Rufus, let *Grandma* put you to bed *this*
   time!
         (*She takes him upstairs.*)

MARY (*Loudly*):   Hello! Will you please talk a
   little louder! I can't hear — I said I can't hear
   you!

JOEL: It's long distance all right.

HANNAH: Oh dear, his father's worse.

ANDREW: At least we know where he is!
         (*They try not to listen, focusing on the
         portrait, but gradually they are caught
         by what they can hear.*)

MARY: Yes, that's better, thank you. Yes, this is
   she, what is it? (*A long silence*) Yes — I heard
   you. (*She stares dumbly at the telephone,
   then rallies.*) Yes, there's my brother. Where
   should he come to? (*Closing her eyes, concen-
   trating, memorizing*) Brannicks — left of the
   Pike — Bell's Bridge. Do you have a doctor? A
   doctor, do you have one? All right then — my
   brother will come out just as fast as he can.
   Thank you — very much for calling. Good-

night. (*She hangs up and stands for a moment,
her hand still on the telephone. Then she
slowly turns to the others.*) Andrew, there's
been an — that was a man from Powell's Station, about twelve miles out towards LaFollette, and he says — he says Jay has met with a
very serious accident. He wants — he said they
want some man of his family to come out just
as soon as possible and — help bring him in, I
guess.

ANDREW: Shall I get Dr. Dekalb?

MARY: He says no. Just you.

ANDREW: I guess there's a doctor already there.

MARY: I guess so.

ANDREW: Where do I go?

MARY: Powell's Station, out on the Pike toward —

ANDREW: I know, but exactly where? Didn't he
say?

MARY: Brannick's Blacksmith Shop. B-r-a-n-
n-i-c-k. He said they'll keep the lights on and
you can't miss it. It's just to the left of the Pike,
just this side of Bell's Bridge.

ANDREW: I won't be any longer than I have to.

MARY: Bless you. I'll — we'll get everything
ready here in case — you know — he's well
enough to be brought home.

ANDREW: Good. I'll phone the minute I know
anything. Anything.

MARY: Bless you, dear.
          (ANDREW *goes*.)

JOEL: Where is he hurt?

MARY: He didn't say.

JOEL: Well, didn't you ask — ?

HANNAH: Joel.

JOEL: No matter.

MARY: Where's Mama?

JOEL: Upstairs with Rufus.

MARY: Keep her up there, will you, Papa — ?
Just a few minutes till I — Make sure Rufus is
asleep, be sure he's asleep, then tell her what's
happened. And talk as softly as you can and
still have her know what you're saying.

JOEL: Would you like us to go home, Mary?

MARY: No!

JOEL: We'll keep out of the way —

MARY: It's not that — it's just that with Mama
it's so very hard to talk.

HANNAH: For heaven's sake, Joel, go along.
          (*He goes upstairs and sits with* CATH-
          ERINE *in* RUFUS'S *room*.)

MARY: What time is it, Aunt Hannah?

HANNAH: About ten twenty-five.

MARY: Let's see, Andrew drives pretty fast,
though not so fast as Jay, but he'll be driving

better than usual tonight, and it's just over twelve miles. That would be — supposing he goes thirty miles an hour, that's twelve miles — let's see, six times four is twenty-four, six times five's thirty, twice twelve is twenty-four — sakes alive, I was always dreadful at figures.

HANNAH: It's only twelve miles. We should hear very soon.

MARY (*Abruptly*):   Let's have some tea.

HANNAH: Why not let me —
        (*She stops.*)

MARY (*Blankly*):   What?

HANNAH: Just let me know if there's anything I can help with.

MARY: Not a thing, thank you. (*She goes into the kitchen, and during the following lights the stove, puts the kettle on to boil, takes down the box of tea, finds the strainer, the cups and saucers.* HANNAH *watches, her hands folded.*) We'll make up the downstairs bedroom. Remember he stayed there when his poor back was sprained. It's better than upstairs, near the kitchen and the bathroom and no stairs to climb. He's always saying we must get the bathroom upstairs but we never do. And of course, if need be, that is if he needs a nurse, we can put her in the dining room and eat in here, or even set up a cot right in the room with him and put up a screen. Or if she minds that, why she can just sleep on the liv-

ing room davenport and keep the door open
in between. Don't you think so?

HANNAH: Certainly.

MARY: Of course it's very possible he'll have to
be taken straight to a hospital. The man did
say it was serious, after all. Sugar and milk —
(*She gets them.*) — or lemon? I don't know if
I have any lemons, Aunt Hannah —

HANNAH: Milk is fine for me.

MARY: Me too. Would you like some Zuzus?
(*She gets them from the cupboard.*) Or bread
and butter, or toast? I could toast some.

HANNAH: Just tea will do.

MARY: Well, here are the Zuzus.
          (*She puts them on the table.*)

HANNAH: Thank you.

MARY: Goodness sakes, the watched *pot*!
          (*She stands by the stove, motionless.*)

HANNAH: I hope you didn't really mind my
giving Rufus that cap, Mary.

MARY (*Vaguely*):   Heavens no, you were good
to do it.

HANNAH: I'm sure if you had realized how
much he wanted one, you'd have given it to
him yourself long ago.

MARY (*Forcing concentration*):   Of course. Oh,
yes. But *Harbisons*, isn't that where you got

it? I hear it's so tough, how did you ever dare
go *in*?

HANNAH: Fortunately, I'm so blind I couldn't
see what might hurt me. I just sailed up to the
nearest man and said, "Where do I go, please,
to find a cap for my nephew." And he said,
"I'm no clerk, Ma'am, I'm a customer myself."
And I said, "Then why aren't you wearing a
hat?" He had no answer to *that,* of course,
so —

MARY: Why didn't he tell me?

HANNAH: Who?

MARY: That man on the telephone! Why didn't
I ask? I didn't even ask! *How* serious? *Where*
is he hurt? Papa noticed it!

HANNAH: You couldn't think.

MARY: Is he living or dead?
           (*She has said it.*)

HANNAH: That we simply have to wait and find
out.

MARY: Of course we have to wait! That's what's
so unbearable!

HANNAH: Try if you can to find a mercy in it.

MARY: A *mercy* — ?

HANNAH: A little time to prepare ourselves.

MARY: I'm sorry, Aunt Hannah, you're quite
right.
           (*She sits at the table.*)

CATHERINE (*Crossing to head of stairs, followed by* JOEL): I'm going down to see if there isn't something I can do for poor dear Mary. (JOEL *stops her.*) But it's my place to, isn't it, Joel? (*She looks at him rather anxiously. He nods. She goes on down the stairs.*)

MARY: I don't know's I really want any tea but I think it's a good idea to drink something warm while we're waiting, don't you?

HANNAH: I'd like some.

CATHERINE (*Going to* MARY): I've decided there is no cause for alarm, Mary dear. Jay is perfectly all right, I'm sure. And Andrew was simply too overjoyed with relief to bother to phone and is bringing Jay straight home instead for a wonderful surprise. That would be like Andrew. And like Jay to go along with the surprise and enjoy it, just laugh at how scared we've been. Of course, we shall have to scold them both. (*She nods brightly, having solved everything, and goes into the living room to sit with* JOEL *on the davenport.*) Joel, what Andrew's doing is coming in with Jay's poor body to the undertaker's. Roberts, probably. Although they do say that new man over on Euclid Avenue is very good. But our family has always used Roberts.

MARY: Did Rufus pick out the cap all by himself?

HANNAH: You don't think I chose that monstrosity, do you? (*She laughs.*) At first he

picked a very genteel little serge, but I smelled
the hypocrisy behind it, and forgive an old
woman, Mary, but I said, "Do you really like
that one or do you just think it will please
your mother?" Then he revealed his true taste.
But I was switched if I was going to boss him.

MARY (*Who has not listened*):   Either he's badly hurt but he'll live. Or he is so terribly hurt
that he will die from it, maybe after a long,
terrible struggle, maybe breathing his last at
this very minute and wondering where I am,
why I'm not there. Or he was already gone
when the man called. Of course it's just what
we have no earthly business guessing about.
And I'm not going to say he's dead until I
know for sure that he is.

HANNAH: Certainly not.

MARY: But I'm all but certain that he is, all the
same. (*After a moment*) Oh I do beseech my
God that it be not so! (*Turning to* HANNAH,
lost, scared) Aunt Hannah, can we kneel
down for a moment? (HANNAH *does not re-
spond.*) Aunt *Hannah* — ?

HANNAH (*Sighing*):   No Mary.

MARY (*Bewildered*):   Why not — ?

HANNAH: It's too easy. As you say, it's one thing
or the other. But no matter what it is, there's
not one thing in this world or the next that
we can do or hope or guess at or wish or pray
that can change it one iota. Because whatever
it is, *is*. That's all. And all there is now is to be

ready for it, strong enough for it, whatever it may be. That's all that matters because it's all that's possible.

MARY: I'm *trying* to be ready — !

HANNAH: Your beliefs have never been truly tested. God has come easily to you. He's going to come harder now. But if you wait until you can't go on without Him, you'll find Him. When you *have* to pray, we'll pray.

MARY: Goodness sakes, why don't I get his room ready.

(*She goes off to back part of the house.*)

HANNAH (*Alone*): It's your turn now.

CATHERINE (*In the living room*): What time is it, Joel?

JOEL: Twelve forty-five. A quarter of one!

CATHERINE: Andrew's had time to get there and back, hasn't he, Joel?

JOEL: Twice!

CATHERINE: Don't shout at me, Joel. Just speak distinctly and I can hear you. (*She crosses to the piano for her ear trumpet.*) Just think, Joel, it will be a posthumous baby.

JOEL: Good — God, woman.

CATHERINE: We haven't had a posthumous birth in the family since — your cousin Hetty was posthumous, wasn't she? Of course, your uncle Henry was killed in the War Between the States.

(MARY, *who has joined* HANNAH *in the kitchen, begins to pray.*)

HANNAH: Our Father, Who art in Heaven — (*As they say the prayer,* ANDREW *enters and rushes to* HANNAH's *arms. He holds her so close that she gasps.*) Mary!

MARY: He's dead, Andrew, isn't he? He was dead when you got there.

ANDREW (*He has withdrawn to the swing.*): He was instantly killed!
   (*She starts to go limp. He rushes to her.*)

MARY: Papa — ! Mama — !
   (*He supports her as best he can into the living room where the others take her from him and seat her on the davenport.*)

CATHERINE: There there there, Mary, dear, there there!

HANNAH (*She goes to get water and then smelling salts.*): Sit down, Mary — !

JOEL: It's hell, Mary, just plain hell!

ANDREW (*Hysterically*): Instantly, Papa! Instantly! (*Snapping his fingers again and again*) Instantly! Quick as that! Quick as that! He was at this blacksmith's shop and they made me look at him! Instantly! This reeking horseblanket and they made me look! I'd never seen a dead man before and it was Jay! Instantly! The flat of the hand! The flat of the hand of death, the flat of the hand — !

*(He is now slapping the seat of a kitch-
en chair.)*

JOEL: For God's sake, Andrew, think of your
sister!

MARY: What happened, Andrew?

HANNAH: Give yourself a minute, Mary, just a
minute —

CATHERINE (*Waving the smelling salts past
MARY's nose*): This will clear your head —

MARY (*Brushing the salts aside*): I don't want
it, Mama, I want to hear what happened! Andrew?

ANDREW (*As if suddenly realizing*): I have to
tell you — ?

JOEL: Tell her!

ANDREW: I can't, I can't be the one — !

JOEL: What *happened*?

ANDREW: I don't even know how to begin — !

JOEL: Just begin!

ANDREW: Where?

JOEL: Anywhere.

ANDREW: Well — he was alone, for one thing —

MARY: Of course he was alone, I *know* that.

ANDREW: I just meant — there was no one else
in the accident, or other automobiles —

MARY: I want to hear about *Jay*!

ANDREW: I'm *trying* to tell you — !

JOEL: *What caused the accident?*

ANDREW (*Shouting*):   A cotter pin!

MARY: What's a cotter pin?

ANDREW: You wouldn't understand, Mary, you don't know about automobiles —

MARY: Papa, make him tell me!

ANDREW: All *right*, it's just something that holds the steering mechanism together like this — (*Holds up his knuckles*) There'd be a hole through the knuckles and that's where the cotter pin goes like a hairpin and you open the ends flat and spread them —

MARY: I *understand!*

ANDREW: *The cotter pin fell out.*

MARY: What happened then?

ANDREW: Nobody was there, we can't say. He just lost control of the auto!

MARY: Who found him?

ANDREW: The man who telephoned you.

MARY: Who was he?

ANDREW: I don't know his name.

MARY: I wish you did.

ANDREW: He was driving in toward town about nine o'clock and he heard Jay coming up from behind terrifically fast — All of a sudden he said he heard a terrifying noise and then dead silence. He turned around and drove back —

MARY: Where was this?

ANDREW: Just the other side of Bell's Bridge —

MARY: Where you come down that sort of angle?

ANDREW: That's the place. He'd been thrown absolutely clear of the auto as it ran off the road. And the car had gone up an eight-foot embankment, then tumbled back, bottom-side up, right next to him, without even grazing him. They think when the cotter pin fell out, he must have been thrown forward very hard, so he struck his chin one sharp blow against the steering wheel, and that must have killed him . . .

MARY (*Putting her hand to his mouth*):   Killed — (*Then, after a long moment*) I'll never see him again. Never. Never, never, never, never. (*She moves into the living room. The others watch helplessly, unable to comfort or even touch her, for when they try, she tears herself away from them, then she falls to her knees in front of* JAY's *portrait in the armchair. She is completely dissolved, moaning and crying.* CATHERINE *kneels beside her and puts her arms around her.*)

CATHERINE: There, there, Mary. We're all here.

MARY (*Now completely drained*): Thank heaven for that, Mama. (*Weakly*) Andrew, I want whiskey.

HANNAH: It'll do her good.

JOEL: Do us all good.

ANDREW: I'll go down home and get some.

MARY: No — (*She points vaguely to the hall closet.* HANNAH *gets the bottle as* ANDREW *is getting glasses. In his haste, he drops one into the sink and it breaks. They pour some for* MARY *but she holds up her glass for more. Then she gulps it several times. Eventually . . .*) Did you — what did he look like — ?

ANDREW: His clothes were hardly even rumpled.

MARY (*Nodding*): His brown suit.

ANDREW (*At a loss*): He was lying on his back.

MARY: His face?

ANDREW: Just a little blue bruise on the lower lip.

MARY (*Hurt*): Is that all?

ANDREW: And a cut so small they can sew it up with one stitch.

MARY: Where?

ANDREW: The exact point of his chin.

MARY (*Touching her father's chin*): Point of the chin, Papa.

ANDREW: The doctor said death was instantaneous. Concussion of the brain. (*She turns away and he stops for a moment. Then she gulps her whiskey and turns back.*) He can't have suffered, Mary, not a fraction of a second. I asked about that very particularly because I knew you'd want to be sure. I saw his face. There wasn't a glimmer of pain in it. Only a kind of surprise. Startled.

MARY (*Nodding*): I imagine so.

ANDREW: It was just a chance in a million. Just that one tiny area, at just a certain angle, and just a certain sharpness of impact on the chin. If it had been even half an inch to one side, he'd be alive this minute.

JOEL (*Watching* MARY): Shut up, Andrew.

ANDREW: What'd I say, Papa?

MARY: Have a little mercy! A little mercy!

ANDREW: I'm so sorry, Mary —

HANNAH: Let her cry.

ANDREW: I'm so sorry.

MARY: O God, forgive me! Forgive me! Forgive me! It's just more than I can bear! Just more than I can bear. Forgive me!

ANDREW: Forgive *you*! I say, O God if you exist, Goddamn you!

HANNAH: Andrew! (*A silence*) Mary, listen to
me. There's nothing to ask forgiveness for.
There's nothing to ask forgiveness for, Mary.
Do you hear me, do you hear me, Mary?

MARY: I spoke to Him as if He had no mercy.

HANNAH: Andrew was just —

MARY: To *God*. As if He were trying to rub it
in. Torment me! That's what I asked forgiveness for.

CATHERINE: There, there, Mary.

HANNAH: Listen Mary, Our Lord on the Cross,
do you remember?

MARY: My God, my God, why has Thou for-
saken me?

HANNAH: Yes. And then did He ask forgiveness?

MARY: He was God. He didn't have to.

HANNAH: He was human too. And He didn't
ask it. Nor was it asked of Him to ask it. No
more are you. And no more should you. You're
wrong. You're terribly mistaken. What was it
He said instead? The very next thing?

MARY: Father, into Thy hands —
    (*She stops.*)

HANNAH: Father, into Thy hands I commend
my spirit.

MARY: I commend — (*She stops again, then*

after a moment, looks up at HANNAH *deeply hurt and bewildered.*) You've never had anything *but* God, Aunt Hannah. I had a husband. I was married to a *man*. I won't *have* God in his place. (*She turns away to find herself facing the picture.*) Nor that picture, Andrew. I never saw that face in my life before tonight. Jay's face had eyes and mouth. Put it in the hall closet, Papa.

> (JOEL *takes the portrait from the room.*)

CATHERINE: Try not to suffer too much, Mary.

MARY (*With a sudden, irrational anger*): That's right, Mama, keep your ear trumpet in your lap! Shut out whatever might be unpleasant! Think of having voices to hear and not listening! (*Stopping, again with that ununderstanding hurt*) I want more whiskey.

HANNAH: Let me fix you one good hot toddy so you'll sleep.

MARY: I want a *lot* more whiskey!

ANDREW: You'll make yourself drunk, Mary.

MARY (*Grabbing the bottle angrily*):   Let me!

HANNAH: You've tomorrow to reckon with!

MARY (*Pouring herself a good drink*): What's tomorrow! I'm going to get just as drunk as I can.

> (*She gulps silently, broodingly for a long moment.*)

CATHERINE (*Suddenly very cheerful, rather chatty*): Mother always said that in times of stress, the best thing to drink was buttermilk. (*They look at her and each other in astonishment, and then* MARY *begins to laugh.*)

MARY: Buttermilk!
(ANDREW *laughs, and then* HANNAH. JOEL *returns and is caught into the contagion of this somewhat hysterical laughter, and they all roar, laughing their heads off, while* CATHERINE *sits disapproving of the levity and somehow uneasily suspecting that for some reason they are laughing at her, but in courtesy and reproof, and in an expectation of hearing the joke, smiling and lifting her trumpet. The laughter quiets down.*)

JOEL: What are we laughing at?
(*And they are off again, giving themselves to their laughter, willing it to continue.*)

ANDREW: Buttermilk!

JOEL: What's so funny about buttermilk?
(*And they laugh all the harder.*)

HANNAH: Now this is terrible! We're not going to laugh anymore! We're going to stop it!

MARY: Aunt Hannah's right! Andrew, stop making me laugh!

ANDREW (*Tickling her*): *You* stop making *me* laugh!

MARY: You started it!

HANNAH (*Clapping her hands*): Children! Children! (*They made a great effort to stop, and suddenly thoroughly enjoy giving in to it again. Finally they quiet down, holding their sides, moaning and drying their eyes, unable to laugh any more.*)

CATHERINE (*Very primly rising to get the whiskey bottle, corking it, and putting it away*): I have never in my life been so thoroughly shocked and astonished.
(*And they are off again, laughing harder than ever, hugging* CATHERINE, *kissing her, petting her, leaning on each other, trying to catch their breaths.*)

MARY (*Suddenly, loudly*): Listen!
(*All the laughing stops and they look to her.*)

ANDREW: What is it?

MARY: Just listen.

JOEL: What's up?

MARY: Quiet, Papa, please. There's something.

ANDREW: I can't hear anything.

HANNAH (*Who has been watching her closely*): Mary does.

ANDREW: There is something.

MARY: It's in the kitchen.

ANDREW: I'll go see —

MARY: Wait, Andrew, don't, not yet.

CATHERINE: Has somebody come into the house?

ANDREW: What made you think so, Mama?

CATHERINE: Why, how stupid of me. I thought I heard. Footsteps. I must be getting old and dippy.

ANDREW: Sssh!

MARY: It's Jay.

HANNAH (*Watching her*):   Of course it is.

JOEL (*Thundering*):   What — !

MARY: Now he's come into the room with us.

ANDREW: Mary — !

MARY: It's Jay, Andrew, who else would be coming here tonight so terribly worried, so terribly concerned for us, and restless. Feel the restlessness.

ANDREW: You mean you can —

MARY: I mean it simply feels like his presence.

ANDREW: Do you feel anything, Papa?

JOEL: I feel goose bumps, of course. But that's from looking at your faces.

MARY: He's going upstairs.

JOEL: You've got to stop this, Mary.

MARY: Quiet, Papa! He's in Rufus's room.

JOEL: For God's sake, Mary, you're having hallucinations.

HANNAH: Joel, I know that God in a wheelbarrow wouldn't convince you, but Mary *knows* what she is experiencing.

ANDREW: I believe it! I really do!

JOEL: I see you've decided whose son you are.

MARY: Please stop talking about it, please. It just means so much more than we can say. I'd just like to be quiet in the house, by myself.
(*She goes upstairs singing "Sugar Babe" softly. The others start to leave.*)

HANNAH: Andrew, when you get home, telephone Jay's people and tell them how it happened.
(MARY *is in* RUFUS's *room. She suddenly calls down to them as they cross the yard.*)

MARY: Andrew! (*They stop and look up at her.*) Where is he? Dear God, where is he?

ANDREW (*Vaguely*):   What d'you mean?

MARY: Where did you take him?

ANDREW: Oh. To Roberts.

MARY: Roberts. Yes. Bless you. (JOEL, CATHERINE, *and* ANDREW *go.* HANNAH *sinks wearily to*

a chair in the kitchen. MARY *turns into her
own room, wandering, hopefully, half frightened.*) Jay, darling? Dear heart? Are you
here? (*She has moved around and now stands
on the threshold of* RUFUS's *room again.*) Jay?
(*She stops, seeing the little boy sitting up in
bed, staring at her. She sinks to the trunk.*)
Dear God.

          Curtain.

ACT III

RUFUS *is alone in his bedroom, dressed in a black suit and cap.*

He goes into his mother's room, down the stairs, into the kitchen, then into the living room. No one is around. He takes off his cap, puts it on the sofa, then from under his jacket takes out his gaudy cap, puts it on, and goes out into the street. The boys enter from down right on their way to school. The first boy runs past.

RUFUS: My daddy's dead! (*The boy ignores him.*) My daddy's dead!

SECOND BOY: Huh! Betcha he ain't!

RUFUS: Why he is so.

SECOND BOY: Where's your satchel at? You're just making up a lie so you can lay outa school.

RUFUS: I am not laying out, I'm just staying out, because my daddy's dead!
            (*The third boy has joined them.*)

291

THIRD BOY: He can lay out because his daddy
   got killed.
> (RUFUS *looks at him gratefully. And the
> third boy seems to regard him with
> something like respect.*)

FIRST BOY: How do *you* know?

THIRD BOY: 'Cause my daddy seen it in the paper. Can't your daddy read?

RUFUS: (*Astounded*):   *The new*spaper — ?

THIRD BOY: Sure, your daddy got his *name* in
   the paper. Yours too.

FIRST BOY (*With growing respect*):   *His* name's
   in the paper? Rufus'?

THIRD BOY: Him and his daddy both, right in
   the paper.

RUFUS: He was killed instntly.
> (*He snaps his fingers.*)

THIRD BOY: What you get for drivin' a auto
   when you're drunk, that's what my daddy says.

RUFUS: What's drunk?

SECOND BOY: What's *drunk*? Drunk is fulla good
   ole whiskey. (*He staggers around in circles,
   weak-kneed, head lolling.*) 'At's what drunk is.

RUFUS: Then he wasn't.

SECOND BOY: How do *you* know?

RUFUS   Because my daddy never walked like
   that.

THIRD BOY: How'd he get killed if he wasn't drunk?

RUFUS: He had a fatal accident.

SECOND BOY: How'd he *have* a fatal accident if he wasn't drunk?

RUFUS: It was kuhkushon.

SECOND BOY: Hell, you don't even know what you're talkin' about!

FIRST BOY (*Simultaneously*): Don't even know how his own daddy got killed!
> (*They scoff and jeer.* RUFUS *begins to think he has lost his audience.*)

THIRD BOY: My daddy says we gotta feel sorry for Rufus here 'cause he's an orphan.

RUFUS: I am?

THIRD BOY: Sure, like the Belgian kids, on'y worse, 'cause that's *war*, and my daddy says any kid that's made an orphan just 'cause his daddy gets drunk is a *pore kid*.

FIRST BOY: He says his daddy *wasn't* drunk.

SECOND BOY: Yeah.

RUFUS: Maybe he was a little.

FIRST BOY: Izzat so?

RUFUS: I remember now.

THIRD BOY: Sure he was.

SECOND BOY: Good ole whiskey.

THIRD BOY: Pore kid. My daddy says his ole Tin
Lizzy run up a eight foot embankment —

RUFUS (*Bravely*):   That's all you know about it.

FIRST BOY (*To third*):   Let *him* tell it.

SECOND BOY: Yeah, *you* tell it, Rufus.

THIRD BOY: Well, come on and tell us then.

RUFUS: Well — it wasn't any old Tin Lizzy he
was driving, in the first place, it was a — a
Chalmers. And my daddy was going like sixty!

SECOND BOY: 'Cause he was drunk.

RUFUS (*Nodding*):   Good ole whiskey.

THIRD BOY: Pore kid.

RUFUS (*Now completely confident*):   And then
the auto didn't run up any eight foot em-
back — emb — what you said — either, it ran
up a — a pole.

THIRD BOY: A *pole*?

RUFUS (*Jumping up on the swing*):   A hundred feet high!
        (*Doubts have now set in among the
        the three boys.*)

SECOND BOY: Aw, what kinduva pole is that?

RUFUS: The *north* pole. (*They stare at him
blankly to see if it is an old joke, but he is too
excited to notice. He points off.*) Out there! If
you squint your eyes you can see it! (*He
squints searchingly, and the three boys look at*

*one another. One makes circles with his fore-
finger at the side of his head, another silently
blubbers his lower lip, another rolls his eye-
balls back so that only the whites are showing.)* Can you see it?

THE THREE BOYS: Oh yeah! Sure, Rufus! We see
it! So that's the North Pole! Hmmm! Always
wondered where it was!

RUFUS: And my daddy's auto ran up it and fell
right back on top of my daddy like — *(Suddenly he jumps from the swing.)* — whomp!
And that joggled his brain loose in his head
and it — fell out and the hand of death came
down out of the sky and scooped it up. *(Now
somewhat out of breath)* And that's kuhkushon.

FOURTH BOY *(Running on)*:   Hey, I'm waitin'
on you.

FIRST BOY *(Edging off)*:   Yeah. Sure, Rufus.
Well, we gotta go. *(RUFUS quickly puts out his
hand with supreme confidence. The first boy
shakes it hurriedly.)* S'long, Rufus.

SECOND BOY *(Shaking RUFUS's hand)*:   That's a
nice new cap you got, Rufus.

THIRD BOY *(Shaking hands)*:   We'll be seeing
yuh, Rufus.

> *(They hurry off, looking back over
> their shoulders at him, talking among
> themselves, one saying "Whomp!" and
> clapping his hands together, another
> blubbering his lower lip, another stag-*

*gering, whether in imitation of a drunk
or an imbecile, it is hard to say.* RUFUS
looks after them, beaming with pride.)

RUFUS: P-r-o-u-d. (*He scuffs into the living
room, making up a bright little song, almost
jigging.*) B-r-a-v-e-p-r-o-u-d! (*He puts one of
his father's pipes in his mouths, finds a newspaper, and sits in the Morris chair to read.*)
"He is sur-sur-vived by his wi-wife, Mary."
Mama has her name in the paper. "And a son
Rufus." Me. (*He thinks for a moment, then
carefully folds the newspaper. He stops, suddenly struck.*) My daddy's dead. Whomp. (*He
swings his legs, thinking it through.*) He can't
ever come home. Not tomorrow or the next
day. Or the next day or the next day or the next
day. Or the next day or the next day or the
next day or the next day or the next day or the
next day. (*As he continues the odd chant, he
begins to cry. He throws the pipe, the newspaper, and the ash tray.*) Whomp! Whomp!
Good ole whiskey! Whomp! (*He kicks the
Morris chair, bangs at the furniture.*) Good
ole whiskey! Good ole whiskey! Good ole
whiskey!

> (MARY, *in her dressing gown, comes
> from the back part of the house, fol-
> lowed by* HANNAH *in deepest mourn-
> ing.*)

MARY: Rufus!

RUFUS (*Escaping her, running into the kitchen,
hiding under the table*):   Good ole whiskey!
Good ole whiskey! Good ole whiskey!

MARY (*Pulling him out from under the table, sitting in a chair, cradling him*): Darling, who have you been talking to?

RUFUS: My daddy's dead. It says so in the newspaper.

MARY: Oh darling, darling! Now Rufus, Aunt Hannah is going to take you down to Grandma Lynch's for the rest of the morning. Mama will come by later, and then we'll go and see Daddy just once more, so you can say good-bye to him. (*She kisses him.*) You be very good and very quiet.

RUFUS: How could he have a fatal accident if he wasn't drunk.

MARY (*Suddenly turning away from him*): Hannah.

> (HANNAH *takes* RUFUS *by the hand, and they go off.* MARY *looks after them, then goes into the back part of the house. After a moment,* RALPH's *voice is heard, off.*)

RALPH: Don't you fret, ever'body, I'm goana see us through this grievous day! (*He enters, followed by* JOHN HENRY *and* JESSIE, SALLY, *and* JIM-WILSON. *At the same time,* JOEL, CATHERINE, *and* ANDREW *enter from the other side of the stage. All but* SALLY *are in deepest black, and she is self-conscious in navy blue.*) Get in here, Jim-Wilson, you're goana spend th'afternoon with your cousin Rufus and you play nice with him! Andrew, m'Chalmers is

right out front and I'm goana drive Mary and
Paw and Maw and you follow me with the
others. You all right, Paw? Try to be brave,
Maw, try to be brave.

JESSIE (*Making* JOHN HENRY *comfortable in the
living room*):   Leave me be, Ralph.

RALPH: Cry your heart out, Maw. It's natural at
a time like this. I'm goana be two sons to you
now. I'm goana be as many sons as you want.

JESSIE (*Wearily*):   Jes' leave me be.
(*The two families are now seated in
the living room.*)

RALPH (*Awkwardly*):   Well, if anybody needs
me, I'll be right outside.
(*He goes to the yard and sits on the
swing. He takes out his bottle and has a
good swallow.*)

SALLY: I feel so bad about my dress, Mother
Follet.

JESSIE: You look fine, Sally.

SALLY (*Ashamed*):   I wish it was black.

JESSIE: Imagine bein' young enough not to
have a black dress. Imagine that Miz Lynch.

CATHERINE: What is it, Joel?

JOEL: *Black dresses.*

CATHERINE: Oh. (*She looks around the room.*)
Is anybody speaking?

JOEL: No, Catherine.

CATHERINE: When I was a girl in Michigan, the dressmaker and the milliner used to come to the house. They were almost the first to arrive. After the priest, of course, but before the undertaker. They filled in that gap. Nobody ever knew how they *knew* when to come, for they were never summoned — they just appeared, as if they had an extra sense about such things. And they always wore purple to show they weren't *of* the tragedy but in sympathy to it. (*She looks from one to the other. They seem to be waiting. She nods and smiles.*) I've finished.

JESSIE: If a woman has a usual life, one black dress will see her through it.

CATHERINE: Beg pardon?

JESSIE (*Sympathetically*): She really *don't* hear good, do she?

JOEL (*After a pause*): In Japan they say white is the color of mourning.

JESSIE: Now that wouldn't seem right.

JOEL: Black wouldn't seem right to them.

JESSIE: You all right, Paw?

JOHN HENRY: There's Granmaw sittin' up on that mountain for a hundred and three years. And here's me with two attacks to m'credit. And still, Jay's the one that gets took. (*He shakes his head sadly.*) Not Jay. Never Jay.

JESSIE: Now, Paw.

JOHN HENRY: I was all *ready* to go.

> (RALPH *sits up in the swing and hides his bottle as* HANNAH *and* RUFUS *enter the yard, followed by* MARY *and* FATHER JACKSON. RALPH *struggles to his feet.*)

RALPH: There he is, the poor little fatherless child.

RUFUS: I saw my daddy, Uncle Ralph.

RALPH: Don't you cry, honey, your Uncle Ralph is here.

MARY: Ralph, I'd like you to meet Father Jackson. This is my brother-in-law, Mr. Follet.

JACKSON: How do you do?

RALPH: How do you do, sir. Can I — take your hat?

JACKSON (*Taking off his hat*):   Thank you.

HANNAH: That won't be necessary, Father. We're leaving again directly.

RALPH: Was everything all right down to Roberts', Mary? (*To* FATHER JACKSON) What d'you think of that, sir? With the deceased's only brother an undertaker and willin' to do the generous thing, free of charge, still she puts him in the hands of a stranger. Did y'ever hear of such a thing's that?

JACKSON: It's right for your brother to be buried here, Mr. Follet, where his home was.

RALPH: Now that just plain don't make sense!

Jay spent over two-thirds of his life in La-
Follette and less'n one-third in Knoxvul! I
figgered it out! (*Turning on* MARY) You just
didn't think of me! You never even thought of
me, did yuh?

MARY: No.

RALPH: My own brother! My only brother!

MARY: My own — only husband.

RALPH: All right for you, Mary. (*He stumbles
upstage, taking out his bottle.*) All right for
you.

> (*He mumbles under his breath.* MARY
> *looks at him for a moment, then the
> procession continues into the living
> room.*)

CATHERINE: There's little Rufus!

RUFUS: I saw my daddy!

JESSIE: Come to Granmaw, Rufus.

CATHERINE: Come sit on Grandma's lap.

JESSIE: Well, I never!

JOEL: She didn't hear you, Mrs. Follet. No
offense.

JESSIE: I keep forgettin'!

JOEL (*Rising*): Is it time, Mary?

MARY: Yes, Papa.

SALLY: I'll put Jim-Wilson in Rufus's room for
his nap, if that's all right, Mary.

MARY: It's all right, Sally. (SALLY *takes* JIM-
WILSON *upstairs.*) Rufus, Mama has to leave
you now. You're to be a good boy and stay
with Grandma Lynch.
   (JOEL *offers his arm to* MARY.)

RALPH (*In the yard, his mumbling reaching a
shout, he smashes his bottle against the back
fence.*):   I'm glad he's dead!
   (MARY *has started to take* JOEL's *arm.
Now she suddenly turns out of the room
and into the yard to confront* RALPH)

MARY: Was he drunk?

HANNAH (*Following her*):   Mary!

RALPH: On top of ever'thin' else, a priest.

MARY: Was my husband drunk?

RALPH: A Follet in the hands of a priest!

MARY: *Was he drunk!* I have to know. You
were with him all afternoon. Tell me!

RALPH: I ain't goanna tell yuh, Mary.
   (*She strikes out at him, but he catches
her wrist.*)

RALPH: You thought of me all right, the night
he died, even. And you just didn't want me. I
ain't goanna tell you nothin'!

HANNAH: We must go, Mary!

RALPH: I ain't goana tell you nothin'!
   (MARY *returns to the living room,
stands a moment, then goes quickly up
to her room.*)

JOEL (*As* HANNAH *starts up after* MARY):
What's she going to do — ?
>   (HANNAH *gestures silence without stop-*
>   *ping. She goes up to find* MARY *in her*
>   *room.*)

SALLY (*Running out to* RALPH, *handing him his*
bowler): Are you all right to drive, Ralph
— ?

RALPH: Well — nobody else is goanna drive my
Chalmers, let me tell you!
>   (*He goes off followed by* SALLY.)

HANNAH: Mary, the service is due to start in a
few minutes.

MARY: I'm going to stay here in this room.

HANNAH: Shall I send Father Jackson up to
you?

MARY: No.
>   (ANDREW *has come up the stairs.*)

ANDREW: Is she coming?

HANNAH: The rest of you get in the cars. We'll
come when we can.
>   (ANDREW *goes back downstairs, and dur-*
>   *ing the following, all but* CATHERINE
>   *and* RUFUS *file out.*)

MARY: Why don't they all leave. You, too,
Hannah. For I'm not going.

HANNAH (*Touching her shoulder*): I'm staying
here.

MARY: If you are, please don't touch me. (*In a sudden rage*) That miserable Ralph! Damn him! You were right, Hannah, God is coming harder to me now. And Jay, too! I can't seem to find either one of them. (HANNAH *stands back quietly*. MARY *gets a necktie from the bureau and scrutinizes the label.*) This necktie was bought in Chattanooga some place. When, do you suppose? Sometimes when he went off like that, he said to be seen as far as Clairborne County. But Chattanooga — Whatever made Jay do it, *ever*! The night we moved into this house, where did he *go*! And when he first went to work in Papa's office — ! (*Stopping, remembering, more softly*) Not when Rufus was born, though. He was very dearly close to me then, very. But other times, he'd feel himself being closed in, watched by superintendents, he'd say, and — There was always a special quietness about him afterwards, when he came home, as if he were very far away from where he'd been, but very far away from me, too, working his way back, but keeping his distance.

HANNAH: Let the man rest, Mary.

MARY: I want him to rest.

HANNAH (*Angrily*): Aren't you even going to attend the funeral!

MARY: Do you think he'll rest simply by lowering him into the ground? I won't watch it. How *can* he when he was *lost* on the very day he died!

HANNAH: You don't know that he was *lost*, or drunk, or *what* he was.

MARY (*After a moment*): No. That's just what I don't know.

HANNAH: And *that's* what you can't bear.

MARY (*After an even longer moment*): I never knew. Not for sure. There were times we *all* knew about, of course, but there were other times when it wasn't always the whiskey. He'd be gone for a night, or a day, or even two, and I'd know he hadn't touched a drop. And it wasn't any of the other things that come to a woman's mind, either, in case you're thinking that.

HANNAH: I wasn't thinking that.

MARY: Those are easy enemies. It was Market Square. And talking to country people about country secrets that go way on back through the mountains. And anyone who'd sing his sad old songs with him. Or all night lunch rooms. What's an all night lunch room for, he'd say, except to sit in all night. And drink coffee so strong it would burn your ribs. And it was locomotives, I suppose, and railroad people, and going fast, and even Charlie Chaplin. What's wrong with Charlie, he'd ask me, not because he didn't know what I'd say, but to make me say it. He's so nasty, I'd say, so vulgar, with his nasty little cane, hooking up skirts. And Jay would laugh and go off to see Charlie Chaplin and not come home. Where

he went, I can't even imagine, for he'd never
tell me. It was always easier to put everything
down to whiskey.

HANNAH: To put it down to an enemy.

MARY: Why couldn't I let him have those
things, whatever they were, if they meant
something to him. Why can't I let him have
them now. The dear. He always worked his
way back.
    (ANDREW *runs in, to the foot of the*
    stairs.)

ANDREW (*In a loud whisper*):   Aunt Hannah,
we can't wait any longer.

HANNAH (*At the top*):   All *right*, Andrew.
    (ANDREW *goes off again.*)

MARY: They must be suffocating in those cars.
(*She smooths the bed for a moment, then
straightens up.*) I'm glad Ralph didn't tell
me. I must just accept not knowing, mustn't
I? I must let Jay *have* what I don't know. (*She
picks up her hat and veil and looks at them.*)
What if he was drunk. What in the world if
he was. Did I honestly think *that* was a gulf?
This is a gulf! (*She tears a rent in the veil.*)
If he was drunk, Hannah, just *if* he was, I
hope he loved being. Speeding along in the
night — singing at the top of his lungs — racing because he loved to go fast — racing to us
because he loved us. And for the time, enjoying — revelling in a freedom that was his, that
no place or person, that nothing in this world

could ever give him or take away from him.
Let's hope that's how it was, Hannah, how he
looked death itself in the face. In his strength.
(*She puts on the hat and pulls the veil over
her face, goes down the stairs.* HANNAH *follows her into the yard.*) That's what we'll put
on the gravestone, Hannah. In his strength.
(*They go off.*)

> (CATHERINE *comes downstage into the
> living room, looks to make sure that no
> one is around, sits on the bench at the
> piano, and carefully opens the keyboard
> cover. She is silently running her fingers
> over the keys when* RUFUS *comes
> into the room and taps her back.*)

RUFUS: Look, Grandma!
(*He shows her a drawing he has just
made.*)

CATHERINE: Oh, that's very nice. Is it you?

RUFUS: It's a Belgian.

CATHERINE: Isn't he wearing your new cap?

RUFUS: He's an orphan.

CATHERINE: What are all these riches coming
down from the sky?

RUFUS: Those are letters and presents from
children all over the world because they feel
sorry for him.

CATHERINE: Why, some day, Rufus, you may be
an artist like your Uncle Andrew. For the
time being, of course, I think it would be

polite for you to *say* you want to go into law,
as your grandfather did and as your dear father was doing. Just for a time. That would only
be showing *respect*.

> (JOEL *and* ANDREW *come into the living
> room.* JOEL *bangs his hat on the end
> table.*)

JOEL: Priggish, mealy mouthed son-of-a-bitch! I
tell you, Andrew, it's enough to make a man
retch up his soul!

CATHERINE (*To* ANDREW):   Was it a lovely funeral, dear?

JOEL: That Jackson! *Father* Jackson, as he in-
sists on being called! Not a *word* would he
say over Jay's body, let alone read a service!
Because he'd never been baptized. A rule of
the Church! Some church!

CATHERINE: Andrew, is there something I
should be hearing?

ANDREW: Absolutely not, Mama! Come on,
Rufus!

> (*He takes* RUFUS *into the yard where
> the swing is.*)

JOEL: You come to one simple, single act of
Christian charity, and what happens! The
rules of the Church forbid it! He's not a member of our little club! I only care, mind you,
for Mary's sake!

> (*He sits beside* CATHERINE *on the daven-
> port.*)

CATHERINE: Joel, I don't know what you're saying, but I wish you wouldn't say it. Wait until
we get home, dear, where what you say won't
matter.

JOEL: Good God!
    (*In the yard,* ANDREW *lifts* RUFUS *over
    the back of the swing and seats him.*)

ANDREW: I tell you, Rufus, if anything ever
makes me believe in God, or Life after Death,
it'll be what happened this afternoon in
Greenwood Cemetery. There were a lot of
clouds, but they were blowing fast, as there was
lots of sunshine too. Right when they began to
lower your father into the ground, into his
grave, a cloud came over and there was a shadow just like iron, and a perfectly magnificent
butterfly settled on the coffin, just rested there,
right over the breast, and stayed there, just
barely making his wings breathe like a heart.
He stayed there all the way down, Rufus, until
it grated against the bottom like a — rowboat.
And just when it did, the sun came out just
dazzling bright and he flew up and out of that
— hole in the ground, straight up into the
sky, so high I couldn't even see him any more.
Don't you think that's wonderful, Rufus?

RUFUS: Yes, sir.

ANDREW: If there are any such things as mir-
acles, then *that's* surely miraculous. (*Slowly
shaking his head, under his breath*) A damned
miracle.

(*The* FOLLETS *enter the kitchen.* SALLY
goes up to RUFUS's *room to sit by the
sleeping* JIM-WILSON. JESSIE *and* JOHN
HENRY *sit at the kitchen table.* RALPH
enters just as MARY *and* HANNAH *come
in from the other direction. When he
sees* MARY, *he takes refuge in the bathroom.* HANNAH *goes upstairs while*
MARY *stops in the living room to speak
to her father.*)

MARY (*Lifting her veil back*): So many people
there, Papa, did you notice? I didn't know half
of them. We don't always realize, do we, how
many others love the people we love. (*She goes
upstairs to join* HANNAH, *removes her hat and
looks at herself in the mirror.*) Rufus says my
face looks like my best china teacup. You
know, Hannah, the one Jay mended for me so
many times. He's beginning to say things like
that now, and I don't know where he gets
them. (*She starts to put the hat away, but
stops.*) People fall away from us, and in time,
others grow away from us. That is simply what
living is, isn't it?

(*She puts the hat on the bureau.*)

HANNAH (*Now sitting on the bed*): Why don't
you rest?

MARY: You're the one, you haven't stopped for
three days.

HANNAH: I'm not tired.

MARY: You must be dead — the words that come to mind.

HANNAH: Not dead. Older perhaps. I'm content to be.

MARY: Well, you're going to lie down for just a minute.

HANNAH: There's supper to be fixed for that mob.

MARY: Not yet.

HANNAH: Perhaps just for a moment.
(*She lies down.*)

MARY: Hannah, I love and revere everyone in this world who has ever suffered. I truly do, even those who have failed to endure.

HANNAH: I like the way you call me Hannah now, instead of Aunt Hannah.

MARY: We're that much closer.

HANNAH: Will you let me know when it's time to get started again?

MARY: I'll let you know.
(*She takes* HANNAH's *glasses off, puts them on the bureau, looks in on* SALLY *and* JIM-WILSON *in* RUFUS's *room. During this,* RALPH *comes out of the bathroom, goes into the yard and off stage.*)

SALLY: He sleeps too much, Mary. He just sleeps and sleeps.

(MARY *leaves them, stops in front of the stairs as if looking out of upstairs hall window.*)

MARY: Be with us all you can, my darling, my dearest. This is good-bye.
    (*During the following,* MARY *comes down the stairs, takes the portrait of* JAY *from the hall closet.*)

CATHERINE (*In the living room*):   I quite agree with you, Joel.

JOEL: I didn't say anything.

CATHERINE: Somebody did.

JOEL: What did they say?

CATHERINE (*Primly*):   They said how fortunate we have been, you and I, to have lived so many years without losing each other.

JOEL: I did say it.

CATHERINE: I must have been mistaken.

JOEL: You weren't mistaken, Catherine. That's-what-I-said!

CATHERINE (*Patting his hand several times*): Never mind, dear.
    (JOEL *and* CATHERINE *watch* MARY *as she enters with* JAY's *portrait, but she seems unaware of their presence. She places it on the music rack of the piano, steps back and gazes at the picture.*)

JESSIE (*In the kitchen*):   How's your breath, Paw?

JOHN HENRY: Pretty fair.

> (MARY *squeezes* JOEL's *hand, touches* CATHERINE's *cheek, goes into the kitchen where* JESSIE *and* JOHN HENRY *are sitting. She kisses his forehead and the top of* JESSIE's *head, then goes out into the yard where she hugs* ANDREW.)

MARY: You can actually *feel* summer coming on.

ANDREW: At last.

MARY: There's just one more thing, Andrew. Would you keep an eye on Ralph for the rest of the day? (ANDREW *groans.*) He has to drive his family back to LaFollett tonight, and goodness sakes, we don't want any accidents.

> (ANDREW *goes off to hunt for* RALPH. MARY *sits on the swing beside* RUFUS.)

MARY: My, you can see all the way to North Knoxville.

RUFUS: Mama?

MARY: Yes?

RUFUS: We sur — sur —

MARY: What are you trying to say?

RUFUS: We sur — *vived,* didn't we, Mama?

MARY: Why yes, darling, we survived.

RUFUS: Am I a norphan now?

MARY: An *orphan* — ?

RUFUS: Like the Belgians?

MARY: Of *course* you're not an orphan, Rufus. Orphans haven't got *either* a father or a mother.

RUFUS: Am I half a norphan then?

MARY: Rufus, orphans don't have anybody to love them or take care of them, and you *do*! Oh darling, Mama's wanted to see more of you these last days, a lot more. But you do know how much she loves you, with all her heart and soul, all her life — you know that, don't you?

RUFUS: Will we still get the surprise, Mama?

MARY: I promised you, didn't I? Did you ever know me to break a promise? (*He shakes his head. They get up from the swing.*) Well then, the surprise will come, just as I said. And do you want to know what it's going to be, Rufus?

RUFUS (*Eagerly*):   What?

MARY: A baby. (*He considers this, not too enthusiastically, and looks down at the ground.*) You're going to have a baby sister. Or it may turn out to be a brother, but I dearly hope it will be a sister. Isn't that wonderful?

RUFUS (*Figuring it through*):   If I'm half a norphan, Mama, then the baby will be half a norphan, and the two of us together will be a *whole* norphan.

MARY (*Impatiently*): Rufus, you're to stop *wanting* to be an *orphan*! Goodness sakes! You be thankful you're not! They sound lucky to you because they're far away and everybody talks about them right now. But they're very, very unhappy little children. Do you hear?

RUFUS: Yes, Mama.
(*Retaining, however, a few private hopes*)

MARY: Good.

RUFUS: Why can't we get the baby right away?

MARY: The time will pass more quickly than you think, much more quickly. And when it does — when she does come to us, you must help her all you can.

RUFUS: Why?

MARY: Because she'll be just beginning. She'll have so much to learn, and I'm counting on you to teach her, because you're so much older and have had so much more experience. She'll be very small and lost, you see, and very delicate.

RUFUS: Like a butterfly?

MARY (*Somewhat mystified*): Why, that's a very grown-up way to put it.

RUFUS (*Excitedly*): Look Mama, there's a train crossing the viaduck!

MARY: It's time to go home, darling.

RUFUS: Let's just watch that train go by. (*He watches excitedly. She looks off, not in the same direction. Pointing at the train, he slowly walks across the stage and sings "Get On Board Little Children," under his breath.*) Where's the baby now, Mama?

MARY: Up in Heaven . . . (*She changes her mind, walks towards him and puts her hand to her waist.*) Right here. (*She takes his hand and places it on her waist.*) Yes, darling. Right here. (*She kneels down to him and holds him by the shoulders.*) You see, Rufus, when a grown man and woman love each other, truly love each other, as Daddy and Mother did, then they get married, and that's the beginning of a family. (*The lights are now up full on the house with all the* FOLLETS *and* LYNCHES *in the various rooms.* MARY *turns and leads* RUFUS *home as the curtain begins to fall.*) It will happen to you one day, before you know it, so I want you to listen very carefully to everything I'm going to tell you because I think it's time you knew about it, and I want you to ask questions if you don't understand. Will you do that, darling?

The Curtain Is Down